DEADLY JUSTICE

A DETECTIVE JANE PHILLIPS NOVEL

OMJ RYAN

Published by Inkubator Books
www.inkubatorbooks.com

ISBN (eBook): 978-1-83756-127-8
ISBN (Paperback): 978-1-83756-128-5

PROLOGUE

As he stared out of the lounge window over the expansive garden, the sunset cast an orange glow across the late evening sky. Today had been unseasonably warm for early May, and the forecast for tomorrow promised more of the same. It would be an ideal morning to finally tackle the lawn. It was well overdue for a proper cut, and he would enjoy navigating the ride-on mower in the sunshine. Once that was done, he could head to the golf club for a late lunch and a catch-up with his fellow members.

A smile spread across his face; he had learnt to enjoy retirement much more than he had ever anticipated. Of course he missed the cut and thrust of the courtroom and the immense power that came with being a Crown Court judge, but even after almost ten years away from the bench, he still wielded a high level of influence within Manchester's legal and political communities and was a regular guest at many of the charity balls that littered the calendar each year. Plus, after receiving his knighthood a little over twelve years ago, he absolutely adored the fact everyone had to call him Sir.

There was no finer feeling. Yes, life for *Sir* Walter was very good indeed.

Turning away from the window, he moved gingerly across the room and began examining the contents of his drinks cabinet. With the clock ticking towards eight, it was time for a good drink, a fat cigar, and a catch-up on the day's news. After a few minutes of deliberation, he settled on the Hennessy XO cognac he'd procured on his last visit to Harrods in London, and poured a large measure into his favoured Waterford Crystal brandy glass. Next he opened the mahogany cigar humidor and selected a Cohiba Maduro, which he held to his nose and sniffed deeply to savour the aroma before clipping the end with a cigar guillotine.

Everything was in place. A moment later the leather of his favourite armchair creaked as he sat down, placing his glass on the small table to his right before lighting the large cigar. White smoke billowed into the air around him as he puffed vigorously. Flicking on the TV, he soon found the news channel and relaxed while the opening titles played. As soon the program began, the male newscaster wasted no time in painting a picture of the financial Armageddon that had recently decimated the UK economy after yet more mismanagement by the British Government. Interest rates were set to rise again, and more and more 'typical' families were set to pay more for their mortgages and energy bills. 'Fuck 'em,' he mumbled as he took a long drink of the Hennessy. 'Serves them right for being scroungers.'

He, of course, as a retired judge no longer had a mortgage to worry about, and with a large portfolio of investments at his disposal, high interest rates were the gift that kept on giving to his monthly dividends. He grinned as yet another irate member of the public appeared on-screen, complaining about the state of British politics.

The program continued, and his glass was soon empty.

Getting up from the chair, he returned to the drinks cabinet and poured another large drink. It was then that he felt the draft of air rushing into the room as the door to his left opened. That bloody dog must have nudged open the back door again, he reasoned. He promised himself he'd kick the wretched mutt into the middle of next week, but he'd need to do it before his wife returned from the theatre later this evening, so he could dish out the punishment without the usual histrionics from Lady Venables.

Placing his glass down on the small table next to the armchair, he wandered out of the lounge and along the darkened hallway towards the rear of the house and the source of the draft. Turning right into the kitchen, as expected, he found the back door open, its old hinges creaking against the wind. 'Fucking dog,' he mumbled as he pushed it closed, noting the sound of the loud click as it locked in place. Shaking his head, he turned on his heel and headed back along the hallway to the lounge. The sound of the news program's closing credits filled the air as he stepped through the doorway and made his way towards the chair and retook his seat. Puffing on the cigar once more, he watched the end glow orange and smoke billow from his mouth in one satisfying motion. *Bliss.*

'Hello, Sir Walter,' said a voice from behind him.

The shock he felt was like a living thing exploding inside him. With his adrenalin spiking, an icy shiver ran down his spine as he swivelled in the armchair, craning his neck to see the intruder. 'Who the fuck—' he managed to mumble before the cord tightened around his throat.

'Goodbye, Sir Walter,' the man repeated as he pulled it tighter.

THE JUDGE WAS SURPRISINGLY strong for a man in his seventies, and his bony fingers fought hard against the cord. Gripping the ligature ever tighter, he pulled him back against the armchair, dropping to his knees as he did, using his own weight to ensure the old man was starved of oxygen. Sir Walter kicked and squirmed as he battled for air, but twenty seconds later, his body gradually stopped moving, and silence descended.

He let out a loud breath as he released his grip on the cord and stepped up. Standing over the judge, his heart raced as the enormity of what he'd done began to sink in. Whilst he'd been planning tonight for a very long time, he'd never fully imagined how he would feel having taken a man's life. His biggest fear had been that he'd lose his nerve at the last minute, but here he was now, staring down at a dead man, a former Crown Court judge no less. Adrenalin coursed through his veins as he moved around the chair to stand across from Sir Walter's body. The old man's face was filled with the terror of his death throes.

When he'd first begun to plan the events of this evening, he'd read a lot about how your nervous system reacts when you kill another human being for the first time: the urge to vomit, an immediate and overwhelming sense of guilt, or the desire to get away from the scene as quickly as possible. None of which had affected him. Quite the opposite, in fact. He felt excited, powerful and absolutely certain he had what it took to pull off the rest of the plan. As his mind wandered to the others on his list, he allowed himself a smile.

Just like Sir Walter, they had all become complacent: certain that they were untouchable, each of them hiding in plain sight with their crimes never brought to light. Until now, that is. Sadly for them, they'd not counted on his raging desire for justice, and he would not let any of them get away with it any longer.

Scanning the room, he noted the variety of framed photographs of the judge hanging on the walls. Pictures of him flashing that self-congratulatory smile, captured next to his wife, and in and amongst who he presumed were his kids and grandchildren. Were they aware of his crimes? he wondered. Did they know he was a sexual deviant, a bully, and a fraud? Maybe, maybe not. It didn't really matter now either way. All that mattered was that Sir Walter was dead, and justice had finally been served.

1

Detective Chief Inspector Jane Phillips reclined in her office chair and sighed loudly into the phone.

'You okay, babe?' asked Adam.

'Yeah, just a long day of paperwork.'

'Can you get off home soon? It's after nine.'

She yawned. 'I know, but I should probably stay another hour and get the decision logs updated. I hate going home when they're not finished.'

'All right, but promise me no later than ten. That place gets more than its money's worth from you.'

'I will. Scout's honour.'

Adam laughed.

'What about you? How's your shift been?'

'Just like every other day in A&E,' said Adam. 'Too many patients and not enough staff to see them all.'

'What time do you think you'll be home in the morning?'

'I get off shift at seven, so with traffic, I'm guessing about eight thirty.'

Just then Sergeant Hicks from the comms team knocked on her door, his expression grave.

'Hang on a sec, Adam,' she said as she pulled the phone against her chest. 'Everything all right, Dennis?'

Hicks took a step forward into the office. 'Something's just come in, ma'am. It's big.'

Phillips nodded and returned the phone to her ear. 'Sorry, love. Gotta go. One of the guys needs me.'

'Aw, bugger,' Adam replied. 'So much for you getting out of there soon.'

'Yeah,' she said, distracted.

'Be careful, Jane.'

'I will,' she said, then ended the call.

Hicks moved to stand in front of her desk.

'What is it, Dennis?'

'A suspected homicide. I know you're not the on-call SIO tonight, but based on who the victim is, I thought you might want to be across it.'

'Go on.'

'Sir Walter Venables.'

Phillips felt her face crumple. 'As in *Judge* Venables?'

Hicks nodded. 'He's retired now, but yeah, Judge Venables.'

'And you say he was murdered?'

'According to the uniform team on the scene, it looks like he was strangled. His wife found him when she got home an hour ago.'

Phillips took a moment to digest what she was hearing. Sir Walter Venables was one of the most influential Crown Court judges ever to sit on the bench. If the first responders were right and he *had* been murdered, this was a case she'd do well to avoid. The pressure from all angles to get a result would be immense from the get-go.

'So do you want it?' asked Hicks.

Phillips remained silent as she imagined what lay ahead, and in spite of herself nodded. She knew only too well that by stepping into that crime scene she was opening the door to a world of pain from above – as well as the media – given the nature of the victim, but there was something inside her that was drawn to the challenge of a case of this magnitude. If she handed it over to another team, she knew she'd regret it. Plus, in twenty years of policing she hadn't shirked from a case yet, and she wasn't about to start now. Besides, the Major Crimes Unit was made up of some of the best detectives on the force.

Hicks handed over the address details. 'Want me to call in the CSIs?'

'If you don't mind?'

'Not at all.'

Phillips picked up her phone. 'Thanks, Dennis.'

'No problem, ma'am,' he said, then turned and left the room.

Phillips scanned through the favourites in her iPhone and a moment later called Jones.

Her second in command answered promptly. *'Guv, everything all right? It's never good news when you call at this time of night.'*

'I hope you weren't getting comfy. I need you out at a potential murder scene in Altrincham.'

'But we're not on call tonight.'

'I know, but the victim is Sir Walter Venables.'

'You're shitting me?' Jones was incredulous, his tone made even more so by his South London drawl.

'I wish I were.'

'Jesus. What happened?'

'Uniform reckons he was strangled,' said Phillips.

'Where?'

'At home. Have you got a pen? I'll give you the address.'

'Give me a second,' replied Jones, clearly on the move at the other end.

Phillips was already itching to get on the road.

'Right, go for it,' Jones said finally.

'It's number 39 St Margaret's Drive, Altrincham. Postcode is whisky-13, 5 uniform golf.'

'Got it. You want me to call in Evans and the team?'

'Sergeant Hicks is already on it,' said Phillips. 'So just meet me there as soon as you can.'

'Google Maps reckons it'll take me half an hour.'

'Should be the same for me. See you soon,' said Phillips and ended the call.

2

As Phillips turned the British racing green Mini Cooper down St Margaret's Drive, the flashing blue and red lights of the uniformed patrol car, along with the ambulance, came into view. Parking up outside Venables's address, she took a moment to work through her time-served ritual of cleaning her glasses before pulling her dark ponytail tight against her head.

Just as it did at the first sight of every crime scene, her stomach churned with nervous energy as she opened the driver's door and stepped out of the tiny car.

Jones was waiting for her, standing next to the patrol vehicle.

'You been in yet?' she glanced towards the house behind him.

'No. Just arrived myself.'

Phillips nodded as she handed over a pair of purple latex gloves. 'Right, let's see what we've got, shall we?'

As they made their way to the front door, a tall, well-built uniformed officer approached. 'Ma'am, sir, I'm Sergeant Nowak. I'm the one who called it in.'

'Sergeant Hicks from the comms team said the wife discovered the body,' said Phillips. 'Is that right?'

'Yes, ma'am. She came home from dinner just after nine thirty and found him in the lounge.'

'And where is she now?'

'In the kitchen, ma'am. The paramedics are treating her for shock.'

'I see. Well, we'd better get in there.' Phillips lifted the blue and white police tape blocking the open front door and stepped over the threshold.

Inside, she was struck by the strong odour of cigar smoke that hung heavy in the air. The entrance hall was double height with a wide mahogany staircase running up the right-hand wall to the first floor. As she followed Nowak along the gloomy hallway, it was evident the house had not been painted or renovated for some time, with the decor dating back to the late 1980s. As Phillips entered the lounge where the victim had been found, the stench of cigar was even more pervasive. Standing just inside the door, the back of Venables's head was visible, poking out above the armchair containing his body. Making her way around the old chair, she took in the scene.

'Bloody hell,' muttered Jones as he moved next to her.

'Definitely looks like strangulation,' added Phillips, staring at Venables's face, his eyes wide with terror, a thick purple bruise circling his throat.

'What a way to go,' said Jones. 'And he never even finished his brandy.'

Phillips glanced down at the full glass sitting on the table next to the body, then turned her attention to Nowak. 'Any sign of forced entry?'

He shook his head. 'No, ma'am. We checked all the doors and windows and couldn't find anything. Although the back door *was* unlocked when we arrived.'

Jones tutted his disgust. 'I'll never understand why people don't lock their doors at night in this city. If they did, *our* job would be a lot bloody easier.'

Phillips remained silent as she scanned the room. 'Do you know what time and where Mrs Venables went out for dinner?'

Nowak glanced down at his notepad. 'She left just after six, a local Italian place, Sale Pepe in town.'

Phillips nodded.

'Any sign of the CSIs?' asked Jones.

'Sergeant Hicks radioed through just before you arrived, sir,' replied Nowak. 'They should be here any minute.'

'Good,' Phillips replied. 'Okay, you'd better take us through to see Mrs Venables.'

Nowak nodded, then led them out of the room and along to the back of the house.

The kitchen was as dated as the rest of the home, and as Phillips stepped inside, she noted the brown vertical wall tiles nestled amongst the beige Formica worktops, which were framed with dark wood veneer detailing. Phillips herself had grown up in Hong Kong until the age of fifteen, but in that instant, she felt as if she'd been transported back to her childhood and her grandparents' Manchester home.

Mrs Venables, who was slightly built with close-cropped white hair, was sitting on a metal-framed chair, the fabric most likely fake leather, thought Phillips.

A paramedic zipped up a green and white bag beside her, then excused herself.

Phillips stepped forward. 'Mrs Venables, I'm Detective Chief Inspector Phillips, and this is Detective Inspector Jones. We're from the Major Crimes Unit.'

'It's *Lady* Venables, thank you very much,' she spat back. 'My husband didn't sit on the bench for all those years for me to be called *Mrs*.'

Phillips had zero patience for the pomp and ceremony of the English upper class, but at the same time, the woman had just discovered her husband's body, so she bit her tongue. 'Do you mind if we take a seat?'

'Go ahead,' said Lady Venables.

They sat down opposite her, and Jones pulled out his notepad and pen.

'We understand you left the house at around seven this evening,' said Phillips.

'That's right.'

'Where did you go?' Phillips already knew the answer but preferred to hear the facts for herself.

'Sale Pepe in the town, just along from the train station.'

'And who did you meet there?'

'A couple of my friends from bridge, it's a monthly thing we do.'

'We'll need their names and numbers for verification,' said Jones.

Lady Venables glared at him. 'What on earth for? You don't think *I* had anything to do with this, do you?'

Phillips forced a thin smile as she spoke. 'We just need all the details for the investigation. Purely procedure. I'll ask Sergeant Nowak to make a note of them when we're done.'

Lady Venables didn't respond.

'What time did you return home?' asked Phillips.

'As I've already told the *other* officer, I came back just after eight-thirty.'

'And did you go into the lounge straight away?'

'Pretty much, yes. The dog was barking in the back garden, so I let her in, then went through to see how Walter was doing and...' Her words tailed off.

'We know this must be very difficult for you,' said Phillips softly.

Lady Venables dabbed her eyes with a tissue.

Phillips continued carefully. 'Did you see anyone near the house this evening? Anything suspicious, either on your way out or when you came back?'

'Not that I noticed, no.'

'And did your husband have any enemies that you knew of?'

'He was a Crown Court judge,' Lady Venables scoffed. 'He sent the dregs of society to prison year after year. I'm sure you could take your pick.'

Phillips ignored the remark. 'Had anyone ever made threats against him?'

'If they had, he certainly didn't tell me about it.' She shifted in her seat. 'Walter was a very private man. Kept himself to himself.'

'What about calls to the house? Anything out of the ordinary of late?'

'No.' Lady Venables locked eyes with Phillips. 'Absolutely *nothing*.'

Phillips sensed there was little point in continuing the questions. Lady Venables was understandably in shock and in no fit state to deal with the details of her husband's death right now. It was time to wrap things up for the moment. 'I'm not sure if Sergeant Nowak mentioned this to you already, but as the house is a crime scene, you won't be able to stay here tonight.'

'He didn't.' Realisation seemed to dawn across Lady Venables's face. 'But this is my home.'

'I know it's not ideal, but our crime scene investigators will be arriving shortly, and they'll need to check the house for any evidence that can help us catch whoever did this to your husband. Is there anyone you can stay with?'

Lady Venables's eyes were filled with sadness as she shook her head. 'My boys both live down south. What am I going to tell them?' she mumbled.

Phillips waited a beat before continuing, 'What about your friends from tonight?'

'No. I wouldn't want to impose on them.'

'In that case, we can provide a hotel if that would be better.'

Lady Venables dabbed her eyes with the tissue again before finally nodding.

'Okay. Sergeant Nowak will make the arrangements, and we'll also organise a family liaison officer to meet you there and see you have everything you need.'

'I'll have to pack a bag.'

'That won't be possible, I'm afraid,' said Phillips gently. 'Like I said, the house is now a crime scene, so you won't be able to remove anything from it, but we can sort toiletries and fresh nightclothes for you. That won't be an issue.'

Tears came in earnest now, the gruff exterior suddenly gone.

Phillips placed a reassuring hand on the woman's wrist. 'We're very sorry for your loss.'

A minute or so later, the tears subsided. When Lady Venables had finished blowing her nose into a fresh tissue, Phillips passed across her card. 'If you think of anything else or need anything – anything at all – please get in touch, day or night.'

Lady Venables stared at the card cradled in her hand.

'We'll leave you with Sergeant Nowak,' said Phillips, standing.

Jones also stood. A minute later as they made their way back to the front door, Evans appeared up ahead. 'Where do you want me?' he asked as they came close.

Jones thumbed over his shoulder down the hallway. 'The lounge. He's ready for his close-up.'

Evans cracked a half smile. 'I'll keep you posted on anything I find.'

'Thanks, Andy,' said Phillips and headed outside.

Back on the drive, they both turned and took in the enormous house.

'Looks like they have CCTV.' Phillips pointed to the cameras above the front door.

'The only modern thing in the place, by the looks of it.'

'We'll need copies of tonight's footage, as well as the last week, to start with.'

Jones nodded. 'I'll give Evans the heads-up.'

Phillips pulled out her phone. 'While you're doing that, I'd better call Carter so he can update Fox. She'll have a coronary when she hears about this one.'

'Won't she just.' Jones smiled wryly. 'You never know. With a bit of luck, it might just finish her off.'

Phillips returned his smile as she placed the phone to her ear. 'If only we were that lucky.'

3

The next morning the team gathered in the MCU conference room at 7:00 AM. In light of the early start, Phillips had organised breakfast rolls, pastries, and hot drinks for everyone, which she placed in the middle of the large conference table.

'Help yourself,' she said as she removed the plastic lid from her steaming coffee.

As ever, DC Bovalino, a mountain of a man, wasted no time in filling his plate, greedily taking a bite of his bacon roll as he dropped back into his seat.

DC Entwistle, in contrast, examined the plates of food in front of him with a keen eye.

'Just pick one, Whistler,' Bovalino said through a mouthful of bacon. 'It's a plate of food, not a bloody crime scene.'

'Piss off, you big lump,' Entwistle shot back with a grin as he patted his washboard stomach. 'Some of us care about what we put in our bodies.'

'And that's why *you* get all the ladies, mate,' added Jones, picking up a pain au chocolat, along with his favourite peppermint tea. 'Ashton House's answer to LL Cool J.'

Entwistle laughed. 'I'll take that,' he replied before finally picking up a plain croissant and taking a seat.

With everyone's plates full and cups charged, Phillips and Jones got to work bringing Bov and Entwistle up to speed on the events of the previous evening. Evans had already sent through pictures of the crime scene, now displayed on the large screen at the end of the room via Entwistle's laptop.

'It's enough to put you off your breakfast,' mumbled Bovalino as he stared at the enlarged image of Sir Walter's body sitting in the old chair, his face locked in death, the bruising on his neck clearly visible.

'And you say there was no sign of forced entry?' Entwistle asked.

'Nothing,' replied Jones. 'We'll need to wait for the post-mortem, but Evans thinks he was strangled from behind whilst sitting there. According to the first responders, the wife said the TV was on high volume when she found him, so there's a good chance he may not have heard his intruder's approach.'

Phillips drank a mouthful of coffee. 'Any joy from forensics on the CCTV at the house?'

Entwistle nodded. 'Came through on email in the early hours of the morning.' He clicked open his inbox, which appeared on the big screen, then took a moment to locate the file. 'According to the message from Evans they've found footage of someone going in and out of the house but his face is obscured.'

A moment later, Phillips and the team watched on as the CCTV video played on the big screen.

'This is the feed from the front of the house. No sign of anyone on this, according to forensics.' Entwistle clicked open another file. 'But they *did* spot someone on this feed from the back of the house. Apparently someone can be seen moving about on this feed just before eight PM.'

It took a few minutes for Entwistle to find the relevant time frame displaying what appeared to be a male moving slowly towards the rear of the house across the garden, face obscured by a hood and scarf. A dog could be seen padding past the intruder in the opposite direction and showing little interest in him.

'That's some guard dog,' Bovalino said sarcastically.

As the video unfolded, the intruder could be seen opening the back door without resistance before stepping inside. The time stamp in the corner of the screen stated it was 7:58 PM. Aside from the dog wandering back into shot and cocking its leg against a small tree in the corner of the garden, nothing else appeared in the frame for approximately ten minutes. Then at 8:11 the back door opened once more, and the killer stepped back into the garden, hurrying out of shot a moment later.

Phillips stared at the time stamp on-screen. 'In and out in ten minutes flat.'

Jones nodded. 'By the way he approached that back door, it looks to me like he knew it would be unlocked.'

'I thought that,' replied Phillips.

'So, what? Are we thinking he's been to the house before?' asked Entwistle.

Phillips nodded. 'Possibly. Have we got any ANPR cameras around the address?'

'I haven't had a chance to look yet,' Entwistle replied. 'But it's on my list to do first thing this morning.'

'Good. We're looking for any cars coming in and out of that area around the time of death, as well as any vehicles that appeared regularly in the last month, but had not been captured on camera before that. See if we can spot him staking out the place.'

'That's a lot of footage, guv,' said Entwistle. 'We'll need some extra help to get through that.'

'Draft in PC Lawford from the uniform support team; she's a smart cookie.'

Entwistle made a note in his pad. 'I'll call her as soon as we're done here.'

Phillips stared at the CCTV footage still playing on the large screen without speaking, then turned back to the team. 'So who do we think could have had it in for old Venables?'

Bovalino was the first to respond. 'As I recall, he had a reputation for being a bit of a zealot when it came to sentencing; maybe one of his overly long convictions has come back to haunt him?'

'Wow. Zealot?' Entwistle shot back playfully. 'That's a big word for you, Bov.'

'What can I say?' The big man winked. 'I'm one of life's great orators.'

Phillips relished the back-and-forth between the guys because it helped to keep the team relaxed. The pressure from the top brass would be coming soon enough – she knew that better than anybody. 'Let's get a list of any prison-leavers in the last few months who were sent down by Venables, as well as anyone who received an unusually long sentence while he was on the bench.'

'That'll be a lot of people, guv,' said Bovalino. 'It'll take some pulling together.'

'I know,' she replied. 'Draft in whatever support you need. I'm certain Carter will be happy to sign off the overtime for this one.'

'Does Fox know about Venables yet?' asked Jones.

'I'm assuming she does. Carter was calling her last night straight after I spoke to him.' Phillips exhaled loudly. 'I've been called to a meeting with them both at eight thirty.'

Jones folded his arms across his chest. 'I can just imagine how she took it.'

'Well, I'll find out soon enough.' She looked at her watch. 'Right, guys, let's get to it.'

Each of the men nodded.

Phillips stood. 'I'd better get going. I don't want to make it any worse by being late.' With that, she headed for the exit.

4

Phillips found Carter waiting for her on the landing that led to the fifth-floor corridor. His expression was grave, and his normally bold posture seemed diminished, his six-foot-two frame appearing shorter than normal.

'Everything okay, sir? You look like you've got the weight of the world on your shoulders.'

Carter offered a faint smile. 'Let's just say Fox didn't take the news very well last night.' His accent was soft, northeast and matched his gentle face and salt-and-pepper hair.

'Which is ridiculous in itself. We didn't bloody kill Venables!'

'Of course not, but we also know how she gets when she thinks the force's reputation is about to be dragged through the media.'

Phillips shook her head. 'Just once, it'd be nice for her to worry less about her precious image and instead focus on supporting us in catching the guy who did it.'

'I know, Jane, and I share your sentiment, but Fox is Fox.'

'She drives me mad.'

'I hear you,' said Carter. 'But let's just play nice in there and get through the meeting as quickly as possible, hey?'

'Is this you subtly telling me not to bite back, sir?'

Carter's smile returned, stronger now. 'Ever the detective.'

Phillips nodded. 'I'll do what I can.'

'Thank you.' Carter reached for the door to the corridor, then looked back at Phillips. '"Once more unto the breach, dear friend..."'

A few minutes later Fox's assistant, Miss Blair, waved them through to her inner office, with her usual dour expression.

Phillips resisted the overwhelming urge to tell her to cheer the hell up as she passed by.

Inside, Fox was sitting behind her large smoked-glass desk, staring at her PC monitor in silence, her half-rimmed spectacles perched on the end of her overly tanned nose. Her dyed blonde hair was notably much brighter today than when Phillips had seen her last week.

Fox remained silent as Phillips and Carter took two of the three seats opposite her desk. A few seconds later, Rupert Dudley, director of communications for the Greater Manchester Police, arrived and sat in the remaining empty chair.

Fox moved her eyes from the screen back towards Phillips and Carter. 'I've asked Rupert to join us to see if we can stave off what is sure to be a *huge* PR issue for us.' Her voice was agitated. 'I don't have to tell you how this will go once the media get hold of it. Sir Walter Venables was one of the most decorated and respected Crown Court judges in the country. The police and crime commissioner has already been on the phone asking for a face-to-face meeting later this morning, which is never good.'

Dudley unzipped his large leather portfolio, which he laid flat on his knees before pulling out his pen. 'Do we have a timeline on when we can release his identity to the press?'

'Lady Venables is due to identify the body later this morning,' replied Phillips. 'One of our family liaison officers is looking after all that.'

'So in that case,' replied Dudley, 'we could potentially name Sir Walter by the middle of the afternoon?'

'No,' Fox cut in. 'That's too early. The later we do it, the less chance the mainstream media have of putting anything meaningful out today.'

'With respect, ma'am, if we delay it, they'll just make a bigger splash tomorrow,' said Phillips.

Fox glared at her. 'This process needs careful management, DCI Phillips, and if the story lands *today*, then it'll make things look ten times worse in the eyes of the commissioner. If we can push it back twenty-four hours, it gives me time to work on her, to try to mitigate the damage.'

Phillips took a silent breath as she remembered her promise to Carter on the stairs.

Fox continued, 'And *nobody* speaks to the press about any of this without my express permission. Is that understood?'

'Absolutely,' Dudley shot back in a flash.

Carter nodded. 'Of course, ma'am.'

'My lips are sealed,' said Phillips.

Fox locked eyes with Phillips. 'I do hope so, DCI Phillips. I don't want you giving your usual special favours to Don bloody Townsend. That man has been given far too much information about this force over the years, and I want it to stop now.'

Phillips took a moment as she considered her words carefully. 'Again, with respect, I think that could be a mistake, ma'am. As you said yourself, this is an incredibly high-profile case. The level of media interest it'll generate will be enormous.'

'Townsend gets nothing,' said Fox. 'I'm tired of the force's innermost workings being splashed all over the city by that two-bit hack.'

'I totally agree that he's gone too far at times in the past, but I do believe it's better to have someone like Townsend onside. He's much easier to manage that way, and I worry that if you cut him out of the loop, well, who knows what he might write about the whole thing.'

'Pah,' scoffed Fox. 'The less he has, the less damage he can do.'

'But, ma'am—'

'That's my final word on the matter.' Fox cut her off. 'He gets *nothing*.'

Phillips opened her mouth to respond but thought better of it.

'When we do announce it, I think a piece to camera would be best,' said Dudley.

'As in a press conference?' Fox asked.

'No, it doesn't need to be as big as that,' replied Dudley. 'Just a short piece from a senior officer in front of the building. That should be enough for now.'

'I'd be happy to do that, ma'am,' Carter cut in.

Phillips breathed a silent sigh of relief. She hated talking to the media.

Fox remained silent and appeared deep in thought. 'Actually, I think DCI Phillips would be best placed to do it in this instance.'

'Really, ma'am.' Phillips was shaking her head as her pulse began to race. 'The chief super is far better than me at these kinds of things.'

'That's as may be,' replied Fox, 'but like it or not, your profile is very high in the city, and the commissioner is a fan thanks to your exploits over the years. If she sees *you* making the announcement, it might go some way to limiting the impact of Venables's death.'

Phillips glared at Carter, her eyes silently begging him to get her out of it, but it was no use.

'That settles it, then.' Fox grinned, revealing her bright white teeth, which Phillips was convinced were caps.

'So did we agree on a time?' asked Dudley.

'Four o'clock should do it,' said Fox firmly. 'DCI Phillips, any objections?'

'No, ma'am.' Phillips's heart sank. 'Four o'clock will be fine.'

Fox sat forward now and linked her fingers together on the desk. 'I don't need to remind anyone in this room how sensitive this case is and how damaging it could be for all of us if we don't manage it carefully and get a result quickly. Do I make myself clear?'

Phillips nodded without expression.

'Absolutely,' said Carter.

'I'll do everything I can to manage the media, ma'am,' Dudley added.

'Good,' said Fox. 'Dismissed.'

Back along the fifth-floor corridor, Phillips and Carter stopped to debrief. 'I'm sorry you got lumbered with the press statement, Jane,' he said.

'Yeah, you and me both.' Her stomach had already begun to churn just thinking about what lay ahead at 4 PM.

'Are you going to be okay with it?' asked Carter.

'Yeah, sure,' she said without conviction.

'I can help you write the statement if you want?'

'No, no. I'll be fine. Look, I'd better go. I need to get back.'

'Of course. Keep me posted on any developments, won't you?'

'Goes without saying, sir,' replied Phillips, then turned and walked away.

5

'How did that go?' asked Jones as Phillips approached his desk.

'Oh, you know. As usual it was all about Fox and how this case makes her look bad to the PCC.'

Jones let out a sardonic chuckle. 'Nothing like getting the full support of the brass, hey?'

Phillips dropped into the chair at the spare desk, opposite Entwistle's workstation – he himself was nowhere in sight. 'Do you know, to this day I can't decide whether Fox getting promoted to chief constable was one of the worst – or *best* – things that's ever happened to Major Crimes. I mean, in one way, the fact she gets to decide the fate of the entire force is terrifying. But then on the other hand, at least *we* don't have to deal with her every single day now she's out of MCU.'

'Yeah.' Jones nodded. 'That joy falls to Carter.'

'Poor bastard,' said Bovalino flatly.

Phillips allowed herself a smile. 'Whistler was right, you sure have a way with words, Bov.'

'I do me best, guv,' he said with a grin.

Resting her elbows on the desk and her face in her hands, Phillips sighed. The thought of what lay ahead in the next couple of hours filled her with dread.

'You all right, boss?' said Jones.

Phillips dropped her hands. 'Fox wants *me* to tell the press the body we found last night was Venables.'

'Live TV?'

'Yep.'

'Oh shit,' replied Jones. 'I thought that was Carter's domain.'

'So did I. But it seems the police commissioner is a fan of *yours truly* – for reasons unknown to me – and Fox thinks that it'll somehow lessen the blow if I deliver the news.'

'What time are you due to speak?'

Phillips glanced at her watch. 'In a couple of hours, probably around four. Dudley is sorting out the logistics. Said he'd give me the heads-up once it's all booked in.'

'Do you know what you're going to say?' asked Jones.

'As little as possible.' Phillips let out a low growl. 'God, I hate doing press conferences. I'd rather stick pins in my eyes than speak on camera.'

'You and me both, guv,' said Jones. 'I did a couple during your sabbatical, and they scared the shit out of me. I was a nervous wreck each time.'

'I thought you were quite good, actually,' added Bovalino.

Just then, the door to MCU opened, and Entwistle returned to his desk. 'Everything okay?'

'Fine,' said Phillips, standing.

'Before you go, guv.' Entwistle opened his notepad. 'I was able to speak to the manager of Sale Pepe in Altrincham while you were upstairs. He confirmed Lady Venables was there at the time of Sir Walter's death.'

Phillips nodded. 'I figured as much. She hardly looks like the murdering type. Any other updates?'

'Nothing as yet, boss.'

'Okay, well, keep me across all developments as soon as you get them.'

'Of course,' replied Entwistle.

Phillips nodded, then turned just in time to see Rupert Dudley walking through the main door to MCU. She intercepted him just outside her office.

'I've confirmed the announcement for four PM,' he said.

'Okay,' said Phillips. 'I suppose I'd better figure out what I'm going to say, then.'

Dudley offered a reassuring smile. 'Would you like some help?'

'Do you know what? I would, actually.'

'In that case, I'm all yours for as long as you need me.'

Phillips gestured towards her office. 'After you.'

JUST BEFORE FOUR O'CLOCK, Phillips stepped out the front doors of Ashton House and into the late afternoon sunshine. About twenty feet in front of her, a larger-than-expected press pack had gathered from TV, radio, and newspapers. Many journalists held microphones emblazoned with their network's logo, and the heavy-duty TV cameras glared at her ominously from the front of the noisy crowd. As she moved closer, her eyes landed on the familiar face of Don Townsend standing on his own, his arms folded across his chest. He stared intently at her, his eyes narrow, and she wondered if his source-cum-spy within the GMP had already shared with him the content of her announcement. With Fox's warning to keep him at arm's length ringing in her ears, she broke his gaze and stepped into position. Her heart pounded in her chest, and she took a long silent breath in the vain hope of steadying her nerves. As the crowd fell silent with anticipation, Phillips swallowed the lump in her throat and began.

'Thank you all for coming at such short notice. I'm Detective Chief Inspector Phillips from the Major Crime Unit. I'm sorry to inform you that last night, officers from the Greater Manchester Police were called to the Altrincham home of Sir Walter Venables at around nine PM. Shortly afterwards, paramedics attended the scene and a short time later confirmed that Sir Walter had died at home earlier in the evening. At this stage we are treating his death as suspicious, and we would urge anyone in the area who may have seen anything unusual last night to come forward. A full investigation into the cause of his death is now underway, and we hope to be able to update you on developments in due course. In the meantime, if you have any questions, please direct them to our press team through the usual channels. I will be making no further comment.'

Despite her saying clearly that she would not be commenting, a barrage of questions erupted from the crowd. Following the advice given to her by Rupert Dudley in her office, she resisted the temptation to make eye contact with any of the journalists and instead simply said, 'Thank you,' then turned on her heel and marched back through the front doors of Ashton House. As usual, she took the stairs back to the third floor, and as she reached the doors to MCU, her phone beeped. She paused as she pulled it from her pocket. Sitting on the home screen was a text message from Don Townsend, which she opened.

I think it's time we had a drink.

Every fibre in her being told her that ignoring him was the wrong way to handle the situation, but Fox had been adamant, and she needed to pick her battles with the chief constable. Against her better judgement, she closed the message app, pushed her phone back into her pocket, and stepped back into MCU.

The only thing that mattered now was catching the killer.

6

A couple of hours later, Phillips headed home. Traffic was mercifully light, so it wasn't long before she pulled the Mini onto the gravel drive of the new home she and Adam had recently bought together. She smiled as she spotted his car parked up in front of the double garage.

Phillips had adored her previous house, a boutique Chorlton terrace that she'd lovingly renovated and called home for well over a decade. When Adam had moved in after just six months of dating, it seemed as though life couldn't get any better, but that had all changed when he became the victim of a near-fatal knife attack just yards from their front door. Following that fateful night, the house had felt tarnished – a constant reminder of how close he had come to death. As they both struggled to come to terms with what had happened, talk had turned to making a fresh start somewhere new. Three months later Phillips found herself being carried over the threshold of a spectacularly remodelled 1920s semi-detached house located just a few streets away from the old one. Now they had the best of both worlds, a bigger house but still within walking distance of her beloved Chorlton village green.

After locking the car, she headed inside and, as she opened the front door, was met by the most wonderful aroma of garlic and spices. Moving through to the kitchen, she found Adam hard at work, cooking up a storm.

'Hey, babe,' she said as she placed her laptop bag on the kitchen bench.

He turned and smiled. 'I thought I heard the front door.' He stepped closer and kissed her.

'Something smells delicious.'

'Just a quick Thai red curry. I don't know about you, but I'm starving.'

Phillips nodded. 'Ravenous. It's been a really long day.'

'Anything you want to share?'

'Not right now.' She glanced at the bubbling pot on the stove. 'How long will dinner be?'

Adam checked the clock on the wall. 'About twenty minutes.'

'In that case, would you mind if I took a quick shower?'

'Not at all. It'll be ready by the time you're done.'

She smiled, then leaned in for another kiss. 'Have I ever told you how much I love you?'

'Once or twice,' he said, returning her smile. 'But I never get tired of hearing it.'

'Well, I do love you,' she replied, patting him on the chest before making a beeline for the stairs.

A few minutes later, Phillips stepped into the gargantuan walk-in shower and thrust her head under the powerful jet. With her neck bent, she stared down at her toes as the water snaked between them, then away towards the drain. She stood that way for the next ten minutes before mustering up enough energy to wash her hair. Then finally, after fifteen minutes in the steaming shower, she reluctantly switched it off and stepped out into the main bathroom.

Towelling herself dry, she slipped on her dressing gown and slippers and made her way back downstairs.

Adam was plating up the curry as she walked back in.

'I thought we could eat at the table tonight. Have a catch-up.'

Phillips took in the dining area that annexed the kitchen and nodded.

A couple of minutes later as they sat down to eat, Phillips took Adam by the wrist. 'This is such a treat after the day I've had, thank you.'

'You're welcome.' He poured them both a glass of iced water.

'But if you don't mind, can we skip the catch-up and watch a bit of TV while we eat? I feel like I've done enough talking for one day.'

Adam offered a sympathetic smile as he picked up the remote. 'Sure.'

As the TV burst into life, Phillips took her first forkful of the curry, and Adam did the same.

For the next ten minutes they ate quietly, both of them engrossed in a documentary exploring train travel across Australia's outback.

Phillips pointed her fork at the screen. 'I always regret not going there when I had a chance.'

'Australia?' asked Adam.

'Yeah. I mean, I grew up in Hong Kong, for heaven's sake. It's only seven hours' flying time.'

'But that wasn't your fault, Janey. It was your mum and dad who kept coming back here for the holidays.'

Phillips swallowed a mouthful of rice. 'Dad never was very adventurous.'

Adam appeared taken aback. 'Are you kidding? He was a

captain in the Royal Hong Kong police and spent his days taking on the Triads. That sounds pretty adventurous to me.'

'I guess so.' Phillips shrugged. 'I just wish he and Mum had travelled a bit more, you know. When they were young enough to enjoy it.'

Adam placed his fork down on his now-empty plate. 'You're never too old for travel, babe. Maybe they just need a little encouragement.'

'Maybe,' replied Phillips as she too finished her curry.

Neither of them said anything for the next few minutes as the TV show's host recapped his travels from the episode, followed with the promise of more of exciting adventures at the same time next week.

As the credits rolled, Adam got up from the chair and began clearing the plates.

'Why don't we go?' Phillips said, turning to get his attention.

'Go where?'

'Australia.'

'Seriously?'

'Yeah,' Phillips replied eagerly. 'I've got loads of holiday time owing to me; we could go later in the year. Do it properly and take three or four weeks. Christmas maybe, when it's hot down under.'

Adam nodded. 'I'd love to, but do you really think Fox and Carter would let you go for that long?'

'Why not? I took a nine-month sabbatical, and they survived.'

'That is true,' said Adam, placing the dishes in the sink.

Just then the opening titles for the local news appeared on-screen.

'Oh. God, I'm not watching this,' said Phillips, reaching for the remote.

Adam's brow furrowed. 'Why? What's up?'

Phillips pointed to the TV once more as the news anchor appeared on-screen, looking serious as he previewed the upcoming stories. 'I did a presser today about Judge Venables's death.'

Adam raised his eyebrows. 'On camera?'

Phillips nodded sombrely. 'Yeah.'

Adam kept his eyes on the screen as the news presenter opened the show.

'Good evening and welcome to this edition of Northwest Evening News. Tonight's top story: Police officers investigating the death of a retired crown court judge at his home last night have today announced they are treating his death as suspicious. Our chief crime reporter, Sinita Chowdhury, reports.'

A smartly presented woman, seeming in her early thirties, filled the screen, talking to the camera against the backdrop of Ashton House.

'Seriously, I can't watch this—'

'No, no, no,' Adam cut in. 'Leave it, please. I want to see it.'

Phillips shook her head as she got up from the table, 'Well, you can watch it by yourself,' she said as she passed him the remote and headed for the lounge.

Closing the door to block out the sound of the TV, she spotted her cream Ragdoll cat, Floss, curled up asleep on the sofa. Dropping down next to her, Phillips pulled out her phone in a fruitless attempt to distract herself from Adam's viewing in the other room, cringing at the thought of him watching her speak to the camera.

For the next few minutes, she mindlessly scrolled through Facebook, looking at nothing in particular as she waited for the story to finish and for him to deliver his verdict.

When he finally appeared a few minutes later, his expression was stoic.

She cringed as she grabbed the cushion next to her and held it against her chest, 'Oh, God, was it really that bad?'

He pursed his lips and nodded sombrely, saying nothing for a long moment before a broad smile flashed across his face. 'I'm just messing with you. I thought you were brilliant.'

'Oh, shut up. You're just saying that.'

'Honestly, I'm not.' He dropped into the seat next to her. 'I don't know what you were so worried about. Seriously, I thought you smashed it. Strong, sincere, authoritative. It was spot on.'

Phillips closed her eyes and let out a loud sigh of relief. 'Yeah, but you're biased.'

'Maybe I am, but either way, I thought you did an amazing job. Honestly, I couldn't do anything like that.'

Phillips smiled. 'Thanks, love. Coming from you, that means a lot.'

Adam wrapped his arm around her shoulder and squeezed her tightly. 'Your problem is, you don't know how good you actually are.'

Phillips let out a sardonic chuckle. 'I'm sure all these years of working for Fox haven't helped.'

'Not at all.'

Phillips dropped her head onto his shoulder. Taking in his scent, she was reminded just how close she'd come to losing the only man she'd ever truly loved.

Kissing her on the top of her head, he squeezed her tightly. 'I don't suppose you fancy an early night, do you?'

Lifting her head, she locked eyes with him.

'Cos I've never done it with a celebrity!' he added mischievously.

'Oh, piss off!' she said with a cackle before launching the cushion against his head.

7

The next day the early morning inner-city traffic was heavy as usual, and it took Phillips almost an hour to drive the four miles from her home in the boho suburb of Chorlton to Manchester's Royal Infirmary situated on the very edge of the city centre. After finding a parking spot on the top floor of the über-busy multi-storey car park, she locked the Mini Cooper and made her way down the stairs to the ground floor.

Ten minutes later she pressed the buzzer at the entrance to the mortuary located in the basement of the main hospital building, the scene of Sir Walter Venables's post-mortem, due to start in the next fifteen minutes. She didn't have long to wait, and was buzzed through the heavy door a second later.

Inside, the familiar smell of disinfectant and formaldehyde hung heavy in the air.

Further along the corridor she spotted Jones sitting on a chair, scrolling on his phone.

He looked up as she approached, then stood. 'Morning, guv,' he said, slipping the handset into his pocket.

'Have you seen Tan yet?' she asked, referring to the chief pathologist, Dr Tanvi Chakrabortty.

'Briefly. She arrived about the same time I did but disappeared into her office; said she had an urgent email to send, but she reckoned she be ready to start on schedule at half-eight.'

Phillips checked her watch: 8:27 AM.

A couple of minutes later, the door to Chakrabortty's office opened, and the doctor stepped out into the corridor, head to toe in perfectly pressed, green surgical scrubs that made her look taller than ever. At five feet eleven, she cut an imposing figure. As usual her jet-black hair was pulled back into a long ponytail that fell between her shoulder blades, and her elegant face appeared fresh. 'Morning, guys,' she said cheerfully as she handed them a plastic surgical apron each. 'And how are we feeling this morning?'

A smile flashed across Phillips's face, knowing full well the question was aimed at Jones, who had a notoriously weak stomach when it came to post-mortems.

'Couldn't be better,' said Phillips playfully.

Jones swallowed hard and wiped his mouth. 'Fine.'

Chakrabortty smiled broadly. 'Right, in that case, let's get cracking, shall we?'

Soon after, Phillips found herself standing next to Jones, opposite Chakrabortty. Between them was the almost grey body of Sir Walter, laid out on a heavy-duty stainless-steel table, naked apart from a green surgical sheet covering his torso and groin. Staring down at the body, she noted the thick bruising around his neck, appearing more pronounced than when she had first seen it a couple of days ago. Probably due to the powerful lighting above, she thought.

Chakrabortty pulled back the surgical sheet and folded it carefully, so it sat just above the pelvic bone, before picking up a large scalpel, which glistened under the lights. She glanced in turn at Phillips and then Jones. 'Are we ready?'

'As I'll ever be,' said Phillips.

Jones nodded silently.

'Okay, here we go.'

Phillips had witnessed hundreds of post-mortems in her twenty-year career, and they still remained very difficult to be part of. Luckily Chakrabortty was considered one of the finest pathologists of her generation, and her careful, deferent approach made the whole experience completely professional and almost businesslike. But she still could never shake the thought that cutting into another human being to find out what killed them seemed the ultimate indignity – a cold and clinical end. Today was no different, so she was more than relieved some ninety minutes later when Chakrabortty announced the procedure complete.

'Let's recap in my office, shall we?' suggested Chakrabortty, pulling off her plastic, bloodstained apron.

Phillips and Jones followed her out of the examination room and back along the corridor to her incredibly tidy office.

'How do you keep this place so clean, Tan?' asked Phillips as she took a seat opposite Chakrabortty's desk.

Tan flashed a smile. 'I'm more than a little bit OCD, I'm afraid. Just ask my Tom,' she said, referring to her husband.

'My office usually looks like I've been burgled,' joked Phillips as Jones took the seat next to her.

A few moments passed as Chakrabortty logged into her PC, found what she was looking for, then turned to face them. 'So. It's clear the cause of Mr Venables's death was strangulation using something flexible, an inch and a half thick.'

'Any ideas what that might be?' asked Phillips.

'No, not at this stage.' Chakrabortty glanced at her

computer screen, then back at Phillips. 'But I can see from Evans's initial crime scene report that the CSIs are testing fibres they found on the neck, which should help narrow it down.'

Phillips nodded. 'Does it say when we'll get those results?'

'Depending on what it turns out to be, twenty-four to forty-eight hours.'

'Okay,' she replied.

'As I mentioned in there, the traces of powder on the body suggest the killer wore latex gloves. Again, Evans will be able to ascertain the exact compound he found, which may help you trace the brand used.'

'For all the good it'll do,' added Jones. 'Hundreds of thousands of latex gloves are sold each week in Manchester.'

Chakrabortty raised her palms in surrender. 'Don't shoot the messenger, Jonesy.'

'You mentioned there was quite a bit of liver damage,' Phillips cut back in.

'Yeah. Not to an alcoholic level, but I think it's fair to say the honourable judge liked a drink or two.'

'We found a large glass of brandy next to the body, along with a huge cigar,' Phillips said.

'Sounds about right for Venables,' Chakrabortty said sardonically.

Phillips felt her brow furrow. 'Did you know him?'

'Only by reputation, really. Tom came across him a few times in court and was never a fan.'

'Really? Why so?'

Chakrabortty took a deep breath before linking her fingers on the desk. 'Look, there's no proof of this, and Tom was just a junior lawyer back then, but rumour has it Venables was somewhat of a bigot during his time on the bench. Not a fan of anyone from ethnic minorities or poor backgrounds. So much so, in fact, it was widely believed that he regularly used his influence as the judge to sway juries towards guilty verdicts, guilty or not.'

'Surely someone would have pulled him on that kind of thing?' Phillips protested.

Chakrabortty shrugged. 'He was a very powerful Crown Court judge – had the ear of a lot of important people, and a lot of defence attorneys feared the repercussions of taking him on directly.'

'He was on the bench for decades,' said Jones. 'If that's the case, he could have sent potentially hundreds of innocent people to prison in that time.'

'That's pretty much what Tom said when he saw Jane talking on the news last night.' Chakrabortty locked eyes with Phillips now. 'By the way, I meant to say earlier, I thought you looked good on camera.'

Phillips felt herself blush. 'Kind of you to say so. Not true, of course, but thanks all the same.'

'No, honestly. You did well; I certainly wouldn't want to do something like that. Anyway, as I was saying, Tom saw you talking about Venables and the fact it was being treated as suspicious, and it all came flooding back to him. He reckons there's loads of people who have been very happy to find out the judge was dead.'

'And any one of them could have strangled him,' pointed out Jones.

Phillips remained silent for a time before finally sighing loudly. 'If that's the case, it looks like we've got our work cut out on this one.'

'So what's new?' asked Chakrabortty with a wry smile.

'Quite,' replied Phillips. 'How long will it be before you send through the full report?'

'The bulk of it's done. It just needs inputting into the system, which one of the team will start as soon as we're done here.'

'Okay, in that case, we'll get out of your hair.' Phillips stood.

Jones did the same a second later. 'Thanks, Tan. As ever, incredibly thorough.'

'That's my job,' replied Chakrabortty.

'We'll see ourselves out,' said Phillips before heading for the door.

Fifteen minutes had passed by the time they stepped out into the sunshine-soaked top floor of the MRI carpark, and Phillips's phone began to ring. Pulling it from her pocket, she cursed under her breath when she saw the name on the screen. 'Don Townsend.' She hit the cancel command on-screen. 'He's the last person I want to talk to right now.'

'He's like a bad penny, that guy,' said Jones.

A moment later, her phone beeped again, indicating she had a voicemail. Flicking the phone to speaker so Jones could hear what was being said, she held the handset between them.

'DCI Phillips.' Townsend's voice had a husky tone, likely brought on by his forty-a-day habit. *'If I didn't know better, I'd say you're ignoring me, and it's really not like you to keep me in the dark. I'm hoping it's a simple oversight on your part as opposed to a deliberate ploy of some kind, so if you could call me back, I'd appreciate it. You know what I'm like, Jane. I need to feel loved and well informed. Otherwise I can end up going off-piste and writing whatever shit falls out of my very vivid imagination. You know where I am. Feel free to get in touch sooner rather than later. After all, I'm always on a deadline, and real-time information is the key to whether a Don Townsend piece lands in a positive or negative way. I'm sure you catch my drift. You take care now, Jane.'* The message ended.

'Fucking prick,' growled Jones. 'Who the hell does he think he is?'

Phillips stared at the phone. 'I need to call him back.'

'That's not a good idea, boss. You heard what Fox said. He gets nothing.'

'Sod Fox,' replied Phillips. 'She's the world's worst communicator. She knows bugger all about managing the press or dealing with someone like Townsend. He can be an incredibly powerful ally or an equally dangerous enemy. If I keep ignoring him, it's not gonna end well for us.'

'That's as may be,' said Jones, 'but whatever shit he prints will be nothing compared to what Fox will do to you if you disobey a direct order. Like you say, she knows nothing about dealing with the press. Maybe Townsend going off the deep end will teach her a lesson. Let *her* cop the consequences of tangling with him for once.'

Phillips shook her head. 'But it won't be Fox who cops it, will it. It'll be Carter and me and you and the rest of the guys.'

Jones shrugged. 'Better that than you sticking your neck out for a snake like Townsend.'

Phillips exhaled loudly. She knew he was right – of course he was – but it didn't make it any easier to stomach. Leaving Townsend on the loose with half a story was like dangling chum in front of a hungry shark. She knew full well it was only a matter of time before someone got chewed up.

8

Two hours later, Phillips called the team into the MCU conference room for an update on the investigation so far. After bringing them up to speed on the findings of the post-mortem and Chakrabortty's feedback around Venables's controversial time on the bench, the room fell silent as each of them digested the new information.

Eventually, Bovalino broke the silence. 'So how long was Venables a judge?'

'I'm not entirely sure,' said Phillips.

'Gotta be over fifteen years,' Jones added.

'Give me a second and I'll tell you.' Entwistle began typing furiously into his laptop as the team watched on. A minute or so later he found what he was looking for. 'Here we are, Sir Walter Venables, appointed to the Crown Court in 1991, retired in 2015. So that's twenty-four years.'

'If Chakrabortty's theory rings true,' said Bovalino, 'then we've got even more ex-cons to vet than we first thought. And that's a big enough list as it is.'

'I know, Bov.' Phillips laid her hands flat against the table.

'Let's not get overwhelmed though. We can only do what we can do.'

'Try telling that to *Mein Führer* upstairs,' Bov shot back, pointing to the ceiling.

Phillips did her best to stifle a grin. 'Forget about Fox; this is *our* investigation, not hers. We'll find this guy. We just need to do what we always do and follow the evidence.'

Bovalino nodded. 'Sure, boss.'

'So. Any joy with the prison-leavers checked so far?'

Bovalino opened his notepad. 'A couple of names stood out. I've found one, and Whistler flagged another.'

Phillips sat forward. 'Okay, tell me about yours.'

'The guy we're looking at is called Darren O'Hare. Originally from Dublin, he moved to Manchester in the mid-eighties. Venables handed him an eighteen-year stretch for manslaughter after he killed a man in a bar fight. One punch and the guy had a massive brain bleed. Never came round.'

Jones cut in now. 'Eighteen years seems a long sentence for a bar fight.'

'Yeah,' replied Bovalino. 'According to the court records, O'Hare was known as a big drinker and bit of a fighter – nothing major, no convictions, but he liked a scrap. Venables said it was clear he had little control over his drinking and would more than likely do it again. He said he was handing out the maximum term in order to save lives in the future. It didn't help that O'Hare was rumoured to have had direct links to the IRA before he came to England.'

'So when did O'Hare get out?' asked Phillips.

'Four months ago. He served nine of the eighteen. Currently living in a halfway house in Longsight.'

'Okay.' Phillips turned her attention to Entwistle. 'What about your guy?'

'I came across a fella called Muhammad Abdeel, convicted of stalking a woman with fear of violence four years ago. Even though it was his first offence and some of the evidence was circumstantial, Venables gave him the *maximum* term of eight years. Apparently during sentencing, he said Abdeel was clearly a man capable of escalating his behaviour, and the public needed to be protected from him. But what's really interesting is that when Abdeel was taken down from the court, he shouted, "*Aap is ke leyay adaeegi kare gey*," which is Urdu and when translated into English means, *You will pay for this*. He's also in a halfway house, but this one's in East Manchester.'

Phillips remained silent as she digested the information. 'Any other potentials we should be looking at more closely?'

'PC Lawford is working through the list as we speak,' replied Entwistle.

'Okay, while she's doing that, I suggest we split up and pay these two a visit. Jones and I will take O'Hare; you two take Abdeel.'

Each of the men nodded.

'Right.' Phillips stood. 'No time to waste.'

9

Jones steered the squad car into a space at the side of the road, not far from the entrance to the halfway house, located in the inner-city suburb of Longsight. The street around them was lined with red-brick terrace houses in varying degrees of disrepair.

'Charming spot,' said Jones, his tone sarcastic.

Phillips glanced out the window. 'I'm not sure which is worse, prison or these halfway places.'

'I hope I never have need to find out.'

'Me either,' replied Phillips before opening the passenger door.

A minute later, Jones pressed the video buzzer fixed to the side of the double door marked 'Beacon House', and they waited.

It wasn't long before a thin voice crackled through the intercom in front of them. *'Yes? Can I help you?'*

Phillips placed her badge in front of the small camera. 'DCI Phillips and DI Jones from Major Crimes. We'd like to speak to Darren O'Hare.'

'One moment, please.'

A second later, the door buzzed, then popped open a fraction.

'Come on through.'

Phillips led the way inside to the large open space where a woman who appeared to be in her early fifties, with shoulder-length blonde hair, was sitting behind a curved reception desk. Her name badge indicated she was called Sal.

'It's not often we get a visit from the heavy mob,' said Sal through a wide smile. 'I hope none of our lot are in trouble.'

Phillips refused to take the bait. 'We just need to speak to Darren, if he's about.'

Sal nodded. 'You've come at the right time cos he's been off scheme all morning, but he's just come back in about half an hour ago.' She picked up the reception phone. 'I'll call his room.'

Phillips and Jones waited as the call connected.

'Hiya, Darren, it's Sal on reception. I've got the police here, love. They want to talk to you.'

There was a pause as she listened to the response. 'I dunno. They haven't said. Just asked to talk to you.'

Another pause.

Sal nodded. 'Okay, I'll tell them.' With that, she ended the call and replaced the handset. 'He's coming down.'

Phillips produced a thin smile. 'Thank you.'

A couple of minutes later the secure door to the side of reception clicked open, and a tall, heavyset man with a shaved head and a ruddy complexion stepped through. He was wearing a black Adidas tracksuit and white Nike trainers.

'Here he is,' said Sal cheerfully.

'I done nothing wrong,' O'Hare mumbled as he approached them. His accent was clearly Mancunian, but the Dublin twang was still present.

Phillips presented her credentials. 'I'm DCI Phillips, and this is DI Jones. We're from the Major Crimes Unit.'

'What's this about?' asked O'Hare.

'Is there somewhere we can speak in private, Darren?' asked Jones.

O'Hare nodded towards the entrance to the building. 'Best talk outside.' He led them out onto the street, where he immediately pulled out a bag of tobacco and papers and began rolling a thin cigarette as he wandered ahead of them. When he finally came to a stop, he lit it and inhaled deeply.

Phillips got straight to the point. 'Where were you on Tuesday night, Darren, around eight o'clock?'

O'Hare took his time exhaling smoke through his nostrils before answering, 'Why do you want to know?'

'Just answer the question, mate,' said Jones.

'I ain't your mate,' O'Hare shot back before taking another long drag. 'Just being seen with you could cause me some major aggro in there.'

Phillips folded her arms across her chest. 'Look, Darren. We can do this one of two ways: either here, or down the nick. It's your choice. Doesn't matter to us.'

O'Hare remained silent as he exhaled more smoke.

'So I'll ask you again. Where were you on Tuesday night, around eight o'clock?'

He shrugged. 'Where I always am. *Here*.'

'Can anyone vouch for you?' asked Jones.

O'Hare scoffed, then bent down and pulled up the left leg of his tracksuit.

Phillips stared down at the thick, black bracelet locked around his ankle.

'I'm still on tag and under curfew. Where I go, this thing goes – more's the fucking pity. You can check with Sal on reception cos she's been on the late shift all week. She signed me in, and I was back by seven.'

Phillips glanced at Jones, who was clearly trying to hide his disappointment.

'And you can check with my probation officer, too,' O'Hare added, pulling his tracksuit leg back down. 'She'll have the tag data.'

'We'll do that,' said Phillips.

O'Hare took one final drag on the cigarette before flicking it away. 'You gonna tell me what this is about?'

'Judge Venables,' said Jones.

'That prick?' O'Hare snarled. 'What's that gobshite got to do with me?'

'He was killed on Tuesday night,' Phillips replied.

'Killed how?'

'We're treating his death as suspicious,' replied Jones.

A wide grin spread across O'Hare's face in an instant. 'Ha. Couldn't have happened to a more deserving bastard.'

Phillips studied him for a moment.

O'Hare pointed back at his ankle. 'I can honestly say it wasn't me.'

Phillips nodded. An awkward silence descended.

'So are we done?' asked O'Hare eventually. 'Can I go?'

'Sure,' said Phillips. 'But we may need to speak to you again.'

O'Hare affected a mock salute and clicked his heels together before setting off back towards Beacon House.

Phillips's eyes never left him as he made his way along the street.

'Cocky bugger,' Jones muttered, moving next to her.

She nodded. 'Cocky bugger with a cast-iron alibi.'

'If his tag checks out, that is.'

'You ever known one not to?' asked Phillips.

Jones sighed. 'No.'

Just then O'Hare stopped at the entrance to Beacon House and turned to face them. 'By the way,' he shouted.

Phillips and Jones remained stoic.

'If you catch the guy who did it, tell him I owe him a

drink!' He clapped his hands together and laughed, then unlocked the door with his key fob and stepped inside.

BACK AT ASHTON HOUSE, the team debriefed on their respective visits. Phillips and Jones went first, relaying their frustrating exchange with O'Hare, with Bov and Entwistle listening intently.

When they'd finished, Bov shared his and Entwistle's experience with Abdeel. 'Pretty much the same as you guys, by the sounds of it. Abdeel is an angry man, and he certainly has no love for Venables, but like O'Hare, he was locked up in the halfway house from seven PM.'

'He also has a tag on his ankle,' Entwistle added.

'Do we know how reliable tags are?' asked Phillips.

Entwistle frowned. 'How do you mean, guv?'

'Well, can they be hacked? Or removed, even?'

'I doubt it,' replied Entwistle.

Phillips continued, 'We need to be certain. Get onto the probation service and find out if there are any cases of them being tampered with. If there are, we'll be talking to O'Hare and Abdeel again.'

'One of my old uni mates works for them,' said Entwistle. 'I'll ask her.'

Bovalino chuckled. 'Another of Whistler's lost loves, no doubt. Just sitting by the phone, waiting for him to call.'

'Piss off, Bov,' Entwistle shot back playfully. 'It is possible to be mates with a woman and not have a relationship with them, you know.'

'What? Like friends with benefits, you mean?' the big man shot back.

Entwistle shook his head but smiled. 'I give up.'

Phillips cut back in, 'Have we heard anything from digital

forensics on the identity of the guy captured on Venables's CCTV?'

'I saw a message alert flash up just now while we were talking.' Entwistle opened the email on his laptop and began reading aloud. '"The suspect is believed to be around six feet two and of medium build. Whilst most of his face and hands were covered, we believe the male is either white, mixed race, or Asian".'

'That narrows it down,' said Phillips sardonically.

'Maybe you should pop upstairs and share that with the chief constable, boss,' said Jones, his voiced laced with sarcasm. 'I'm sure she'd be over the moon with such a detailed observation.'

Phillips sucked her teeth. 'At least O'Hare and Abdeel are still in the frame if that *is* the case. Having said that, though, we're still no further forward. We need to double our efforts, guys, okay?'

'Yes, guv,' Bovalino replied.

'On it,' said Entwistle.

Jones nodded.

'I'll be in my office, updating the decision logs, if anyone needs me,' said Phillips, and she stepped up from the chair and headed into her office.

10

For the next few hours, Phillips threw herself into updating her paperwork, making notes of the various junctions within the case and the decisions she had come to at each point, a necessary requirement of modern-day policing. By the time Entwistle knocked on her door, the clock on the wall was showing three o'clock.

'You got a second, guv?' Entwistle's expression was grave.

Phillips sat back in the chair. 'What's up?'

'I get updates from the *MEN* app on my phone, and I thought you might want to see this?' He handed over his mobile.

Phillips took it and stared down at the headline on-screen.

MANCHESTER – A CITY OF MURDER AND MAYHEM! ARE THE STREETS NO LONGER SAFE? BY DON TOWNSEND.

'Shit. That's all we need.' She continued reading in silence.

'It doesn't paint Fox in a particularly positive light,' said Entwistle. 'She's not going to like it.'

Phillips shook her head. 'Bloody hell. What is Townsend playing at? I mean, listen to this. "Since taking the reins of the Greater Manchester Police, Chief Constable Fox has overseen a fifteen percent rise in violent crime, burglary, sexual assaults, and homicides combined. And despite her promise to end gun- and drug-related crime when she first took the post, gangs continue to do battle on the streets of Manchester, with hundreds of innocent victims' lives destroyed each year. It begs the question, is our chief constable being outfoxed by the criminals, and is it time for new leadership within the force?"' She passed the phone back. 'Fox will go postal when she sees this!'

At that point Jones walked in, holding his mobile in his hand. 'You seen the article in the *MEN*?'

'Just been reading it,' replied Phillips. 'I *knew* Don would pull something like this.'

'He's a bloody snake!' said Jones.

Phillips grabbed her own phone and scanned through the contacts until she found Townsend's number, then hit the green call icon.

A few seconds later the phone began to ring at the other end before he answered. *'DCI Phillips? Well, this is a pleasant surprise. I thought you were ignoring me.'*

'What the fuck is that article about, Don?'

'You've read the piece, then?'

'Too right I have,' said Phillips. 'Have you lost your mind?'

'Just saying it how I see it.'

'I thought our days of being on opposing teams were behind us.'

'So did I, Jane. And I did warn you; if you continued to keep me in the dark on Venables, then I'd be forced to use whatever means

necessary to fill my column. After all, this isn't a game for me – I have a job to do.'

'So do I, Don. And you just made it a hell of a lot harder to do that job. Fox is going to go ballistic.'

'The truth hurts sometimes,' Townsend shot back. *'And the reality is, the facts don't lie – crime rates are much higher now than when Fox first took over. It's a shit show, Jane, and you know it.'*

'I'm part of that so-called shit show, Don.'

'Your words, not mine,' he replied.

'Go to hell,' said Phillips as she ended the call.

Entwistle was staring at her with his mouth slightly open and appeared unsure of how to react to what he'd just heard.

'That sounded like it went well,' said Jones, evidently trying to defuse the tension in the air.

'Bollocks,' spat Phillips, dropping the phone on the desk. 'I shouldn't have let him get under my skin like that.'

'Hard not to, guv. He's a first-class arsehole.'

Phillips shook her head. 'I really thought we were past this, though. You know, after everything that's happened over the last couple of years.'

'A snake will always slither, boss, it's in its nature. No matter what's gone on between you two, Don Townsend will always eventually return to type.'

'You're right,' replied Phillips. 'I know you are, but it really pisses me off.'

Just then Carter appeared at her office door, his brow furrowed. 'I take it you've seen it, then?'

'Yes, sir. I've just this minute finished giving Don Townsend a piece of my mind.'

Carter got straight to the point. 'Fox wants to see us both immediately.'

'I thought she might.' Phillips stood.

Carter's shoulders appeared to sag. 'Come on, let's get this over with.'

Phillips nodded and followed him out.

FOX WAS SITTING behind her desk when they arrived, a paper copy of the *MEN* open in front of her.

A sheepish Rupert Dudley had taken the farthest of three chairs opposite.

Phillips and Carter filed in in silence and took the other two seats.

Fox wasted no time in venting her fury. 'What the *actual fuck* is going on here, people?'

'Ma'am?' said Carter.

She stabbed her index finger down on the paper. 'How is Don Townsend allowed to print this rubbish?'

Dudley cleared his throat before speaking. 'Well, ma'am, unless he libels you or says anything slanderous, there's little we can do to stop him writing whatever he wants.'

Fox glared at Dudley; her nostrils flared. 'So you're just going to let him get away with it, are you?'

'As I say, I'm not sure what I can do to stop him.'

'I'm sorry, but that's totally unacceptable, Rupert. The PCC will have a field day with this one, and even more attention from her is the last thing I need right now.'

Dudley shifted uncomfortably in his seat.

Phillips knew remaining silent was likely her best option to get out of the meeting unscathed, but she couldn't just sit by and let Fox turn this into their problem. 'With respect, ma'am, I did try to warn you that keeping Townsend on the outside would cause issues.'

Carter's chin dropped towards his chest next to her. It was slight, but Phillips had spotted it.

Fox turned her murderous gaze to Phillips now. 'Are you saying this article is somehow *my* fault, Chief Inspector?'

'No, ma'am, that's not—'

Fox was clearly in no mood to let her finish. 'Let me remind you, DCI Phillips, that *I* am the chief constable of the Greater Manchester Police, and I answer to the police and crime commissioner. Not a tabloid hack like Don fucking Townsend. If I want to keep him at arm's length, then I'll do just that.'

'Which means he'll just write more of the same.' The words fell from Phillips's mouth before she could stop them.

Fox glared at Phillips, and a snarl formed on her top lip. 'So you *are* saying this is down to me?'

'No, ma'am. That's not what I'm saying. It's just Don Townsend has a reputation for going rogue if he doesn't get his own way.'

'So what? I'm supposed to check in with him before I make all future decisions, am I?'

Carter cut in now. 'Ma'am, I'm sure all DCI Phillips means is that we could potentially adopt a more strategic approach to how we communicate with him. Wouldn't you agree, Rupert?'

Dudley evidently wasn't expecting the question and suddenly resembled a rabbit in headlights. 'Er, well...' He swallowed the lump in his throat. 'That is one option, yes.'

Fox remained silent, rage simmering in her eyes. Finally she turned her focus to Phillips. 'So tell me, Jane, any chance you've made some progress in the Venables murder?'

Phillips held her gaze. 'We have CCTV from his house that captured the killer.'

Fox raised her eyebrows. 'Really? And did you get an ID?'

'I'm afraid he was wearing a scarf over most of his face.'

'So it's useless, then?' Fox shot back.

'I wouldn't say that,' replied Phillips. 'Digital forensics

have identified the fact the man is around six feet two and likely white, mixed race, or Asian. Definitely not black.'

'Wow. Quite the breakthrough.' Fox's tone was facetious.

Phillips continued unperturbed. 'The post-mortem also confirmed Venables was strangled from behind.'

'And how does that help us catch the killer?'

'Every detail helps us paint a picture of the murder scene,' replied Phillips.

Fox shook her head. 'I don't need pictures, Jane, I need results.'

'And we're doing everything we can to get them, ma'am.'

'Well, do more!' growled Fox.

It took every ounce of self-control for Phillips not to react. Instead, she took a long silent breath before responding, 'Yes, ma'am.'

'I want this case put to bed ASAP,' Fox continued. 'So you're to drop everything else and find the guy who did this to Venables. Understood?'

'Of course,' said Phillips.

'We'll do everything we can,' added Carter.

Fox folded the newspaper into a baton and pointed it directly at Dudley. 'Any more of this shit, Rupert, and I'll be looking for a new comms director. You got that?'

Dudley nodded nervously. 'Yes, ma'am.'

'Good.' Fox tossed the paper into the bin next to her desk. 'Dismissed.'

Phillips shot up from her chair and out of the office, with Carter not far behind. Further along the corridor, they stopped to debrief.

'She's got a bloody nerve,' Phillips raged under her breath.

Carter nodded. 'Try not to let her get to you, Jane. We knew she'd react like this.'

Phillips felt like she would explode. 'But all this shit is

down to *her.* She was the one who cut Townsend out, not us. Yet we're the ones copping it.'

Carter slipped his hands into the pockets of his black uniform trousers. 'Look, you know as well as I do that when it comes to Fox, it's *never* her fault. Never has been, never will be.'

Phillips clenched her fists in frustration.

'It's like the saying goes.' Carter flashed a sympathetic smile. 'Success has many fathers, but failure's a bastard.'

11

Sitting at her desk an hour later, Phillips was still stewing over the meeting with Fox and struggling to concentrate. Standing up from the chair, she moved across to the window in the hope it might help her refocus on the task in hand: catching Venables's killer. As she stared out at the car park below, her mind wandered back to the post-mortem and Chakrabortty's conclusion that the man had been strangled from behind whilst sitting in the dusty old armchair. Had he even seen his killer that night? she wondered.

Just then, her mobile began to ring on the desk. Turning back into the room, she wandered towards it and could see it was senior CSI, Andy Evans. She answered it. 'Andy.'

'Hi, Jane. How are things?'

'Oh, you know, shitty.'

'That good, huh?'

'Please tell me you have something of value for me.'

'I do. We've identified the fibres we found on Venables's neck.'

'And?' said Phillips impatiently.

'They came from something made out of horsehair.'

Phillips felt her face wrinkle. 'Horsehair?'

'Yep. Based on the chemical agent used to clean it before it was used to kill Venables, we've matched it to the type used in legal wigs.'

'You're kidding?'

'I'm not,' replied Evans. *'The results just came through.'*

Phillips took a moment to consider the new information. 'So let me get this right; you're saying our murdered Crown Court judge was strangled with horsehair that's normally used in barristers' wigs?'

'Exactly that.'

'Well, that's ironic,' said Phillips.

'It does seem a little poetic when you think about it,' Evans replied.

Phillips remained silent as she cast her mind back to the murder scene and the image of Venables sitting staring in death.

'As soon as we're finished on this call, I'll email the full results over,' added Evans.

'Great. Can you copy in Entwistle, too?'

'Of course.'

'Thanks, Andy. Brilliant work, as ever.'

'We do our best.'

As Phillips ended the call, she checked the time on her phone. It was approaching 6:00 PM. The office was still busy, so she headed out to update the team.

'You look a bit happier than you did earlier, guv,' said Jones as she approached the bank of desks.

'Just had Evans on the phone. He's identified the fibres on Venables's neck.'

She had each of the men's attention now.

'So what are they?' Jones asked.

'Horsehair.'

Bovalino recoiled slightly. 'Do what?'

'Horsehair,' Phillips repeated. 'Like the stuff they make legal wigs from.'

'Well, that's no coincidence,' said Jones.

'My thoughts exactly.' Phillips turned her attention to Entwistle. 'You should have received an email from Evans with the details of what's in the fibres.'

Entwistle clicked on his inbox. 'Yep, just landed.'

Phillips continued, 'I want you to find out where people buy legal wigs in Manchester and the northwest.'

'Sure thing, guv.' Entwistle made a note in his pad. 'I'll get straight onto it.'

'Thanks. So, any updates on the fact Venables may have influenced juries?'

'We've not found anything yet, boss,' said Bovalino. 'There's certainly nothing in any of the case file notes we've reviewed so far.'

'And there won't be. I'm pretty sure of that. In my experience, the world of law is a closed shop, so we're going to need someone who worked with him – or even against him for that matter – to hopefully give us the true picture.'

Entwistle opened his mouth to speak but seemed to think better of it.

'What are you thinking, Whistler?' asked Phillips.

'It's probably a daft idea – I mean, she's hardly a friend of Major Crimes or anything, but...'

'But what?' urged Phillips.

'Well, when I was looking into Venables's background, I noticed that Nic Johnson worked for him when she was starting out.'

Phillips raised her eyebrows. 'I'd forgotten she used to work for the CPS before she turned to the dark side.'

Bovalino shook his head as he folded his arms across his chest. 'No way Johnson's going to want to help us.'

'I don't know about that, Bov,' Phillips shot back. 'And

anyway, as we'll be talking to her as part of our official investigation, she won't have a choice, will she?' She checked her watch. 'It's too late to go over there now, but, Jonesy, why don't you and I pay her a visit first thing in the morning.'

'Sure,' he replied. 'Want me to pick you up?'

'Yeah.'

'Eight o'clock?'

'Sounds good.' Phillips stood. 'I don't know about you guys, but I've had enough for one day. Unless you're working on something that absolutely can't wait, get yourselves home. We can start fresh tomorrow.'

Each of the men agreed as Phillips turned and headed for her office.

12

It had been surprisingly easy for him to gain access to the purportedly exclusive Alerton Hall golf club located in the salubrious village of Mere, twenty miles south of the city centre. Luckily it appeared that non-members were actively encouraged to use the course during the week when there were no members competitions running, which meant a wide mix of golfers with varying abilities filtered through the pro shop, clubhouse, and bar on a daily basis.

In order to protect his face from the basic CCTV system in operation – which he'd spotted on his first visit some weeks ago – he had placed a black TaylorMade golf cap low down against his brow. Then, dressed in a blue Callaway polo shirt with black Adidas golf trousers and matching trainers, he had strolled through the main doors of the club that afternoon without so much as a sideways glance from any of the patrons milling about inside. Having recced the place previously, he had been delighted to learn that the four-digit code allowing access to the men's locker room had remained the same week in, week out. Standing now at the entrance to the pro shop, pretending to browse a selection of putters, he glanced to his right as a returning golfer approached the locker room door opposite and tapped in the code on the keypad: 2-0-1-2. Perfect. A few minutes later, he placed the putter he'd been holding back in the display rack, then picked up his small backpack and headed across the hall where he keyed in the code before stepping inside the locker room.

Inside, the changing facilities were spread across a large space with long mahogany lockers standing above cushioned leather seats. Beyond them the shower block was separated by a brightly tiled white wall. To his right, a flat-screen TV fitted to the wall was tuned into the golf channel.

At that moment, two men, with white towels wrapped tightly around their plump middles, wandered from the showers, a trail of steam floating in their wake. They were clearly friends and chatted happily about the round they'd played sometime earlier. Neither man noticed him as they opened their lockers and continued their conversation. Without fuss, he stepped past them and headed for the showers.

He'd chosen the location for this evening's activity precisely because of the layout of the showers. Each unit consisted of a separate cubicle with thick, floor-to-ceiling doors of the same dark mahogany as the locker doors in the changing room. Once inside the shower cubicle, patrons could not be seen. Exactly what he wanted. Satisfied nothing had changed since his last visit, he made his way back through the locker room and along to the bar, careful to hide his face from the CCTV cameras.

Without ordering a drink, he took a seat in one of the lounge chairs that faced the entrance to the bar and did his best to blend in with the early evening crowd.

Twenty minutes later, Jack Todd wandered into the bar,

nodding to a few people around the room, but without actually making conversation. As he'd observed on previous visits, Todd played his rounds solo and drank alone afterwards, propping up the bar as he stared at the large TV screen on the wall whilst nursing his usual tipple, a large single malt. Evidently, he was a man who preferred his own company.

Todd also was a creature of habit, and after his third whisky, he pushed the empty tumbler across the bar before slipping off the stool with a cursory nod towards the barman. A few seconds later Todd headed in the direction of the locker rooms.

He gave it a few minutes before stepping up from the chair as he slung his backpack over his left shoulder. With his head slightly bowed and the brim of the cap covering his face, he followed Todd out.

By the time he reached the locker room, Todd was the only person in sight. He had already removed his shirt, exposing a massive belly hanging heavily over his belt and golf trousers.

Taking up a position on the opposite side of the changing room, he opened the locker in front of him and quickly removed his shirt and hung it on the hanger inside. Next he removed his trainers and socks before slipping his trousers off, which he folded carefully before placing them in the locker. Wearing just his underwear now, he reached into his backpack and removed the cord, which was doubled back on itself, and slipped it inside one of the complimentary towels along with a tiny screwdriver. Then as casually as he could, given what lay ahead, he wandered towards the showers, pausing by the washbasins next to the cubicles.

He didn't have to wait long for a naked Todd to stride through, a towel hanging from his shoulder.

Glancing into the large mirror fixed to the wall above the

basins, he watched Todd choose a shower cubicle and step inside. A second later the water started, and steam began to creep out from under the door. Checking they were alone, he unfolded the towel and took out the screwdriver as he made his way to Todd's cubicle. He knew that for safety reasons, the locks on the showers were fitted with an external mechanism that allowed access from outside in case of emergency. Placing the screwdriver in the slot, he released the lock slowly and silently, then picked up the cord. Gently pulling the door ajar, he peeped inside. Todd stood with his back to him, his head fully under the heavy jet of water. Stepping inside, he closed the door and locked it again.

Gripping the cord tightly in both hands, he moved across the soaking tiled floor, stopping just behind Todd. 'It's time to clean house, Jack.'

Todd jerked his head out of the water. 'What the—?'

Before Todd could finish, he took a step closer and wrapped the cord around his thick wet neck, then pulled tightly from behind as water splashed over both men.

Todd instantly began clawing at the cord with his thick fingers, a guttural rasp escaping from his lips.

He increased his grip on the cord and pulled tighter, then forced his knee into Todd's back, pushing him forwards against the tiles, using the big man's weight to crush his stricken airway.

Todd dropped onto his knees as the water pounded down. Staring at the top of his head, hatred bristled like an electric charge in every fibre of his being. Tightening his grip, he pulled tighter still.

Todd's scrabbling hands began to slow, and a moment later he keeled over sideways onto the shower floor.

Retaining his grip on the cord for the next minute, he continued to stare down at Todd as steam began to obscure his view. Taking a knee, he let go of the cord with one hand and checked the pulse at the neck. Todd was dead.

He took a few deep breaths as he attempted to steady his pulse and calm his racing mind. As had been the case when he had killed Venables, adrenaline was surging through his body, along with that same mix of excitement and satisfaction.

Phase two is complete.

Picking up the small screwdriver, which had fallen onto the floor tiles, he folded the cord back on itself, then removed his now-soaked underwear. He grabbed a flannel from the small vanity cabinet at the side and made sure to wipe Todd's neck where he'd checked the pulse, before using the same flannel to conceal the cord. Next, he grabbed Todd's dry towel from the hook on the wall and wrapped it around his middle. Opening the cubicle door slightly, he peered out and was more than a little relieved to see the locker room was still empty. He stepped out, pulled the door closed behind him, and used the small screwdriver to lock it shut once again. With a glance left and right to ensure no one had been lurking out of sight, he made his way back to the lockers, where he quickly dried off and changed back into his golfing clothes. Five minutes later, with his cap pulled down low over his face and his backpack slung over his shoulder, he walked out of the main entrance to the golf club and disappeared down the side of the old building.

13

Recently, Phillips had been trying not to drink during the week. Opening a bottle of wine as a way of unwinding each evening had become something of a habit, one she knew was not good for her in the long run. However, tonight, when Adam had asked if they could go to the pub, after the day she'd had, she'd been more than happy to make an exception. Their local, the Horse and Jockey in Chorlton, had been one of the venues they'd visited on their first date almost two years ago. They arrived just after nine thirty, and while Adam headed to the bar to get drinks, Phillips grabbed a rare empty table outside overlooking the village green. Sitting there alone for a few minutes, she cast her gaze around the surrounding tables, noting the array of couples, co-workers, and friends sharing a drink in the warm evening air. Her mind was drawn to her own team and the small amount of time they spent together outside of work – they were always so busy with their caseload – and she wondered if that was a good or a bad thing.

Just then, Adam placed a large glass of ice-cold Pinot

Grigio on the table and took a seat on the bench beside her before taking a couple of mouthfuls of his lager.

When he was done, he wiped his mouth and smiled softly. 'How was your day?'

'Not great,' replied Phillips, then gulped down some of the wine.

'What happened?'

Phillips exhaled deeply as the alcohol took effect, allowing her shoulders to soften just a little. 'Fox happened.'

'What's she been up to now?' Adam took another drink.

'Did you see the article in the *MEN* this afternoon?'

Adam shook his head. 'What was it about?'

'Fox and the GMP. Don Townsend wrote it.'

'In that case, I'm guessing it wasn't very complimentary.'

'No, it wasn't,' replied Phillips, fishing her phone from her pocket. A second later she opened the *MEN* App and handed it to Adam. 'Get a load of this.'

Adam took the phone and began reading, and it wasn't long before he physically winced. 'Ouch. I can see why she took it badly. Paints her in a terrible light.'

'Doesn't it?'

'So what's got up Don's nose? I thought he was a friend of the force these days?'

'Fox did,' said Phillips. 'Earlier this week she gave me a direct order to cut him out of the loop on the Judge Venables case. Said he was already getting way too much information on cases—'

'From the mole,' Adam cut back in. '*Not* you guys.'

'Exactly – and I haven't given up on finding that sneaky bastard either – but the way she was going on, you'd think I was handing over my case notes to him every time we spoke.'

'Which obviously pissed you off.'

'Totally,' Phillips shot back. 'Anyway, she was adamant he was getting nothing, which I said was a mistake, and I also made it clear that Townsend was much better as an ally than as an enemy. I warned her something like this would happen if we cut him out, but she was having none of it.'

'Sounds like she got what was coming to her, in that case,' said Adam.

'She did, but then somehow she managed to blame me, Harry, and Rupert Dudley for his article.'

'The comms guy?'

Phillips nodded and took a mouthful of wine.

'So what happened?'

'We were dragged to a meeting and basically told we were all shit and her reputation was suffering because of our incompetence.'

'She's a total narcissist, that one, I'm telling you,' said Adam.

'And the rest,' Phillips shot back. 'I'm convinced she's a bloody sociopath, too.'

'Sounds about right.'

'So when I reminded her that I'd warned her this would happen.' She pointed to her phone. 'Well, you can imagine how she took that.'

Adam chuckled. 'Oh, Jane, you never learn, do you?'

'What was I supposed to do? I'm not going to sit there while she slings mud around at us for something that *she* did.'

'And how did she take you saying that?'

'Badly,' Phillips admitted.

'So what was the outcome of all of this?'

'The usual. It's down to me and the guys to pull her out of the shit with a result – and quickly.'

Adam drained his pint and placed the glass on the table. 'And to think, you'd escaped all of this, and you chose to go back.'

Phillips sipped her wine as she attempted to block out the

attack on Adam, which had led to her taking an extended leave of absence last year.

'I know,' she eventually replied as she placed her glass back on the table. 'And I don't regret that – well, most of the time, I don't – because I love what I do, but the one thing I really cannot stomach is the hypocrisy and duplicity involved in playing police politics.'

Adam shrugged. 'I don't know what to suggest, babe. It's the same in all large organisations, I'm afraid. I mean, we're certainly no exception at the hospital. Our place is full of politics and game-playing upstairs. Thankfully I can stay out of it on the shop floor, so to speak.'

Phillips spotted Adam's empty glass. 'Let me get you another one.'

'Sounds good.'

Phillips headed inside for fresh drinks and, after waiting her turn at the crowded bar, headed back outside five minutes later. 'Sorry, it was three deep in there.' She handed him his lager. 'Anyway, enough of my shit. How was your day?'

Adam took a long gulp and stared out across the green. 'I lost a patient this morning.'

Phillips recoiled. 'Oh, God. What happened?'

'Hit and run. A woman in her thirties. The police think the driver was speeding away from a drug deal that went bad. The car hit her so hard she flew thirty feet into the air. By the time she got to me, she was in a really bad way. I tried everything to save her, but she died before we could get her into surgery.' Adam dropped his chin to his chest.

'Aw, sweetheart.' Phillips wrapped her arm around his back. 'I'm so sorry. I feel terrible now, banging on about my day when you've been through all that.'

Adam turned to face her. 'Don't be daft. It's all relative.'

Phillips offered a faint smile and rubbed her hand on the nape of his back. 'Are you okay?'

'I'm fine,' replied Adam. 'Sadly, it comes with the territory.'

Just then, Phillips's phone began to ring. Glancing down at the bench, she could see it was Jones. 'I'll let it go to voicemail. It's probably nothing.'

'It's never nothing when Jonesy rings. You should answer it.'

'You sure?'

Adam nodded and took a drink.

'Jonesy?' Phillips accepted the call.

'Sorry to bother you, guv, but we could have another strangling on our hands.'

'Shit. Really?'

'Yeah, and you won't believe who the victim is.'

Phillips felt her pulse quicken. 'Who?'

'Chief Constable Jack Todd, retired.'

'Bloody hell. You're kidding?'

'I wish I were.'

'And you're sure it's him? Todd, I mean.'

'That's what the uniform team who responded are saying.'

'Where was he found and when?' asked Phillips.

'In the showers at Alerton Hall golf club in Mere. Uniform was called in about half an hour ago. Sergeant Hicks was on the desk, and with the scene being so much like the Venables case, he passed it straight onto me.'

Phillips glanced at Adam, who stared back. There was sadness in his blue eyes, and her heart sank. In that moment she considered asking Jones to tackle it on his own, but she knew that wasn't an option when it came to the suspected murder of a former chief constable.

Adam silently mouthed the words, 'It's okay.'

'You sure?' she mouthed back.

Adam nodded.

Phillips returned her attention back to Jones. 'I'll meet you there in the next hour.'

'No worries.'

'Can you call in the CSIs?'

'I'll do it now.'

'Thanks, Jonesy.' Phillips ended the call.

Adam exhaled deeply. 'You gonna be okay to drive?'

'I've only had one, but I'll get a taxi, just to be safe,' replied Phillips. 'I'm sorry about this.'

'I know you are, Janey, but don't stress. I knew what I was taking on when we got together.'

'Will you be okay on your own after today?'

'I'll be fine. I'll finish this and then head back.'

Phillips offered a warm smile and hugged him tightly.

'Go on,' said Adam. 'Get yourself away.'

14

Phillips arrived at Alerton Hall half an hour later and was greeted by the usual hullabaloo of flashing red and blue lights.

After quickly suiting up in the prerequisite forensic overall, she headed for the locker room, then through to the showers, where Jones was already waiting for her.

Evans and his team were in situ and busy setting up, placing reinforced plastic stepping plates on the floor, which would allow them to walk around the body without contaminating anything. 'Give me five minutes, and we'll be ready to go,' he said, far too cheerfully for this time of night, as he stepped inside the cubicle.

'Who found him?' asked Phillips as they waited for sight of the body.

Jones glanced at his notes. 'According to the uniform team, the assistant manager, Nathan Gray. He was closing the lockers up for the night when he noticed the shower running, so he knocked on the cubicle door. When he didn't get an answer, he unlocked the door from the outside and found Todd dead on the floor.'

'So what time was that?'

'Around nine.'

'And when was the last time he was seen alive?' asked Phillips.

Jones glanced at his notes again. 'Gray said he came in for his usual post-match drinks about seven, then headed to get changed about forty-five minutes later.'

'Did anyone see anyone else come in with him?'

'Too early to say just yet,' replied Jones, 'but I saw some CCTV cameras around the entrance to the club. Hopefully we can get something off those.'

'Yeah, that would be very helpful,' said Phillips.

Just then, Evans reappeared. 'Ready when you are.'

Phillips nodded and followed him back inside along with Jones.

The cubicle itself was surprisingly large and deep – about two metres – with a separate changing and vanity area just inside the entrance, and an ornate showering space at the opposite end. Todd was lying naked on the floor tiles with his feet facing the door, his massive belly almost hiding his face from their position on the stepping plates.

Evans moved along a few more steps and crouched down, pointing with his gloved finger to the large bruise that ran around Todd's throat. 'Looks very similar to the marks we found on Venables. Chakrabortty will need to confirm, but it certainly looks like another strangling.'

Phillips stared down at the body, which appeared wrinkled and bright white due to the amount of time it had been exposed to the water. She blew her lips. 'I could never have imagined Jack Todd would end up like this.'

'You knew him, guv?'

'Not personally, but our paths crossed every now and again when I was coming up through the ranks. Not wanting to speak ill of the dead, but I never liked him or his methods.'

'Yeah,' added Jones. 'He was chief constable when I joined as a DC all those years ago, but I never met him.'

Phillips turned her attention to Evans. 'Any fibres on the neck?'

'I'll have to check, but the constant flow of water could complicate things.'

'How long will that take?' asked Jones.

'Now I know what I'm looking for, about twenty minutes either way.'

'In that case,' Phillips cut back in, 'we may as well go and speak to Gray.'

Jones nodded before Phillips led them out.

Gray was sitting alone on a stool at the bar, staring into space as they approached.

'Mr Gray?' said Phillips.

Snapping out of his trance-like state, he turned to face them. 'Please, everyone calls me Nate.'

Phillips offered a soft smile. 'We need to ask you a few questions about tonight, if that's okay.'

'Sure.'

Jones held his notepad and pen at the ready.

'I know you explained what happened to the uniform team when they arrived,' said Phillips, 'but could you tell us how the events broke down.'

Gray straightened on the stool. 'Well, like I told them, I was closing up the lockers around nine o'clock when I noticed one of the showers was still running, so I went to investigate. That's when I spotted the clothes in front of the open locker, and I started to panic a bit: worried that someone had had a heart attack inside. We've had a few over the years, and a lot of our older members aren't in the best state of health, if you know what I mean.'

'So what happened then?' asked Phillips.

'I went back to the bar, grabbed a knife from the cutlery tray, and used it to open the lock from the outside.'

Jones scribbled in his pad.

'The steam was incredible, thick like fog, and it took a minute or so before I could see. And that's when I spotted Jack lying on his back on the floor.'

'So what did you do?' asked Phillips.

'I went to check if he was breathing.'

'Did you touch the body?'

Gray paused and appeared nervous. 'Yes. I didn't mean to. I just panicked.'

Phillips raised her palm. 'It's okay. You didn't know he was dead. It just means we'll need to take your fingerprints and DNA for elimination purposes.'

Gray nodded vigorously. 'I'll do whatever you need.'

'And did you move the body at all?'

'No. Once I realised he was dead, I got the hell out of there and called you guys.'

'Which was the right thing to do,' said Phillips. 'Did you notice anyone or anything strange this evening – or over the last few days for that matter?'

'No, nothing.' He shrugged. 'It's just been a normal week.'

'Any new members you've not seen before?' asked Phillips.

Gray shook his head. 'Not that I can think of. The truth is, now we've opened the club up to non-members, we get loads of new faces in every week. It's a really popular course, one of the few championship rounds in Manchester, so we're always busy.'

'How about your CCTV?' said Jones. 'Does it work?'

'Yeah,' Gray replied, 'but it's not very good. Black and white and the picture quality is pretty poor.'

'Even so, we'll need copies,' added Phillips.

'The club manager, David Eccles, will need to sort that for you, but he's not back from his holiday until the morning.'

'What time is he due in?' said Jones.

'Should be opening up about seven.'

'Ok.' Jones made a note in his pad. 'We can sort someone to come and speak to him.'

Gray nodded.

Phillips cut back in, 'Do you know who Mr Todd played with yesterday?'

'I don't, but the golf pro, Steve Southern, will have it in the booking system. He's gone home, but he'll be back in from six in the morning.'

Jones made another note.

She handed over her card. 'Look, we know this will have been a massive shock to you, Nate, so if anything comes back to you or you remember anything you haven't thought of tonight, you can reach me on that number. Okay?'

Gray stared down at the card before looking up again. 'Thank you, I will.'

'We'll send in one of the forensic team to sort your fingerprints and DNA,' Phillips added. 'So if you can just wait here.'

'Of course.'

Phillips signalled for Jones to lead them out.

'I'll get the CCTV and details of Todd's round sorted first thing tomorrow,' said Jones as they walked side by side towards the locker room.

A minute later they once again found themselves standing over the body of the former chief constable Jack Todd. 'Any joy on the fibres?' Phillips asked.

'Definitely something there,' replied Evans, 'and from memory, very similar to those we found on Venables.'

'So potentially horsehair again?' said Jones.

'I'll need to test them, of course, but certainly looks that way.'

'When can we have the results?' asked Phillips.

'Well, it really depends on what time we finish here tonight – or more likely tomorrow – but now we know what we're looking for, I would hope within twenty-four to forty-eight hours.'

'Right,' said Phillips. 'Given who the victim is, the sooner the better, Andy. Fox is gonna want answers yesterday.'

Evans locked eyes with Phillips. 'I'll make sure they're a priority.' He pointed behind her. 'We found what appears to be the victim's phone in his locker. We don't have the access code yet, but we could see from the home screen that he had a number of missed calls from someone called Gilly.'

'Gilly?' said Jones.

'Maybe it's his wife,' Phillips replied, 'wondering where he's got to.'

'We need Todd's address.'

Phillips pulled her phone from her pocket.

'Who you ringing?' asked Jones.

'Control.'

The call connected a few seconds later. *'DCI Phillips,'* said Sergeant Hicks, *'what can I do for you?'*

'I need an address for former chief constable Todd.'

'Sure. Just give me a second.'

She could hear Hicks typing at the other end, and for a long time he said nothing. *'Sorry, ma'am, the system seems to be on go slow tonight.'*

'It's fine,' said Phillips, doing her best to hide her impatience. She was eager to get on.

'Here we are,' he said finally. *'Thirteen Fraser Avenue, Hale Barns.'*

'Can you email me the postcode?' asked Phillips.

'Doing it now, ma'am.'

'Great. Thanks, Dennis.' Phillips ended the call and turned her attention back to Jones. 'Two prominent people of the law, both strangled and potentially with something made of horsehair. Is the killer sending a message?'

Jones exhaled loudly. 'Could well be, guv. But why Venables and Todd?'

Phillips tapped her phone against her thigh absentmindedly. 'I dunno, but we really need to speak to Mrs Todd.'

'I hate telling people their loved ones are dead.'

'Me too,' replied Phillips. 'But someone has to let her know this evening. It might as well be us.' With that, she unzipped her forensic suit and began pulling it off her shoulders.

15

On the drive to Hale Barns, Phillips had called Carter to update him on the events of the night so far. As expected, the similarities between the two deaths had been of grave concern, and he had insisted she keep him abreast of any developments, night or day. Having assured him she would, she had hung up and brought Jones up to speed.

'So what did he say about Fox?'

'Nothing much at this stage, but it was obviously on his mind because he said he was calling her as soon as we were done.'

'First a dead judge,' said Jones, 'and now a dead copper. I don't envy him making that call.'

'Me either,' replied Phillips, glancing out the window at the world whizzing by.

The rest of the journey passed in relative silence, and it wasn't long before they arrived at Todd's address, pulling onto the drive at the front of the large detached house, which had likely been built in the 1930s.

As they came to a stop, Phillips glanced at the clock on the dash. It was approaching midnight.

'There's a light on, so hopefully she's not in bed,' offered Jones.

'Yeah.' Phillips took a deep breath and grabbed the door handle. 'I hate doing these things.'

A minute later, the heavy oak front door was answered by a small, grey-haired woman in a long baby-blue dressing gown. She was frowning.

'Mrs Todd?'

The woman nodded. 'Gillian.'

Phillips presented her credentials. 'DCI Phillips and DI Jones.'

'Is it Jack? Has something happened to him?'

'Can we talk inside?' Phillips said softly.

Gillian nodded and opened the door wide.

Phillips stepped inside first, with Jones just behind, and they followed her through to the lounge located next to the front door.

'I was about to call you lot. I've been trying to get hold of Jack for hours, but he's not answering his phone.' Gillian's voice was laced with panic. 'It's not like him. He always lets me know where he is.'

'Maybe you should sit down,' suggested Phillips.

Gillian complied and took a seat, perching on the edge of an armchair, her eyes betraying her fear.

Phillips and Jones took their positions on the large leather sofa opposite.

'I'm very sorry to have to tell you this,' said Phillips, 'but a man was found dead this evening at Alerton Hall golf club, and we believe it's Jack.'

Gillian inhaled sharply as the words landed, and for a moment she said nothing. 'Jack's dead?'

'We believe so, yes.'

'But...but...I don't understand. He was absolutely fine when he left the house this afternoon.'

'I'm really very sorry, Gillian.'

'Was it a heart attack? He's been having a few problems of late.'

Phillips glanced at Jones, then back at Gillian. 'No.'

'Well, then what was it, then? A stroke?'

'We can't be certain at this stage,' Phillips said as she shifted in her seat, 'but we are investigating the circumstances surrounding his death.'

'What exactly does that mean?'

'All we can say with certainty at the moment is they were suspicious.'

'Suspicious?' Gillian's eyes darted back and forth, and she appeared dazed and confused. 'This doesn't make sense.'

'We're very sorry for your loss,' said Phillips softly.

'Are you sure it's Jack?'

'Yes, we are.'

Her face crumpled, and the tears came now. 'What am I going to do without him?'

Jones jumped up from the sofa. 'Why don't I make some tea?' He headed for the kitchen.

Whilst he was out of the room, Phillips found some tissues, which she handed to Gillian, and did her best to offer words of comfort, but the truth was nothing she could say or do could make this situation better right now.

By the time Jones returned with a tray of teacups, which he handed out, Gillian had regained some of her composure.

'We know this is very difficult for you, but do you think you'd be up to answering some questions?' asked Phillips.

Gillian took a sip of her tea and nodded silently.

Phillips smiled softly. 'Thank you. You said you saw your husband this afternoon. What time was that?'

'Just after midday. He was heading out to the golf club.'

'How did he seem?'

'Fine. Just like usual, I guess.'

'I see.' Phillips took a drink of tea. 'Was he acting any differently lately?'

'In what way?'

'Jumpy, agitated – nervous, even?'

'No. Not at all. Quite the opposite, in fact. He seemed very happy of late.'

Phillips sat forward on her chair a little. 'Did your husband have any enemies that you know of?'

'Probably.' Gillian paused. 'I mean, he was a policeman for thirty years and put a lot of bad people in prison.'

'Did he ever mention anyone in particular?'

'No.' She shook her head. 'He never talked to me about his work; said he didn't want to worry me, which of course only made me worry more.'

'I can imagine,' said Phillips. 'Being a cop can be very hard on loved ones at times.'

Gillian appeared lost in her own thoughts.

A few moments later, Phillips continued, 'Did anyone ever come to the house or approach you or Jack when you were out and about?'

'No. Never.'

Jones cut in now. 'Do you know who he played golf with today?'

'You must be joking,' Gillian scoffed. 'The golf club was his domain and totally off-limits to me from the day he joined. Jack was very clear on that.'

Jones raised an eyebrow. 'So you've never been to Alerton Hall?'

'Not once. On account of it being a men-only club.'

Phillips and Jones exchanged glances. Todd had clearly been lying to his wife.

'Jack was quite traditional in that way, and my place has

always been here, at home.'

'And have you always been a homemaker?' asked Phillips.

'Yes. He liked his tea on the table and expected a clean house and pressed shirts each day. That probably sounds very old-fashioned nowadays, but that's how it was for us.'

The room fell silent.

Phillips decided to change the subject. 'We'll be organising a family liaison officer to come and see you here at the house tomorrow. In the meantime, is there anyone who can come and stay with you tonight? Any family close by?'

Gillian dropped her chin to her chest for a few seconds before looking up again. 'No. We never had children; Jack wasn't keen.'

'In that case, do you have any friends we can call?'

'Not anymore.' Sadness oozed from Gillian's eyes. 'Jack didn't really get on with a lot of my friends, so I had to stop seeing them once he retired. Didn't like me going out without him, and saved a lot of arguments.'

'That must have been difficult for you,' said Phillips.

Gillian cracked a thin smile. 'He was my husband, and I always did what he asked. After all, that's what marriage is about, isn't it, to love, honour, and obey?'

Phillips resisted the overwhelming urge to answer honestly – and very much to the contrary. 'I guess so.'

Gillian dabbed her eyes with a tissue. 'My poor Jack.'

Phillips's heart went out to her. 'Look, if it's okay with you, Gillian, I'd like to organise for a family liaison officer to come and stay with you tonight. I really don't think you should be on your own.'

'Seriously, I don't want to be a bother,' she replied. 'I'll be fine.'

'You won't be a bother, and I'd feel better knowing you had someone with you after a shock like this. We'll sort it out as soon as we're finished here.'

'If you're sure.'

'I am,' said Phillips.

Gillian offered a weak smile. 'Thank you.'

Phillips glanced at Jones. The pensive look in his eyes matched how she was feeling about the elephant in the room. Turning her attention back to Gillian, she sat forward in the chair. 'I know this is the last thing you'll want to do, but we're going to need someone to officially identify Jack. Do you think you could do that?'

Gillian's lip began to tremble before she finally answered, 'I'd like to see him.'

'I know it's not an easy thing to do, but we'll make all the arrangements for you.'

'Thank you.'

Jones stepped up from the chair. 'I'll go and sort out the FLO now,' he said before heading out of the room.

'Okay, well, I think we have everything we need,' replied Phillips. 'Is there anything we can get you while we wait for the liaison officer?'

Gillian dabbed her eyes once more. 'No, I'm fine.'

'I really am very sorry for your loss,' Phillips said softly.

Gillian didn't respond, appearing lost in her own thoughts.

Phillips decided to give her some space and headed out into the hall in search of Jones. She found him talking on the phone in the kitchen.

'Thanks. As soon as you can,' he said before hanging up.

'What's happening?'

'Sergeant Clement is coming over. Reckons she can be here in the next half an hour.'

'Great. Pam would always be my first choice in a situation like this. She knows the drill.'

Jones nodded in the direction of the lounge. 'Is she gonna be okay?'

Phillips glanced back over her shoulder to make sure they couldn't be overheard. 'I hope so. I think the shock is starting to kick in just now.'

'It's to be expected.'

'Let's step outside,' said Phillips before opening the back door that led out into the garden.

Outside, she turned to face Jones, speaking in a low whisper. 'Kept her on a pretty tight leash, didn't he?'

'You're not kidding,' Jones whispered back. 'And lied to her by all accounts. Since when has Alerton Hall been an all-male club?'

'Yeah, exactly. Makes you wonder what else he was keeping from her.'

'Whatever he was up to, he sounds like a total shit. I mean, what kind of man stops his wife from seeing her friends because he doesn't like them?'

'A very controlling one,' said Phillips. 'The way she described their relationship in there sounded borderline abusive. As if he was gaslighting her.'

'Totally. Something's definitely not right with this picture, guv.'

'I agree.' She pulled out her phone.

'Who are you calling?'

'Carter. I'm sure he'll appreciate the heads-up on Todd. While I'm doing that, can you brief Bov and Whistler? 'We're gonna need an early start in the morning.'

Jones nodded, then stepped away.

As she waited for the call to connect, Phillips looked back at the house. Jones was right: first a dead judge and now a retired chief constable, both strangled. Something definitely wasn't right here. What that was, she had absolutely no idea, but she was sure of one thing – however long it took, she would find out.

16

The team, including Chief Superintendent Carter, gathered in MCU's conference room at 7:00 the following morning. Carter had provided pastries and coffees as a bit of a morale booster.

When everyone had gathered their breakfast and preferred hot drink, Phillips began. 'So, as you guys know, Jonesy and I attended what looks like a second strangulation late last night, at Alerton Hall golf club. The victim was Jack Todd – formerly Chief Constable Todd – of the Greater Manchester Police. Retired almost fifteen years now. It appears as though he was attacked and strangled whilst taking a shower after playing golf.'

'The killer took a big risk,' said Bovalino. 'I mean, killing him in a public place. Someone could have walked in at any time.'

'True, but he mitigated the risk. The showers at Alerton Hall are single, self-contained units, with full-height doors, thick tiled walls and very private. In all honesty, the killer could have carved him up in there, and no one would have heard a thing.'

'Yeah,' agreed Phillips. 'Based on where the murder took place, this looks well planned and well executed – if you'll pardon the pun.'

Carter took a sip of coffee. 'How did his wife take the news?'

'As expected, she was shocked,' replied Phillips. 'Especially when we explained his death was suspicious.'

'I felt quite sorry for her,' Jones added. 'Not just because Todd was dead, but because she'd been forced to put up with him for so long. By the sounds of it, I think the killer may have done her a favour.'

Carter frowned. 'How do you mean?'

'It was the way she described him and how he treated her, very controlling, sir.'

'Wouldn't entertain having kids,' pointed out Phillips. 'And made her give up her friends when he retired, because he didn't get on with them. Fifteen years without seeing her friends, alone in that big house, running after him.'

'For some reason, he also lied to her about Alerton Hall being a men-only club,' Jones added.

'Why would he do that?' asked Carter.

'No idea,' replied Phillips, 'But it makes you wonder what else he's been lying to her about.'

Jones cut back in, 'The way she described him, he sounds like a gaslighting misogynist, and she's better off without him, in my opinion.'

Carter cleared his throat. 'I can understand how you feel, Jonesy, but given Jack Todd's history within the GMP, I'd prefer those kinds of remarks were not shared outside of this team.'

'Of course,' replied Jones. 'Sorry, sir.'

Phillips cut back in, 'Evans reckons the bruising on Todd's neck is almost identical to that found on Venables, and he collected fibres from his neck. They're being tested as we speak, but he believes they're very similar to the fibres found on Venables.'

'So horsehair?' asked Entwistle.

Phillips nodded. 'Highly likely.'

'Two victims connected to the law, both strangled with horsehair? That can't be coincidence, surely?' said Entwistle.

Phillips locked eyes with him. 'Whistler, what do I always say when it comes to coincidences?'

'They don't exist in Major Crimes, guv,' he replied sheepishly.

'Exactly. Which makes me think our killer is using it to send some kind of message. What that message is, however, is unclear.'

'So are we definitely thinking it's the same guy for both?' asked Carter.

'Until we can prove otherwise, I think we have to, sir,' Phillips said. 'The similarities are too great for it not to be.'

'I have to agree, sir,' Jones added.

Phillips turned to Bovalino. 'I want you to head out to the club as soon as we're finished here. They have CCTV footage, but we couldn't access it last night. Apparently the general manager, a David Eccles, is returning from his holiday today. He should be able to sort out copies of the tapes for you.'

The big man nodded.

Phillips continued, 'And we also need to know who Todd played his round with yesterday.'

'Did his wife not know?' asked Carter.

Jones chuckled. 'No. He not only lied to her about the Alerton Hall being men-only, but apparently the club and everything that happened in it was off-limits to Gillian as well. That's what I mean about him being so controlling; buggering off for hours on end and she's no idea what he's doing or who he's doing it with.'

Phillips cut back in, 'The golf pro will have all the bookings on his system. And when you're done with him and the general manager, ask around any members or staff you come across. See if anyone noticed anything different or strange yesterday.'

'Will do,' said Bovalino.

Phillips turned her attention back to Entwistle. 'I want digital forensics to go through Todd's phone as a priority.'

Entwistle made a note in his pad. 'I'll get straight onto them.'

'And I think it's worth doing some background checks on Todd,' added Phillips. 'Yes, he was a senior copper for a very long time, but it can't hurt to do some careful digging.'

'Of course,' said Entwistle.

'Any updates on the horsehair stockists?' asked Phillips. 'Any in Manchester?'

Entwistle shook his head. 'No, guv. There are only two places to buy legal wigs in the UK, and both are in London. Stanwick and Lee on Fleet Street, and Ellis and Ravensworth on Chancery Lane.'

'We're going to need samples from each of them.'

'I'll speak to them as soon as they open this morning.'

'Good,' said Phillips.

'Oh, and I got a call from my mate in the probation service last night. She's certain there's never been a case of a tag being tampered with or removed, certainly not in the last five years. The new technology is supposedly bulletproof.'

'Which means O'Hare and Abdeel are off the hook,' said Jones.

'Looks that way,' Phillips said.

'Shame.' Jones folded his arms across his chest. 'I was looking forward to wiping that smug grin off O'Hare's face.'

Phillips drained her coffee. 'He'll keep. Right now, you and I need to pay a visit to Nic Johnson. See if she can give us any insight on Venables.'

'Ready when you are,' said Jones.

'Anything else from anyone before we go?'

Each of the men shook his head.

'In that case, let's get cracking.' Phillips stood, and the rest followed suit.

'Do you have a minute, Jane?' asked Carter.

'Sure.' Phillips waited until Jones, Bovalino, and Entwistle had filed out of the room. 'Is everything okay, sir?'

Carter folded his arms across his chest, his brow furrowed. 'I wanted to talk to you about my call with Fox last night.'

Phillips's heart sank. She'd been so busy this morning she'd managed to forget about Fox. 'Let me guess, she wasn't happy.'

Carter winced. 'That's one way to put it.'

'So what did she actually say?'

'That we need to get our collective fingers out and find whoever is doing this.'

'Which is exactly what we're doing, sir.'

'And that a dead judge and a dead copper could be the death of her as chief constable.'

'We should be so lucky,' Phillips shot back.

Carter ignored the remark. 'She wants a meeting with you, me and Dudley this morning.'

Phillips exhaled sharply. 'What the hell for?'

'To sort out PR and how we manage the message around Todd's death.'

Phillips threw her arms in the air. 'Seriously? In one breath she's telling me to get my finger out, and in the next she's dragging me into a pointless meeting about PR. How am I expected to catch this guy if I'm stuck in meetings all day? I'm supposed to be heading out with Jonesy now to see Nic Johnson.'

Carter stared at her in silence.

Phillips raised her arms in defence. 'I'm sorry, sir. It's just so frustrating at times.'

'I get it, Jane. I really do. But there's no getting out of it.'

Phillips said nothing for a moment, then nodded, saying, 'Understood.'

'There is one more thing,' added Carter. 'Fox is actually on leave today, so the meeting will be off-site.'

Phillips frowned. 'Really, where?'

'Fox's house.'

Phillips burst out laughing, assuming Carter was making a joke, but his deadpan expression suggested otherwise. 'Are you serious?'

'Yes, I am.'

'Oh, wow. I'm not sure how I feel about that,' Phillips replied.

'Can't say I feel massively comfortable with the idea either, but she's the boss.' Carter headed for the door, then turned back as he opened it. 'I can drive us over there, and when we're done, I can drop you in town so you and Jones can still do your visit with Nic Johnson.'

'As long as it's not taking you out of your way, sir.'

'Not at all.' Carter checked his watch. 'So, see you in reception in ten?'

'Of course. I'll update the team and head down.'

'Good stuff.' Carter smiled, then walked out.

17

Fox's house was located in the Cheshire village of Prestbury, an affluent area of South Manchester. The drive up to the house was over fifty yards long and resembled a private road with trees and thick hedges lining both sides of the narrow track. The house itself had been rendered with white paint and appeared to have been constructed in the 1930s or '40s, consisting of two wings built at thirty-degree angles.

'Oh, how the other half live,' mumbled Phillips as they pulled up outside the front door.

Carter made no comment as he killed the engine, and Rupert Dudley seemed so intimidated by being summoned to Fox's private residence that he had lost all power of speech.

A minute later, Phillips and Dudley stood behind Carter as he rang the large, art-deco doorbell.

As they waited for a response, Phillips took in the palatial home and wondered what the monthly mortgage payments must be on a home like this. She knew Fox had been living here for almost thirty years, but the place had to be worth well over a million pounds in today's money.

Just then one side of the large double front door opened, and Fox stared out. She looked almost unrecognisable in her civilian clothes of blue jeans and a white flannel cotton shirt.

'Good morning, ma'am,' said Carter.

'You'd better come in,' she replied without feeling.

Carter stepped in first, with Phillips and Dudley tucked in behind, as Fox led them towards the rear of the property into the sprawling open-plan kitchen with views over the mature garden beyond. Taking up a position next to the island in the middle of the room, she turned to face them, the three of them standing side by side.

'So let's hear it.' Fox folded her arms across her chest. 'Another high-profile murder. What on earth is going on, DCI Phillips?'

'Well, ma'am—'

It seemed Fox was in no mood to wait for answers. 'Do any of you realise what kind of position this puts us in with the media? Not to mention the PCC.'

Phillips clenched her toes in her boots as she attempted to keep the disdain she felt for Fox from her face.

Carter did his best to placate her. 'I think we're all acutely aware of the profile of both cases, ma'am.'

Fox continued unabated. 'This latest death could drag up a whole lot of history for the force that we really don't need, so we must tread carefully.'

'In what way, ma'am?' Carter asked.

'Look, it's no secret that Jack Todd retired under a bit of a cloud, which badly damaged the force's reputation at the time. Since then, it's taken a lot of hard work and effort to regain the public's trust. Trust that we can ill afford to lose right now with Venables's death causing so many waves for us.'

Carter shifted in his seat. 'Forgive me, ma'am, but what

exactly happened with Todd? Obviously, I wasn't in Manchester during his tenure.'

Fox ran her fingers through her bright blonde hair. 'I'd rather not go over old ground, but in short, he was found to have massaged some of his crime figures in order to hit his KPIs over a number of years. The press got hold of it, and he was quickly pensioned off. All a bit over the top, if you ask me.'

'I'm sorry, ma'am, but it was a little bit more than just massaging his KPIs.' Phillips hit back. 'Todd was the one behind the directive that stopped us from reporting domestic violence incidents.'

'Can you expand a little?' asked Carter.

'Because of Todd, officers were told to let couples sort out their domestic issues themselves,' replied Phillips. 'Thanks to his directive, the number of hate crimes against women went through the roof. One woman was murdered by her boyfriend, a man who should have been arrested for the five previous assaults he had committed against her.'

'I'll admit that was unfortunate, and the press had a field day with it at the time,' said Fox, 'but it was an isolated incident, and it's in the past. Right now, all our energy needs to be focused on the present. The last thing we need is to be raking over old coals, Chief Inspector.'

'I'm sorry, ma'am, but that woman's death is on us.'

'Which is exactly my point, Jane. If we go dragging up the past, we'll only serve to remind the public of darker days that once existed within the force. Days that are thankfully behind us now.'

Phillips could feel her jaw clenching in frustration. She was ready for the fight, but she knew she wouldn't win, especially not in these surroundings. Plus, the longer this conversation continued, the longer she would be away from the front line. She decided to bite her tongue.

Fox continued, 'So, your brief is clear; tread very carefully around Todd and his time in the job, no matter how chequered you think it might be.'

It took all of Phillips's strength to say nothing and nod her agreement.

Fox smiled widely, but her eyes remained dark. 'Good. I'm glad we understand each other.' She turned her attention to Dudley now. 'So, what are the plans for going public on Todd's death?'

Dudley stood to attention and opened the leather portfolio in his hands. 'Right. Okay, we'll be releasing a statement this morning saying a man was found dead at Alerton Hall golf course last night. At this stage we will not name the victim as Todd.'

'I see,' said Fox.

Dudley continued, 'I understand from Chief Inspector Phillips that his wife will be ID'ing his body later today.'

Phillips nodded. 'We have a FLO, Sergeant Clement, making the arrangements this morning, ma'am.'

'Once that happens,' said Dudley, 'someone will need to speak to the press, as we did with Venables, releasing Todd's name.'

Fox locked eyes with Phillips.

'I'll do that, ma'am,' Carter cut in. 'I think the chief inspector's time will be best served furthering the investigation as opposed to talking to a few hacks.'

'Agreed,' said Fox flatly.

Phillips's relief was palpable.

'Right, unless there's anything else?'

'Nothing, ma'am,' replied Carter.

Phillips shook her head.

'I have everything I need,' added Dudley.

'Good,' said Fox crisply, dismissing them. 'In that case, get to work.'

18

The offices of Johnson Law were located in Spinningfields, an über-trendy section of Manchester city centre that in recent years had undergone a total regeneration and was now home to bars, restaurants, and large glass-fronted offices with tenants ranging from TV production companies and media agencies to accountants, lawyers, and architects. The area was well known as one of *the* places to be seen in the city.

Johnson Law occupied the top floor of number one Hardman Square, and as Phillips and Jones stepped out of the glass elevator, they were surrounded by a sea of smoked glass and brushed-metal fixtures and fittings. The place oozed money, and knowing how much Nic Johnson charged per hour, Phillips thought it was a fitting tribute to those fees. She wondered if Nic's clients ever felt ripped off because of its opulence or reassured by its obvious cost.

'We'd like to speak to Nic Johnson, urgently,' said Phillips as she approached the smiling receptionist and presented her ID.

The receptionist's smile slipped slightly. 'I'll just see if I can locate her.'

Phillips and Jones stood in silence as the receptionist picked up the handset and dialled.

A second later, the call connected. 'Hi, Ian, it's Chloe. I have the police here, and they need to speak to Ms Johnson. They say it's urgent.' She nodded into the phone for a few seconds. 'Okay, I'll let them know.'

Phillips locked eyes with her. 'Is she on her way?'

'Er, it looks like she's in a meeting. One of her clerks, Ian, is coming through. He shouldn't be long.'

A few minutes later, a man Phillips placed in his mid-thirties, with a long body and close-cropped red hair, walked through the double doors into reception, smiling.

'Ian,' said the man, offering his hand. 'I'm sure Chloe has already explained, but I'm one of Ms Johnson's clerks.'

Phillips shook his hand first, then Jones.

'I'm sorry, but I'm afraid Ms Johnson is in a meeting at the moment,' he said. 'Can I help with anything?'

Phillips did her best to hide her frustration. 'As we're investigating the murder of Judge Venables, I'm sure she can be interrupted.'

Ian's smile never faltered. 'She really can't be disturbed. She's about to go to trial tomorrow and locked in a planning meeting with her KCs.'

Phillips held his gaze.

'I'm happy to check and see if she has any availability later today if you'd like to come back?'

Phillips nodded. 'I guess that will have to do.'

Ian began scanning through his iPhone. 'She has half an hour at twelve thirty, if that's any good?'

Phillips checked her watch. That was an hour and a half away. Resisting the urge to pull rank and demand to see Johnson as a point of law, she opted for the pragmatic approach, knowing it would be her best chance of getting anything useful from their eventual meeting. 'That's fine. We'll come back,' she said, then turned to Jones. 'Let's go get a coffee.'

Jones nodded and followed her out.

A few minutes later they found themselves stood outside in the sunshine, looking back at the building.

'You acquiesced surprisingly quickly in there,' said Jones.

'Took all my strength to not grab him by the collar and force him to take me through to her, but the heavy-handed approach never works with someone like Johnson. She's under no obligation to give us anything of value – and heaven knows we've rarely been on the same side in the past – so I'm hoping by us playing the game, she'll play ball.'

'Smart move,' said Jones.

'Maybe,' Phillips replied. 'Still pissed we have to wait around, though.'

'Come on, let's get that coffee. My treat.'

'Wow. I'm honoured.'

'You never know, I might even stretch to a brownie.'

Phillips recoiled playfully, then pretended to touch the back of her hand against his forehead. 'Are you feeling all right?'

'Very funny,' said Jones.

'Has Sarah met this new philanthropic version of her husband?'

Jones chuckled. 'Ssh. No. And don't you be telling her either. Otherwise she'll be wanting treats all the time.'

Phillips patted him on the back. 'Don't worry, Jonesy. Your secret's safe with me.'

At exactly 12:30 pm, Phillips and Jones walked back into the reception of Johnson Law.

Right on cue, Ian, Johnson's clerk who'd arranged the meeting, appeared through the double doors, which he held open. 'If you'd like to follow me.'

Phillips obliged, with Jones close behind her, and a minute later, Ian ushered them into Johnson's office.

She was on the phone, sitting behind her large smoked-glass desk. She glanced up at her guests. 'Look, I've got to go; someone's just come in. I'll call you back later on, okay?' With that, she replaced the receiver and gestured to the two chairs opposite. 'Please sit down.'

Phillips and Jones took their seats.

Johnson glanced at the large gold Rolex watch on her left wrist. 'I don't have long, I'm afraid. We're going to trial tomorrow, and we have a lot to do to be ready.'

'We understand, and we'll do our best to be quick,' replied Phillips.

Jones took out his notepad.

'So how can I help Major Crimes today?' Johnson reclined in her large leather chair.

Phillips tucked her hair behind her ear. 'We were hoping you could give us some background on Lord Justice Venables.'

'Sir Walter?'

'Yes. We're investigating his death.'

Johnson nodded. 'Yeah, I saw you on the news the other night. You came across well, as it happens.'

Phillips chose to ignore the comment. 'We understand you used to work for him back in the day.'

'For my sins, but that was a long time ago now, back in the CPS.'

'What can you tell us about him?' asked Jones.

'Which version would you like?' Johnson had a glint in

her eye. 'The political-career-enhancing answer, or the truth?'

'Do you really need to ask?'

'Okay.' Johnson screwed her nose up. 'He was an awful man. A total misogynist and a letch. Always making lewd remarks to the females in the chambers, and he absolutely reeked of stale booze and cigars. I remember his disgusting yellow teeth and pungent breath.'

'Sounds delightful,' said Phillips.

'He was also a massive racist and bigot. I hated working for him. In fact, working with him turned me onto private law. I couldn't stand the thought of being stuck with him and his cronies in the Crown Prosecution Service for the rest of my days, so I jumped ship as soon as I could.'

'Did you ever hear of him prejudicing juries when he was on the bench?' Phillips asked.

Johnson answered without pause. 'He did it all the time.'

'But how?' said Jones. 'Surely any one of the defence barristers could have pulled him on it?'

'Some of the stronger and more experienced ones did from time to time,' Johnson replied. 'And he would stop doing it for a while, but it never took very long to start again. If someone went up in front of him whom he didn't like – usually based on the colour of their skin or their social class – he would do everything he could to influence the jury into finding them guilty, and if the barrister wasn't strong enough to stand up to him, he'd usually get what he wanted.'

'That's so wrong,' said Phillips. 'The whole point of a judge is to be impartial.'

'Pah,' Johnson scoffed. 'Venables couldn't even *spell* the word. Then to make matters worse, once he had the guilty verdict, he'd usually dish out the heaviest sentence available.'

'Yeah,' said Phillips. 'We've been looking at some of his old cases. He really did go hard on the sentencing, didn't he?'

'Yeah, but it eventually caught up with him.'

Phillips tilted her head to the side. 'How do you mean?'

Johnson sat forward. 'I'm not sure if this is true, but the rumour around town at the time was that Venables chose to retire rather than being pushed. Apparently a couple of his cases were overturned on appeal, and when the Ministry of Justice looked a little closer at his records, they were worried about how many other rulings could end up going the same way. So they offered him the chance to step down with a full, final-salary pension and his reputation intact. Get him out of the way.'

'So he manipulates the system for years and finally gets caught,' replied Jones. 'But rather than hold him to account, the MOJ gives him a payoff and sends him on his way.'

'I'm afraid that's just how the world works, DI Jones,' said Johnson, shrugging. 'As my dad used to say when he was practicing, never expect the law to be fair or just. Guilty people walk free every day.'

'With a little help from people like yourself,' Jones shot back.

Johnson smiled thinly. 'Everyone is entitled to a defence, Inspector.'

Sensing the tension building, Phillips cut back in before Jones could respond. 'Were there any other rumours circulating about him?'

Johnson pursed her lips for a long moment before responding. 'Again, I can't say for sure whether it's true or not, but it was widely reported that he was a regular at the Purple Door in Whalley Range.'

'The brothel?' asked Phillips.

'I think the official description they use is' – Johnson made air quotes with her fingers – '"massage parlour". But yes, that's the one. He was in there every week, by all accounts.'

Phillips shook her head. 'A Crown Court judge openly using prostitutes.'

'It was another reason I couldn't stand him; he was a total hypocrite. The number of times I heard him preach in court about the importance of good moral fibre, as he called it, and all the time he was paying for sex and discriminating against the poor and people of colour.' Johnson shuddered. 'He was a vile creature, and the world's a better place without him, in my opinion.'

'It would seem a lot of people feel that way,' said Phillips.

Johnson glanced at her watch again. 'Look, I'm really sorry, but I need to get back to my trial planning. Is there anything else I can assist you with, quickly?'

'No. You've been very helpful.' Phillips stood, and the other two did as well. Phillips offered her hand. 'Thanks, Nic. We appreciate your time.'

Johnson shook her hand and then Jones's as well.

'My pleasure," Johnson said. "It's nice to be on the same side for once.'

'Quite,' Phillips replied. 'We'll see ourselves out.'

Back in the lift a few minutes later, Phillips turned to Jones. 'I've never been a big believer in karma, but the more I hear about Venables, the more I think he had it coming.'

Jones nodded.

The lift came to a stop, and the doors opened.

'So what next?' Jones asked as they stepped out.

Phillips checked her watch. It was approaching one o'clock. 'They should be open by now. Fancy a massage at the Purple Door?'

Jones cackled. 'Can I claim it on expenses?'

'We'll have to see if they do receipts.' Phillips cracked a wry grin. 'Somehow, I doubt it.'

19

The Purple Door looked like any other Victorian townhouse in Manchester. Tucked down a residential road in Whalley Range, just off the main drag of Princess Parkway, passersby could be forgiven for thinking the residents were out of town. With blinds and shutters covering all the exterior windows, there were absolutely no visible clues alluding to the activity taking place inside on a daily basis.

With Jones at her side, Phillips stepped up to the front door and pressed the intercom.

A second later a woman's voice crackled through the speaker fixed to the wall next to the door. *'Hello? How can I help?'*

Phillips lifted her badge up to the small camera mounted within the intercom. 'Police. We'd like to speak to the manager.'

There was silence for a few seconds before a buzzer sounded.

'Push the door.'

With an audible click, the door popped ajar, and Phillips pushed it open.

Inside, they were greeted by a long, narrow corridor with purple velvet wallpaper running down both walls above a thick white shag-pile carpet. 'Charming,' said Phillips, her voice brimming with sarcasm.

Making their way along the corridor, they were soon standing in front of a tall, old-school curved reception desk. Behind it sat a professional-looking receptionist. She was pretty with dark black hair cut into a severe bob with a razor-straight fringe millimetres from her eyes. The gold badge on her chest indicated her name was Dee-Dee and that her star sign was Capricorn. 'Welcome to the Purple Door massage parlour. How can I help today?'

'I'm DCI Phillips, and this is DI Jones from the Major Crimes Unit. We'd like to talk to the manager about one of your regulars.'

Dee-Dee smiled, but her eyes remained cold. 'I'm afraid all our clients insist on anonymity. This is a *very* private establishment.'

'I'm sure it is,' Phillips shot back. 'But this client is dead, so I don't think he'll mind too much.'

The smile evaporated as the receptionist picked up a phone on the desk. It appeared to ring a couple of times at the other end before being answered. 'Claudine, it's Dee-Dee. I have two police detectives in reception who say they need to talk to you.' There was a pause. 'Okay, thank you.' She replaced the handset. 'Claudine is on her way down.'

Phillips nodded. 'Thank you.'

A couple of minutes later, the door behind reception opened, and a tall woman with short, cropped platinum hair stepped through. She wore a black pencil skirt that matched her black silk blouse and moved with the grace of a catwalk model as she walked towards them. She offered her hand. 'Claudine Faber. What can I do for you?'

Phillips shook her hand. 'DCI Phillips and DI Jones, from the Major Crimes Unit. Is there somewhere we can talk privately?'

Faber nodded. 'Please follow me.'

A few minutes later Phillips and Jones stepped into what appeared to be an executive lounge, replete with a selection of white Chesterfield armchairs that surrounded a glass coffee table in the middle of the room. Positioned near the far wall was a drinks caddie with various bottles of spirits.

Phillips noted the small CCTV camera positioned in the ceiling in the corner of the room. Glancing at Jones, she nodded towards it.

Following her gaze, he spotted it and nodded back.

'Please take a seat,' said Faber before dropping into one of the armchairs.

They took seats beside each other.

'What can you tell us about Sir Walter Venables?' asked Phillips.

Faber's brow furrowed. 'Walter? Is this about him being found dead? I saw it on the news the other day. Came as quite a shock.'

'We understand he was a regular here.'

'Yes, in fact he was here on Monday night, just gone.'

Phillips sat forward. 'And who did he visit with on Monday?'

'Daisy. Same as always.'

'We'll need to speak to her,' said Phillips.

'Er, okay, let me see if she's in.' Faber checked her watch. 'She starts at two, so she should be here by now. If you can give me a minute, I'll go and see if I can find her.'

'Sure,' Phillips replied.

Mindful of the camera above their heads, they sat in

silence while they waited for the next five minutes before the door opened again and Faber returned. A young blonde woman seemingly barely out of her teens with her hair pulled tightly into a ponytail followed her in. She was wearing a velvet cream tracksuit and tan Ugg boots.

'This is Daisy,' said Faber.

Phillips stood momentarily and offered her hand. 'Hi, Daisy. We just need to ask you a few questions about Walter Venables, if that's okay?'

Daisy frowned. 'Am I in trouble?'

'Not at all. Please have a seat.' Phillips sat back down.

Daisy followed suit.

Phillips turned her attention to Faber. 'Would you mind if we speak to Daisy alone?'

Faber recoiled slightly and appeared somewhat affronted. 'Sure. I'll be in my office if you need anything.'

Phillips waited for Faber to leave, then focused back on Daisy. 'We understand Walter Venables was a regular client of yours.'

Daisy's eyes darted between Phillips and Jones.

'We know what goes on here, Daisy,' said Jones softly. 'Rest assured it's of zero interest to our investigation, so you can speak freely.'

'That's exactly right,' added Phillips. 'You've got nothing to worry about. We just need you to answer a few questions.'

Daisy visibly relaxed as her shoulders sagged slightly.

Phillips continued, 'Did you know Sir Walter is dead?'

Daisy nodded. 'Claudine told me the other day. Said he'd been found dead at home.'

'That's right,' said Phillips.

'Do you know what happened to him?' asked Daisy.

'All we can say at the moment,' Phillips replied. 'is that we're investigating his death.'

Jones cut in now. 'We wondered if he'd ever mentioned

anything to you that might help us. You know, did he seem worried at all? Had anyone threatened him lately?'

'Not that he told me.'

Phillips took the lead once more. 'Did he ever talk about his private life with you?'

'A few things but not much, really. He did mention a couple of times that his wife didn't understand him and that she couldn't satisfy his needs, but then they *all* say that.'

'They?' said Phillips.

'The punters,' Daisy replied. 'It's always the wives' fault that they're here and having to pay for sex.'

'Did he ever mention having any enemies?' asked Jones.

'No, but he was an ex-judge, wasn't he? Plus he could be a nasty piece of work when he wanted to be. I'm sure loads of people had it in for him.'

'I think you're probably right,' replied Phillips. 'By all accounts, he certainly wasn't popular.'

Daisy nodded. 'I never liked him.'

Phillips sat forward in the chair. 'Why was that?'

'Because he was a total arsehole,' said Daisy firmly.

'In what way?'

Daisy took a moment before answering. 'He was a horrible man who liked to degrade me – got off on swearing at me, calling me a bitch and a whore. A lot of the times he'd slap me about or half choke me when he was on top. Pulled my hair really hard and slapped my backside when he was behind me.'

'That can't have been nice for you,' said Phillips, realising as she did that the words weren't adequate.

'I hated it, but I charged him double, so I put up with him for an hour a week. It paid my rent, so I just thought of that when I was with him. You learn to zone out in this job.'

'I'm sure,' said Phillips. 'Did he come at the same time each week?'

'Yep. Nine on Monday evenings. Always drunk as a skunk and stinking of cigars. Made me want to be sick.' She twisted her face in disgust.

'Makes you wonder where his wife thought he was when he was here,' said Jones offhandedly.

'Oh, she knew all about him coming here,' Daisy replied.

Phillips raised her eyebrows. This was a surprise. 'Really?'

Daisy nodded. 'Used to pick him up when he was finished. I'd see her each week, sitting out there in the car, waiting for him.'

'Are you sure about that?' asked Jones.

'One hundred percent. I asked him about it once, and he said that they had an *arrangement,* as he called it. She had her life, and he had his. As long as she got her monthly allowance and he kept it discreet, she didn't care what he did. Slept in separate beds too, by all accounts.'

'He told you that, did he?' asked Jones.

'Yeah. Regularly. He would pretty much tell me the same bullshit stories every week. "My wife doesn't understand me; she's a mean old bitch; she's frigid and hasn't put out for years." That kind of stuff. Like I said, he was a nasty piece of work.'

'Did he ever talk to you about his time as a judge?' Phillips said.

Daisy seemed relaxed now. 'Sometimes.'

'What did he say?'

Daisy shrugged. 'Nothing specific, just that he had been a very powerful man, and he was pissed off they made him retire. Said the raving lefties had pushed him out.'

'Did he say why he was pushed out?' asked Phillips.

'No. Like I say, he never went into detail on anything. Just used to ramble on about it while we were having sex.' Daisy shuddered. 'He made my skin crawl.'

Phillips took a moment to digest the information before

focusing on Daisy again. 'Is there anything else you can tell us about him that might be helpful? Any other thing he used to ramble on about perhaps?'

Daisy paused, then finally shook her head. 'Nothing that I can think of. Like I said before, I'd learnt to zone out. My body was here with him, but my mind was always somewhere else.'

'Okay. We appreciate your talking to us.' Phillips pulled a business card from her jacket pocket and handed it across. 'If anything does come back to you, my number's on there.'

Daisy glanced down at the card. 'Thanks.'

Phillips turned to Jones, signalling that it was time to leave, and they stood up from the chairs in tandem. Daisy stood now too.

'You've been very helpful, thank you,' said Phillips, nodding at her.

Daisy glanced between them both. 'I know this is an awful thing to say, but I'm glad he's not around and I won't have to see him anymore.'

Phillips smiled softly. 'Look after yourself, Daisy, and be safe. Okay?'

Daisy nodded as her eyes glistened with emotion.

'We'll see ourselves out,' added Phillips as they headed for the door.

20

After leaving the Purple Door, Phillips and Jones agreed it was time to talk to Lady Venables to get a clearer picture of who her husband really was, and how much she knew about him. So far, everything pointed to a man whom very few people had liked or respected.

As Jones pulled the car to the kerb outside the Venableses' home, Phillips's phone beeped, indicating a text had arrived. Pulling it from her pocket, she took a moment to read the message.

'Everything all right, guv?' asked Jones.

'Yeah,' said Phillips. 'It's from Carter. Letting me know he's just made the announcement to the press about Todd's death.'

Jones switched off the engine. 'First a Crown Court judge, and now a former chief constable; the press is gonna have a field day.'

Phillips nodded gravely. 'Aren't they just?'

'Can't wait to see what Townsend comes up with next.' Jones's tone was sarcastic.

'God, don't. Fox will go postal if he writes another piece like last time.'

'Which he probably will, the slimy bastard.'

Phillips closed the message and returned her phone to her pocket before grabbing the door handle. 'Time to find out what Lady Venables has to say about her husband's secret life.'

As they reached the large front door, Jones rapped his knuckles against it.

A minute later the door opened, and Lady Venables peered out, her eyes narrow. 'What do *you* want?'

'We need to ask you a few more questions about your late husband,' said Phillips.

'It's not convenient right now. I'm rather busy.'

'It won't take long, and this way we won't have to take you back to the station to talk.' Phillips's tone was polite, but the threat was clear.

Lady Venables tried hard to hide her disdain, but it was evident for them to see on her twisted face. 'If you must.' She opened the door wide and walked back down the hallway towards the kitchen at the rear of the house.

'Quite the welcome,' whispered Jones before stepping inside.

By the time they caught up with Lady Venables, she was perched on a high stool at the breakfast bar in the kitchen. She held a copy of the *Daily Mail* in her hands, which she folded and placed to one side. 'Can we make this quick, please?'

'Of course,' said Phillips. 'We're sorry to have to bring up such a delicate matter, but we're trying to get a better understanding of who your husband really was.'

Venables folded her arms across her chest. 'What delicate matter?' Her voice was like ice.

Phillips paused before answering. 'We understand Sir

Walter was a regular customer at the Purple Door massage parlour.'

Lady Venables flinched. 'Don't be ridiculous.'

'I'm afraid we have it on good authority that he was,' Phillips countered.

Lady Venables seemed incredulous. 'He wouldn't go to a seedy place like that. He was a Crown Court judge, for God's sake!'

'Yes, he was,' replied Phillips flatly. 'Which is why it's vital we know the whole truth about his life *and* his character. If he's not who he purported to be, then that could go some way to explaining who, and why, someone might have wanted him dead.'

Lady Venables remained stoic as she stared back at them both.

Phillips continued, 'To be clear, Lady Venables, we have witnesses who will testify to the fact your husband visited the Purple Door once a week, every week at nine every Monday evening.'

'I don't have to put up with these slanderous accusations.' She grabbed her phone from the side. 'I'm calling my lawyer.'

Phillips exhaled heavily through her nose. She had little patience for this pantomime. 'The same witnesses also identified you picking him up in the car after each of his visits.'

Lady Venables swallowed a lump in her throat, glancing down at her phone for a long moment before slowly placing it back on the bench.

'We know this can't be easy for you,' Phillips continued, 'but it's time to stop pretending and tell us the truth.'

Lady Venables closed her eyes before dropping her chin to her chest. Eventually she lifted her head and locked eyes with Phillips. 'If I tell you, will it stay between us?'

'Look, I can't make any promises. If anything has a bearing on the investigation, we may need to share it with the relevant people, but you can rest assured we'll be as discreet as the law will allow.'

Lady Venables took a deep breath, then nodded as she exhaled. 'It's true. He did go to that place.'

'And were you aware of what was really going on inside?' asked Phillips.

'I'm not an idiot, Chief Inspector,' she snapped back. 'Even though he treated me like I was. I could smell the women on him. It was so humiliating.'

Jones cut in now. 'I'm sorry, but I don't understand. If you were *so* against him going to the Purple Door, then why did you act as his driver every week?'

'To make sure he was discreet about it.' Venables folded her arms across her chest. 'Walter was a fantasist. He was convinced he was all powerful and that he could do what he liked, and no one could hurt him. It was a hangover from his days on the bench when he was pretty much untouchable. But life's not like that anymore. These days every man and his dog have a camera on their phone. All it needed was for one picture to make it in the papers and he'd have been ruined, *as would I*. Can you imagine the headlines? A Crown Court judge using prostitutes on a weekly basis? The shame would've been unbearable.'

'So you were there to help him stay hidden?' asked Phillips.

'Yes,' said Lady Venables. 'I'm not proud of it, but over the years I've built a good life for myself in this community. I have standing and respect, and I wasn't going to let Walter destroy all of that just because he couldn't control his sexual urges.'

Phillips took a moment before continuing, 'The girl he saw at the Purple Door said he was fond of degrading her when they were together, verbally and sometimes physically. Does that sound like your husband?'

Lady Venables remained silent for a moment before answering, 'Yes, it does.'

'Again, I know this is difficult, but it helps us understand who he really was. Did he ever behave like that with you?'

'Once.' Lady Venables closed her eyes briefly. 'Some time ago when we shared a bed. He got a bit rough one night when we were being intimate and started using foul language. I was so shocked I slapped him across the face and locked myself in the bathroom. When I eventually came out, I fully expected him to show some remorse, but he was completely unapologetic. Said it was just a bit of fun, and I had taken things too seriously. I was furious, and I made it very clear I wasn't going to put up with being treated or spoken to like that. It was disgusting and no way to speak to a woman, let alone your wife. He didn't like that, of course, and it wasn't long after that incident that he confessed that he regularly used prostitutes and that he'd been doing so for most of our marriage.'

'Wow. That must have come as a shock,' said Phillips.

'He broke my heart that day.' Lady Venables sighed. 'Our marriage was finished after that, and we became like strangers living under the same roof.'

'I hope you don't mind me asking,' said Jones, 'but why not just divorce him?'

'And do what? Start again at my age? No, it was easier to come to an agreement that suited us both. He didn't need a divorce in his life and neither did I. So we continued living together but pretty much separate lives.'

'I see,' said Phillips.

'In all honesty, now he's gone and those visits to that wretched place have finally stopped, it's something of a relief.' She bit her top lip. 'Sorry, that's not what the grieving widow is supposed to say, is it?'

Phillips shook her head. 'Given the circumstances, I can understand that's how you might feel.'

Lady Venables produced a weak smile.

Phillips changed to a different line of questioning now. 'Last time we were here – the night we found your husband – you said you couldn't think of anyone specific who might have wanted to hurt him. Has that changed at all?'

'How do you mean?'

'Well,' said Phillips, 'have you had any more thoughts about it? Has anyone perhaps come back to you?'

Venables shook her head. 'No, I'm afraid not. As I said the last time we spoke, he sent a lot of very dangerous people to prison for a very long time. I'm sure any one of them could have wanted him dead.'

'Yes, it's certainly starting to look like that,' replied Phillips.

The room fell silent.

'Are we done here?' Lady Venables asked abruptly.

Phillips glanced at Jones, who nodded, then back at Venables. 'Yes, I think we have everything we need for now.'

'Good.' Venables slipped off the stool. 'In that case, I'll show you out.'

Phillips held up her palm. 'No need. We know the way.'

Outside, Phillip's phone began to vibrate. It was Evans. 'Andy,' she answered, 'any luck with the fibres on Todd's neck?'

'Yeah, that's why I'm calling. I've just this minute got the results back from the lab, and they're a match for those we pulled from Sir Walter's neck.'

'So we're definitely looking at the same killer for both murders.'

'Looks that way, yes.'

'Thanks, Andy,' said Phillips, then ended the call. This was getting interesting.

21

Later that afternoon, the team gathered back in the conference room at Ashton House. As ever, Entwistle's laptop was hooked up to the big screen.

Between them, Phillips and Jones debriefed the guys on the conversations that had taken place with Nic Johnson, the girls at the Purple Door, and Lady Venables.

'He sounds like a prime rat bag,' surmised Bovalino when they were done.

'I think that about sums him up,' said Phillips. 'Nic Johnson even made the comment that he got what was coming to him, karma and all that.'

Entwistle sat forward. 'If revenge for a false conviction or a long sentence *was* the motive for his murder, then we'll be looking at a very long list of suspects. He was a sitting judge for over twenty years.'

Leaning back in the chair, Phillips ran her hands through her hair and blew her lips. 'That's exactly what we were saying in the car on the way back, wasn't it, Jonesy?'

Jones nodded.

The room fell silent before Phillips finally spoke. 'We

could tie ourselves up in knots and lose days of the investigation trying to search all those case files, so I think we should pass that stuff over to the support team and focus our energies on the evidence we have so far.' She turned her attention to Bovalino now. 'Any joy with the CCTV from the golf club?'

The big man passed across the DVD.

Entwistle's face wrinkled as he stared down at the disc in his hand. 'What am I supposed to do with that?'

'Play it,' said Bovalino.

'On *what* exactly? I don't know if you've noticed, big man, but it ain't 1998, and our laptops and PCs don't have DVD drives anymore.'

Bovalino sniffed loudly. 'I'm sure a smart cookie like you can figure something out.'

Entwistle shook his head as he inspected the disc before jumping up from the chair. 'I'll go and speak to the IT guys. They must have something we can use. Back in a minute,' he added as he headed for the door.

Bov turned back to Phillips. 'I checked with the golf pro – and I also spoke to the manager –about who Jack Todd played with the day he died. Turns out he was a bit of a cheat and not very popular with the other members. So much so, the committee threatened to kick him out if he carried on.'

'Ouch.' Phillips sucked her teeth. 'Jack would have *hated* that. He never was one for committees and their cronies.'

Bovalino continued, 'After that incident, he stopped playing in competitions completely and started playing alone. I talked at length to both the manager and the golf pro, and I have to say, neither had anything positive to say about Todd.'

'He sounds a lot like Venables in that respect,' said Jones. 'Everyone we've spoken to thought he was an arsehole, including his wife.'

'You might well be onto something there, you know,' said Phillips.

'What're you thinking?' Jones asked.

'Think about it. Both victims, Venables and Todd, were deeply unpopular men by the sounds of it. Obsessed with controlling all aspects of their lives, including the people closest to them. I mean, the way Venables's wife and Todd's missus described their marriages, they were essentially abusive.'

'So what?' Jones frowned. 'The killer was exacting some form of revenge for that abuse? Rebalancing the scales?'

Phillips shrugged. 'Maybe. And if that is the case, then we're looking for someone who knew the pair well enough to know what they got up to behind closed doors.'

At that moment, Entwistle stepped back into the room carrying a small black box with a thick cable hanging from it. He presented it to the room. 'Glen in IT reckons this should do the trick.' Then he sat down at his laptop and began connecting the two machines. A minute or so passed before the screen on the wall changed and the ubiquitous DVD logo appeared on it. 'Am I a genius or what?'

'A regular Einstein,' muttered Bovalino with a chuckle.

Entwistle ignored the jibe and inserted the disc into the DVD drive. The faint sound of the spinning disc could be heard, and a few seconds later the CCTV footage from the golf club appeared on-screen.

'So what are we looking at, Bov?' asked Phillips.

'I got the manager to pull off various angles from different cameras and edit them together. Whistler, if you press Play, we'll see the man I suspect is the killer.'

Entwistle obliged.

Bovalino narrated the action. 'So you'll see Todd here heading into the bar after his round. A few minutes later, this guy, wearing the black cap and carrying the backpack, follows him in. See how he keeps his face hidden from the cameras.'

'Clearly knows they're there,' said Jones.

'Exactly,' Bov shot back. 'Now annoyingly, there's no cameras in the bar – God only knows why – but as you'll see from the time stamp in the corner of the screen, Todd leaves the bar forty-five minutes later. According to the bar manager, the bar staff remembered serving him his usual order of three whiskies before he headed to get changed. As we can see here, the man in the cap follows him out just a minute later.'

'Hiding his face from the screen again,' noted Phillips.

Bovalino nodded. 'Yeah. Now, this next camera angle picks up Todd as he heads into the locker room, and lo and behold, cap and backpack man follows him in.'

'I'm guessing there's no footage in the locker rooms?' asked Entwistle.

'No, not in this case, but then again, you can understand why they don't.' Bovalino continued, 'Again, looking at the time stamp in the corner of the screen, fifteen minutes have passed by the time the cap and backpack man comes back out of the locker room, with his face once again covered from view.'

'Fifteen minutes is easily enough time to sneak into the shower and strangle Todd,' Phillips said.

'This guy has to be our killer, surely,' added Jones.

'I'm certain of it.' Bovalino pointed at the screen with his pen. 'This final footage confirms it for me. It's taken from a camera in the car park. As we can see, cap and backpack guy leaves by the main entrance, but rather than heading for a car or walking to the main road, he turns and heads across the course and disappears into the trees.'

'Yeah,' said Entwistle. 'I mean, how many other members leave by legging it across the fairway?'

'Exactly. And if he's a golfer, where's his clubs?' Jones added.

Phillips stared at the screen for a long moment. 'We should get this footage checked by the digital forensics team so they can compare it to the guy caught on camera at Venables's house. See if they're a likely match.'

Bovalino made a note in his pad. 'I'll get straight onto it, guv.'

'Great work, Bov,' said Phillips. 'Really great work.'

The big man flashed a wide grin.

Phillips turned to Entwistle. 'Where are we at with Todd's background check?'

'I've done some digging, but I can't really find much on him other than he was chief constable for ten years and retired suddenly when one of his directives around crime reporting was leaked to the press.'

'Should have been arrested, not pensioned off,' muttered Jones.

'Why?' asked Entwistle. 'What did he do?'

'I'd only just moved up from London when it came into force,' Jones replied, 'but essentially an order came down from the top that certain crimes were not to be reported. Uniform were to deal with the incidents at the scene, but not bring charges or write them up.'

'Why?' asked Entwistle.

'To keep the crime figures in line with the Home Office's desired KPIs,' replied Jones.

'Violent crimes and domestic abuse incidents went through the roof,' Phillips interjected. 'At least one woman was beaten to death by her boyfriend, who had a history of violence against her.'

Jones nodded. 'It was an absolute fucking joke.'

'It really was,' said Phillips before falling silent as she stared at the screen on the wall.

'What're you thinking, boss?' asked Bovalino eventually.

'The girl who was murdered by her boyfriend. I'm just wondering if she could have something to do with Todd's murder.'

'If we are looking at revenge killing, it would make sense in Todd's case, but how would Venables be connected to her?' said Jones.

'I don't know,' Phillips replied, 'but let's start by finding out as much as we can about her, see if there's anything that can join the dots for us.'

'I can do that,' said Bovalino.

'Thanks.' Phillips turned to Entwistle. 'Any news from the horsehair suppliers?'

'Yes. I've got samples from both being couriered up from London as we speak. Evans has agreed to test them over the weekend.'

'Good,' said Phillips. 'Speaking of which – look, I know this isn't ideal, but we really need a breakthrough on at least one of these cases ASAP. So unless you have something you can't get out of, I'm gonna need you in this weekend.'

Bovalino shrugged. 'Fine by me. I could do with the overtime.'

'I've got nothing on that I can't reschedule,' said Entwistle.

Phillips turned to Jones. 'Is Sarah gonna hate me?'

'Nah.' Jones shook his head. 'We were just going to do some gardening. It'll keep.'

'Thanks, guys.' Phillips checked her watch – it was approaching seven o'clock. 'It's been a long week. Let's call it a day and get an early start in the morning.'

The sounds of yes, guv, filled the room.

'I don't know about you boys,' said Phillips, 'but I could really do with a drink.'

22

The next morning, Bovalino had quickly found the details of Sally Crowther, the young woman murdered by her boyfriend, as a direct result of the directive from Todd.

Soon after, Phillips and Jones made the short trip from Ashton House to the suburb of Denton, located seven miles east of Manchester city centre. It was 11:00 AM by the time they pulled up outside the home of Sally's parents, Jonny and Linda Crowther. Looking out from the passenger seat, Phillips took in the scene. A man, likely in his mid-sixties, with grey hair and a wiry frame, was mowing the lawn in the small garden to the front of the smartly appointed semi-detached house. The sun was shining, and he appeared to be sweating in the heat.

'I wonder if that's Sally's dad,' said Jones.

'Only one way to find out,' replied Phillips, reaching for the door handle. A moment later she flashed her ID as they approached. 'Mr Crowther?'

The man shut off the mower and nodded. 'Yes?'

'DCI Phillips and DI Jones from the Major Crimes Unit. We'd like to talk to you about Sally, if you have a minute.'

A puzzled look flashed across Crowther's face. 'Sally? That was almost twelve years ago.'

'We're aware of that,' replied Phillips, 'and we're sorry to bring it all up again, but we think Sally's death may be connected to one of our active investigations.'

Sadness oozed from Crowther's dark brown eyes as he bowed his head momentarily before looking up again. 'You'd better come round the back.'

With Jones bringing up the rear, Phillips tucked in behind Crowther as he set off down the side of the house, which led to a long, narrow garden at the rear. A small patio was covered with a wicker table and four garden chairs. A large parasol hung above it, cantilevered from the side, offering protection from the mid-morning sun.

Crowther gestured with an outstretched arm. 'Please have a seat. My wife, Linda, will want to hear this.'

'Thank you,' said Phillips as she pulled out a chair. Jones did the same.

'Can I get you both a drink? Tea, coffee? Something cold?'

'Whatever's easiest would be lovely,' replied Phillips. Jones nodded his agreement.

'I won't be a moment,' said Crowther, then disappeared inside.

For the next few minutes, Phillips and Jones sat in silence, taking in their surroundings. Gardening was clearly a passion for someone in the Crowther household. Pink and white roses, as well as bright red and rich purple geraniums in bloom, filled the beds that ran along the side of the immaculately manicured lawn.

A noise from behind caused Phillips to turn in her seat to see Crowther carrying a tray filled with glasses of orange squash. A petite, grey-haired woman in a flowery summer dress followed behind.

'This is Linda,' said Crowther as he placed the tray on the table in front of them.

Linda Crowther smiled as she offered her hand. 'Pleased to meet you.'

'And you,' said Phillips as she shook it.

Jonny passed around the drinks and took a seat next to his wife.

'This is very kind of you,' said Phillips before taking a drink of the juice.

'My husband said you wanted to talk to us about Sally,' said Linda. 'Something about an active investigation.'

'Yes.' Phillips placed the glass down on the table.

Jones pulled out his notepad and pen.

Phillips continued, 'We were hoping you could tell us what you remember about the night she died.'

'I'm not sure I can,' said Linda. 'It was a very long time ago, and to be honest, I've tried to blank it from my mind.'

'I can understand that,' said Phillips. 'But anything you can remember could help us.'

She frowned. 'What does Sally have to do with your investigation today?'

'You may have seen on the news that former chief constable Todd was killed recently.'

'We did,' said Crowther. 'Good riddance, too. If it weren't for that bastard, our Sally would still be here.'

'Jonny!' Linda said, flashing a scolding look to her husband before turning her attention back to Phillips. 'You'll have to excuse his language.'

Phillips offered a warm smile. 'Don't worry. I'm surrounded by it at work all day.'

Linda took a sip of her drink. 'Are you saying Jack Todd's death is connected to Sally?'

'We're not sure at this stage,' Jones cut in, 'but as your husband alluded to just now, we know that one of his directives – namely how domestic crimes were reported at that time – impacted directly on Sally and ultimately may have led to her death.'

'There's no *may* about it,' Crowther shot back. 'If the police had arrested Paul when he first attacked her, or even the second time it happened, he'd have been put in jail, and she'd have been able to break free from his grip. Instead they let him go, and the third time he attacked her, he beat her to death. Todd was totally responsible for that.'

Phillips nodded but remained silent.

Crowther continued, 'Paul was allowed to beat and abuse our daughter for years, and the police did nothing to stop him. I intervened when her bruises became too big to hide from us, but I ended up getting a beating from him too.'

'Which again, the police did nothing about,' added Linda. 'Just told Paul to behave himself and left it at that. Two weeks later, Sally was dead.'

Phillips remained silent as she took a sip of her juice before placing it back on the table. 'This may seem like an odd question, but did Sally have any connection to Lord Justice Venables?'

Linda's brow furrowed, and she turned to her husband. 'Wasn't he the judge at Paul's trial?'

Crowther took a moment to process the question, then nodded. 'Yeah, I think he was. Like we said, it was twelve years ago, and we've blocked a lot of it out, but I'm sure I remember the name Venables from the court case.'

Phillips flashed a knowing glance at Jones, then back to the couple. 'Do you remember anything specific he might have said at trial about Sally or her death?'

'Like what?' Linda asked.

'I don't know, maybe something controversial? Or did you notice him make any remarks to the jury about the case?'

Crowther shook his head. 'Sorry, no. A huge part of that period is just a blur these days.'

'Same for me,' said Linda, and she took her husband's hand, almost as if she were unaware she did it.

'We understand. It must have been very difficult for you both.' Phillips shifted in her seat. 'I can assure you that this next bit is purely procedure and something I have to ask, but, Mr Crowther, where were you between seven and nine on Thursday night?'

He sat to attention. 'Me? Why?'

'It's the time frame for Jack Todd's murder. Like I said, I have to ask.'

Crowther tilted his head to one side before answering, 'I'll probably have been walking the dog after dinner and then watching the cricket highlights. England was playing Sri Lanka that day.'

'He was,' his wife added. 'I can vouch for him.'

Jones scribbled in his notepad.

'Good,' said Phillips. 'Right, well, I'm pretty sure you've got better things to do on a Saturday than talk to us, so we'll get out of your way.' Pulling a business card from her pocket, she placed it on the table. 'If anything comes back to you about the trial, my mobile is on there. Please call me any time.'

'I don't feel like we've been much use to you,' said Crowther as he stood up.

'Not so,' replied Phillips. 'You've been very helpful indeed.'

'And thanks for the drink,' added Jones. 'Much appreciated on a day like today.'

With that, they got up from the seats and headed for the front of the house.

'What do you make of that?' asked Jones when they were back in the car.

'Obviously, we've no proof as yet, but my gut's telling me Sally could well be the connection. I mean, she was murdered because of Todd's directive, and Venables was the judge at her killer's trial? Coincidence?'

'You make a good point, guv,' said Jones. 'So what now?'

'Now we go back to the office and see what we can dig up on the trial of Paul Stillwell. See if we can find anyone connected to that case with links to Todd and Venables.'

'Sounds like a plan,' said Jones, firing the ignition.

Just then, Phillips's phone beeped, indicating she'd received a message. Pulling it from her pocket, she could see it was from Don Townsend and opened it.

We really need to talk, Jane.

'Everything okay?' asked Jones.

'Yeah, just Don Townsend. Says we need to talk.'

'What you gonna do?'

'What *can* I do?' Phillips shrugged as she began typing into her phone. 'Fox made it clear he's off-limits, but I'm also not going to lie, either.

Sorry. Can't. Fox's orders.

She hit Send, then put the phone back in her pocket. 'Let's get back to base.'

23

After a long afternoon of searching through the trial records for Paul Stillwell – the man who murdered Sally Crowther – Phillips sent the team home to get some rest, but she remained for another hour as she attempted to catch up on paperwork, finally leaving the office just after seven.

When she arrived home, it was coming up to eight o'clock. The drive was empty where Adam's car would normally be parked, as he'd agreed to work an extended shift this evening. After unlocking the front door, she was greeted by a purring Floss snaking around her legs, delighted Phillips was home.

Heading into the kitchen, she threw the keys to the Mini onto the bench along with her phone before pouring dry food into Floss's bowl on the floor, who wasted no time diving into her dinner. With the cat munching away contently, Phillips moved across the kitchen to the large American-style double-doored fridge, opened it and quickly scanned the contents of the shelves. Feeling uninspired and too tired to cook, she grabbed an ice-cold bottle of her favoured Pinot Grigio along with a large glass, then wandered into the lounge. Pouring herself a generous measure, she kicked off her shoes and switched on the TV as she settled down on the massive couch. The first few mouthfuls of the cold wine slipped down with ease, and she felt a wave of relaxation wash over her. 'That's better,' she whispered.

A few minutes passed before Floss padded along the carpet and jumped up onto her lap. 'Fed and happy now, are we?' Phillips began stroking her to the rhythmic sound of purring.

For the next hour, Phillips flicked around channels as she attempted to find something to engage with, but she was in one of those moods where nothing seemed to satisfy her, and eventually she gave up and turned it off. The room fell silent aside from the cat's contented purring, and as Phillips lay on the couch, staring out through the French door to the garden, her mind wandered back to the investigations and the potential link between Todd, Venables, and Sally Crowther. They'd not found anything of note during their hunt this afternoon, but tomorrow was another day.

Her attention was suddenly drawn to the sound of her phone ringing in the kitchen. Careful not to wake the now snoozing cat, Phillips lifted her off her knee and placed her gently down on the couch before jumping up and heading off in search of her phone.

As she picked up the handset, she could see it was Don Townsend on the other end. 'Oh, bugger off, will you?' she mumbled as her finger lingered over the call cancel button. But at the very last second – for reasons unknown to her – she had a change of heart and decided to answer it.

'Don.'

'Oh, so you are allowed to talk to me, then?' His tone was facetious.

'It's Saturday night, Don. What do you want?'

'Like I said in my message earlier, to talk.'

'About what?' asked Phillips. 'You know I can't give you any information on my active cases. Fox's orders.'

'That's just it. I might have some information for **you** *this time. Something that could help you with those active cases you're so keen to protect.'*

'Really? And why would you do that?'

'Call it a peace offering. I do hate it when we fight, Jane,' he shot back.

Phillips stayed quiet as she considered what best to do. She had to admit she was intrigued. 'Say I agree to talk – where and when?'

'Your local, the Horse and Jockey, right now.'

'You want to talk *now*?'

'Yep. I'm sitting at the bar as we speak. It's literally five minutes' walk from your house.'

'How do you know where I live?'

'I'm a reporter, Jane. It's my job to know,' replied Townsend, very matter-of-factly. *'Look, it's Saturday night, and I'm sitting in a pub, drinking on my own. Come on, Jane. Keep me company. I promise you won't regret it.'*

Phillips sighed heavily into the phone. 'Aside from the fact this is all a bit creepy – even by your standards, Don – I have to admit I'm curious.'

'You're such a sweet talker.'

'Okay, I'll take the bait. I'll be there in fifteen minutes.'

'Excellent,' said Townsend. *'I'll order you your usual.'*

As Phillips ended the call, she stared down at the phone and considered the ramifications of what she was doing. If Fox found out she was meeting with Townsend, she'd go ballistic. That said, if he *did* have information that could help her investigations, then all would be forgiven. Either way, she said she'd go, and that was exactly what she was going to do.

She'd never liked playing by Fox's rules, and Fox was the least sociable person on the planet. She was hardly likely to bump into her in the Horse and Jockey on a Saturday night, was she?

24

It was dark by the time Phillips set off to meet Townsend, but the night air was still warm around her. So far it had been unusually warm for May, but that seemed to be becoming more common with each year that passed, due in no small part to climate change, no doubt. As she walked through the open door leading into the belly of the Horse and Jockey pub, she spotted Townsend immediately, standing up at the bar. He was a tall man at six feet four. His jet-black hair slicked back against a face that seemed permanently tanned gave him a look of a television New Jersey mobster, and she had to admit he cut an imposing figure.

'Jane,' he said with a broad, tobacco-stained smile as she approached.

'Don,' she replied, scanning the room, suddenly fearful of being spotted with him.

Townsend passed over a large glass of white wine. 'One Pinot Grigio as promised.'

Phillips took the wine and nodded in the direction of an

empty table positioned at the rear of the pub. 'Why don't we sit somewhere a little more private?'

'As long as you keep your hands to yourself.' Townsend laughed, clearly a few whiskies to the good.

Ignoring the remark, Phillips led the way, and a moment later they both slid into the booth out of sight of the main bar.

'This all suddenly feels very clandestine, Jane.' Townsend had a twinkle in his eye.

'Just making sure we're out of the way. I'm under strict orders not to talk to you from Fox, so if I want to stay on her good side, I need to be careful.'

'Does she have one?' Townsend shot back.

Phillips decided to cut to the chase whilst he was still relatively sober. 'So what's this information you have for me?'

'What?' Townsend waved her away. 'No foreplay?'

'Look, cut it with all the innuendo, will you, Don? It's creeping me out.'

'Spoilsport,' he mumbled.

'So come on, what was so important it couldn't wait until Monday morning?'

'All in good time, Jane.' Townsend took a mouthful of whisky. 'So how are the investigations going?'

Phillips stared him dead in the eye. 'You know full well I can't talk to you about any of that.'

'Fox's orders, right?'

'Yeah.'

Townsend shook his head. 'What's she got against me all of a sudden?'

'Er, maybe the story you wrote saying she was the worse chief constable in a generation and that it was time for her to step down?'

'She takes things far too seriously,' he said with a grin.

'Seriously, Don. It's been a long week, and I'm knackered. Either share the information you have, or we're done here.'

'Bit of a shock about Jack Todd, wasn't it?'

Phillips eyed him with suspicion. 'Yeah. It was.'

'Like you say, must have been one hell of a week for you. First a Crown Court judge is murdered, then a retired chief constable. Both strangled in the same way.'

Phillips tried not to react. The information on the cause of Venables and Todd's deaths had not been released yet.

'Oh, don't look so surprised, Jane. You know I have my sources.'

'A bloody spy more like,' spat Phillips. 'Who the hell is passing on this information to you?'

Townsend smiled thinly. 'So they *were* both strangled?'

'That's none of your business, Don.'

'Look, here's the thing, Jane.' Townsend sipped his drink. 'After Carter went public about Todd's death, my editor came to see me. He's keen to do a colour piece on the life and times of the former chief constable. A follow-up to the Fox piece, something along the lines of the GMP not only being rotten to the core today but going all the way back to the eighties and nineties when things were really bad. Very much warts n'all.'

Phillips glared at him.

'So I started doing a bit of digging into Todd. Spoke to an old mate of mine who was a bit of a mentor when I first came to the *MEN*.' Townsend tapped the side of this glass with his index finger. 'And it seems Jack Todd used to be a bit of a lad back in the nineties, when he was chief superintendent in serious crimes.'

'Where's this going, Don?' Phillips was struggling to hide her frustration.

Townsend continued, 'Fond of playing fast and loose when it came to securing confessions, I'm told. Apparently, a lot of innocent men ended up in Hawk Green thanks to Jack Todd.'

'Do you have any proof of this?'

'Not yet, but thanks to my mate, I know where to look, and he's convinced I'll find enough to go to print with it all.'

'And what good will dragging up the past do?' asked Phillips.

Townsend leaned back against the booth. 'Now that sounds like Fox talking, not DCI Phillips.'

She didn't respond.

'In fact, I bet Fox said *exactly* the same thing when Todd was murdered, didn't she?'

'Again, where is this all going, Don?'

'Did you know Todd and Venables were mates back in the day, too?'

'I didn't, no.' Phillips folded her arms across her chest.

Townsend nodded. 'Big golfing buddies, by all accounts, when Todd was chief super and Venables was head of the CPS in Manchester. Apparently across the nineties they worked very closely and put a lot of folks behind bars – many of whom still protest their innocence to this day. By all accounts, a lot of people would have had good reason to want them dead.' He drained his glass. 'You do know their deaths are connected, don't you, Jane?'

Phillips took a moment before replying. 'It's certainly a possibility I've considered.'

'Another thing that might interest you is that at the same time Todd and Venables were locking up innocent people in Hawk Green, Todd was supported by a very ambitious DCI who to this day is still working for the police as a high-ranking officer.'

'And who might that be?' she asked.

'All in good time, Jane.' The twinkle was back in Townsend's eyes. 'According to my mate, that same DCI was equally fond of playing fast and loose and is alleged to have been heavily involved in soliciting false confessions when needed.'

'Are you going to tell me the name or not, Don?'

'You're the detective, Jane; surely you can figure it out.'

Phillips took a moment to think of all the current senior officers on the force. She suddenly had a suspicion – but hoped to God she was wrong.

Townsend continued, 'Why do you think Fox told you to stay away from digging into Todd's background? Who's she really protecting by asking you to leave the past alone?'

Playing for time, but with her suspicions rising, Phillips answered, 'I'm just trying to think...Carter wasn't around back then, Chief Superintendent McKenzie in Serious Crimes would have been working for Police Scotland back in the nineties, and Chief Superintendent Bagshaw is too young to have been a DCI then.'

Townsend took a slug of whisky and smiled. 'Which leaves...?'

Now she knew for sure. 'You've gotta be kidding?'

Townsend's smile was even wider now.

'Fox,' she said, still taking it in. *Fox was Todd's DCI.*

'Bingo!' He lowered his tone and continued, 'Which is the reason Fox warned you off digging into Todd – because she's likely as crooked as he was.'

Phillips shook her head. Her stomach was churning. 'I don't believe this.'

'Believe it, Jane. It's real, and it's happening. A serving chief constable is trying to suppress a murder investigation because she's frightened it could expose her corrupt past.'

'Can you prove any of this?' she asked.

'Not as yet, but again, my mate has told me where to look. If it's there, you know I'll find it.'

Phillips was lost for words, and her head was spinning.

She didn't want to believe any of this, that Fox had deliberately told her to tread carefully around Todd to protect herself – but she knew the chief constable well enough to know it was very likely true.

'I told you you'd want to hear what I had to say,' said Townsend.

'Who else knows about this?'

'Just me and my mate, but he's long since retired and has no desire to take on a sitting chief constable.'

'And what about you, Don?' Phillips locked eyes with him. 'Do you want to take her on?'

Townsend offered a lopsided grin and ran his hand through his slicked black hair. 'That depends.'

'On what exactly?'

'On whether or not I'm welcomed back into the fold, Jane. This is one hell of a story and would be a sensational piece to write, no doubt about it. But I'm a long way off retirement, and I want regular content I can use.'

'Which means what?'

'Which means if you go back to giving me the exclusives, I'll keep this story under wraps.'

'Permanently?' asked Phillips.

'I can't promise that, but I can make sure it stays buried for a very long time to come.'

Phillips stared at him in silence as she considered the offer. She had little interest in protecting Fox's reputation, but the last thing she needed right now was the force being dragged through the mud. Her job was hard enough as it was without Don Townsend turning the city against the police. Plus, if Fox *was* involved in Todd's past misdemeanors, as those came to light, the chief constable would answer to the proper authorities.

'Okay.' She nodded. 'I'll give you back your exclusives, but I need one more thing from you besides burying this story.'

Townsend cocked his head to one side. 'And what's that?'

'The name of your informant. The mole inside the GMP who's sharing information on cases.'

'No can do, Jane. They're off-limits, and that is *non*-negotiable.'

Phillips could feel her jaw clenching as her anger threatened to boil over. 'I want the name of your informant.'

Townsend drained his glass and placed it back on the table. 'Not happening, Jane. I have my journalistic integrity to consider.'

'Oh, fuck off, Don. You don't know the meaning of the word.'

'That hurts my feelings,' said Townsend, pretending to pout.

Phillips stared back in silence.

'What's it gonna be, Jane? Do we have a deal? Do you want me to bury this story? Or is Fox about to get what's coming to her?'

Phillips swallowed hard. 'We have a deal.'

'Excellent!' replied Townsend, grabbing his empty glass. 'Can I get you another wine to celebrate?'

'No, thanks.' Phillips pushed her drink across the table. 'I need to get back.'

'You can't leave me to drink on my own,' said Townsend. 'Not now we're back to being friends.'

Phillips slipped out of the booth and stood. 'Any word of this gets out, Don, and I *will* make sure you regret it.'

'You have my word.' Townsend performed a three-finger salute and smiled. 'Scout's honour.'

Phillips didn't reply, just turned on her heel and marched out of the pub.

The walk home seemed to take forever as Townsend's accusations weighed heavy on her mind. Had Fox been involved in soliciting false confessions when she was working for Todd? Had she cooperated with him and Venables to send innocent men to prison? Could Chief Constable Fox, the highest-ranking police officer in the Greater Manchester Police, be that corrupt? Just the idea that it might be true was unthinkable.

As she reached her driveway, she sat on the garden wall and took a moment to try to clear her head. If Townsend's revelations were true, they could obliterate trust in the police in one fell swoop, destroying the legacy of hundreds of coppers in the process. And even if the rumours were just that, with little grounding in reality, they could be just as damaging if they made it into print. Knowing Townsend was out there with that kind of information in his pocket scared the crap out of her – she shuddered at the thought of the headlines he could produce.

With her head no clearer and her stomach churning, she pulled her phone from her pocket. Something this big went way beyond her paygrade. It was time to call in the cavalry.

25

Heaton Park was located just fifteen minutes from Ashton House, and the carpark was surprisingly busy for nine o'clock on a Sunday morning. Phillips pulled the Mini Cooper into a space next to a large SUV. The owner of the gargantuan vehicle had the boot open and was tending to a large black Labrador that appeared impatient to get going on whatever walk had been promised. Slipping out of the driver's seat, Phillips closed and locked the door, then set off towards the agreed rendezvous point, ten minutes away on foot, and well out of the way of prying eyes.

Most of the walk to her destination was uphill, and by the time she reached Carter, she was sweating under the glare of the early morning sunshine.

'Morning, Jane,' he said cheerfully, looking incongruous in his civilian clothes – a blue Polo shirt and dark blue jeans over brown boating shoes.

'Morning, sir,' she replied, out of breath. 'And thanks for agreeing to meet me here.'

'I have to say I'm intrigued to know what's so important it

warranted meeting on a Sunday morning a mile inside Heaton Park.

Phillips moved to stand next to him and took in the view down over the rest of the park. 'I'm sorry I couldn't say on the phone, but I wanted to make sure that what I tell you stays between us. Information seems to leak out of Ashton House like a sieve.'

Carter's eyes narrowed. 'What's going on, Jane?'

Phillips's pulse had finally slowed after the exertion of the climb up the hill. 'I met with Don Townsend last night.'

'Oh god, that's all we need. If Fox finds out, she'll skin you alive.'

'I know, sir. It wasn't planned, I promise. He'd been messaging earlier in the day, saying we needed to meet, and I'd ignored him. Then he called last night, and for some reason, I answered it.'

'What was he after?'

'Nothing. Well, that's not strictly true—'

'I'm sure it's not,' Carter cut in.

'What I mean is he wanted to give *me* some information.'

'Really? What kind of information?'

'For a start, he knew Venables and Todd had both been strangled.'

'How?' asked Carter. 'That detail's not been released to the press.'

Phillips nodded. 'His source told him.'

'The mole, you mean?'

'Yeah. Whoever it is, they're still passing over information.'

'We need to find them, Jane. This is getting out of hand now.'

'I agree, sir, but we have a slightly more pressing development to deal with first, which is the other thing he wanted to tell me.'

Carter's face wrinkled. 'Which is what?'

Phillips took a deep breath and exhaled sharply. 'Townsend told me he spoke to his now-retired mentor from his early days at *MEN*. A friend who worked there when Jack Todd was chief super in the Serious Crimes Unit and when Venables was in charge of the CPS.'

'And?'

'This friend said it was widely known that the pair were in cahoots together and between them put a lot of innocent people in Hawk Green.'

'But why would they do that?'

'To massage their conviction rates. As we know, Todd was known for fudging his figures, even when he was chief constable.'

'True,' said Carter. 'So if Venables and Todd were connected like he suggests, could that be why they were killed in the same way? Someone from their past getting their own back?'

'That's where my head went,' replied Phillips. 'But that's not the worst of what he told me, sir.'

Carter sighed. 'Why do I have a feeling I really don't want to hear what's coming next?'

'Because you don't.'

He turned to face her. 'Okay, what *is* the worst of it?'

'Townsend's mentor told him about a DCI who was on Todd's team back in the nineties who played as fast and loose as he did. Apparently they were rumoured to be heavily involved in coercive behaviour to secure false confessions.'

'Right. And how does that affect us?'

'That same DCI is still a serving police officer in a very senior rank.'

'What?' said Carter. '*How* senior?'

Phillips stared him straight in the eye. 'Chief constable – senior.'

'Fox?' Carter did a double take. 'This is a joke, right?'

Phillips shook her head. 'I wish it were, sir.'

'I don't believe what I'm hearing.'

'I felt the same last night, for a while at least, and then, the more I thought about it, the more it started to prey on my mind. It might explain why Fox is insisting I back off looking into Todd's background.'

'I hear what you're saying, but that could also just be Fox doing her job, protecting the force as well as the reputation of a former senior officer.'

'True, but my gut's telling me there's something in what Townsend's saying.'

Carter rubbed his hands down his face, causing the skin to redden. 'These are serious allegations, Jane. I mean, does he have any proof to back it up?'

'Not yet,' said Phillips, 'but he's one hundred percent confident he can get it *if* he starts digging.'

'We can't let that happen. If there's anything in what he told you last night, then this situation needs managing carefully and through the appropriate channels as opposed to click-bait for the local rag.'

'I believe I can manage him, sir.'

'And how do you propose to do that?' asked Carter. 'We're talking about Don Townsend here.'

'Yes, we are. And knowing how he operates, I've persuaded him to keep it under wraps, for now at least.'

'How?'

'I made him a deal,' replied Phillips. 'He keeps quiet about it, and in return I give him exclusive insight on our cases.'

Carter winced. 'Fox will never go for that.'

'She won't know. And besides, would she *really* prefer the alternative?'

Carter said nothing as he stared down across the park. A

couple was walking their dog at the bottom of the hill. 'Who else knows about this?'

'Just you, me, Townsend, and his informant.'

'Do we know who this fella is?'

'No,' Phillips replied. 'But I don't think we need to worry about him. Townsend reckons the guy is long since retired and has no desire to get involved in something as big as this.'

'Jesus, Jane. This is a *massive* problem.'

'I know, sir. So what do we do?'

Carter blew his lips. 'In all honesty, I don't know. I need some time to think.'

'I understand.'

'For now, let's keep it between us. Nothing to the team, okay?'

'I'd like to bring Jones in on it. He's my number two, and there's no secrets between us.'

'I understand why you'd want to do that, but no.' Carter shook his head. 'We need the team focused on catching whoever killed Venables and Todd. Not distracted by the fact the regime could be severely compromised.'

'Jones can handle it, sir, and stay objective. I'm certain of that.'

'Sorry, Jane. I'm pulling rank on this one. No one is to know outside of you and me.'

Phillips said nothing before finally nodding. 'If that's what you want.'

'It is,' replied Carter.

'What about Entwistle?'

'What about him?'

'He's currently doing a background check on Todd. If I tell him to back off, he'll get suspicious.'

'Then don't tell him to back off. In fact, don't say anything at all, just leave him to it.'

'But what if he finds something?'

'We'll just have to hope he doesn't, but if he does, we'll deal with it as it happens.'

Phillips nodded. 'If that's the case, I have an idea that could kill two birds with one stone.'

'What're you thinking?'

'We both agree we need to find this mole of Townsend's, so I can put Entwistle on that as his main priority – task him with finding out who has had access to each of the compromised crime scenes. That could be a decent distraction *and* help us find the bastard who's been passing over confidential information.'

'Sounds like a plan,' said Carter.

'I'm heading into the office now. I'll brief him as soon as I get in.'

'Great.' Carter slipped his hands into his pockets. 'Sometimes I wonder why I left the relative serenity of the north-east. Life was never this complicated up there.'

'That's the life of a murder cop in Manchester, sir,' said Phillips.

Carter nodded. 'Indeed.'

'Right. I'd better catch up with the team. We have a lot to do.'

'Tread very carefully on this one, Jane.'

'I will, sir. I know what's at stake.'

26

The rest of Sunday had passed by in a blur as the team buried themselves in the finer details of Venables's and Todd's murders. If truth be told, Phillips had struggled to concentrate all day, as her mind was constantly filled with images of a young DCI Fox working alongside Todd to coerce confessions to massage their conviction rates and further her career. The more Phillips considered Townsend's allegations about the now chief constable, the more plausible it seemed to be. Fox had risen through the ranks based on the results she'd achieved as detective in the Serious Crimes squad and even managed to form her own department on the back of that success, Major Crimes. Had her beloved unit really been founded on the back of police corruption? If it had, the reality didn't bear thinking about.

After a fruitless day in the office, Phillips had headed home – and with Adam working the night shift once more – had run a hot bath and gone to bed early in the hope of getting a good night's rest. Sadly, the opposite had happened, and she'd spent most of the night in and out of a fitful sleep filled with wild dreams involving Fox and Todd acting as

Gestapoesque interrogators to a young police constable Phillips back when she was in uniform. By five o'clock she had given up trying to sleep and headed for the shower and an early start in the office.

She arrived just after seven. An hour later, Jones appeared at her office door, carrying a steaming takeaway coffee, which he passed over before taking a seat opposite. 'How're you doing this morning?' He took a tentative sip of his own drink.

'I'm knackered after a terrible night's sleep,' she replied as she savoured the aroma of the fresh coffee. 'Nothing that this can't fix though.'

'What time's Todd's post-mortem?'

'Scheduled for ten,' replied Phillips.

'Want me to tag along?' Jones asked.

Phillips took a drink of her coffee. 'Yeah, otherwise I think I might fall asleep at the wheel.'

The room fell silent as they both concentrated on their drinks before Jones finally spoke. 'It's a strange case this one, isn't it, boss?'

'Yeah, it is.'

'I mean, Sally Crowther has to be the link between the two men's murders: it's too much of a coincidence otherwise. But no matter where we looked over the weekend – and we've looked in every file there is – we just can't find anyone who fits the description of the cap and backpack man.'

Phillips placed her cup down on the desk and sat back in the chair. 'I know. I've been updating the decision logs this morning, and it's ridiculous how little we have to go on. Zero leads as to who he might be and why he wanted to kill them. Venables was strangled six days ago, and we're no further forward.' She glanced at her watch. 'I'm expecting a call from Carter any minute, summoning me to see Fox to explain why we have so little.'

'God, that's all you need.'

Just then, the desk phone rang. Phillips grabbed the receiver. 'DCI Phillips.'

'Jane, it's Andy Evans.'

'Hey, Andy. Any updates on the horsehair samples from London?'

'I do, but it's not good news, I'm afraid. We've spent the weekend looking at both samples that came from the manufacturers, and neither is a match for those we found on either body.'

Phillips sighed heavily, drawing an inquisitive look from Jones. 'Okay. That wasn't what I was hoping for, but I appreciate you guys taking the time to rush them through.'

'Not a problem,' said Evans. *'I'm just sorry we couldn't be more helpful.'*

'Thanks anyway,' Phillips replied before hanging up.

At that moment Entwistle knocked on the door. 'Morning, guys.'

'Evans just called,' said Phillips. 'Neither of the samples from London were a match for those found on Todd or Venables.'

'You're kidding.'

'I wish I were.'

'Bollocks,' said Jones. 'So we have no idea where they came from, then?'

Phillips shook her head. 'Nope, not a clue. So we're back to square one.' She focused on Entwistle. 'So I need you to figure out where else someone might be able to source enough horsehair to make a ligature.'

'Of course. I'll get straight onto it,' replied Whistler. 'I also wanted to let you know I've started on that list of staff for you, but with everything else going on, it's gonna take some time.'

'I know, but it's vital we get to the bottom of it.'

'Understood,' he said, then headed for his desk.

Jones locked eyes with Phillips, his eyebrows raised. 'Staff list, guv?'

Phillips cleared her throat, feeling very uncomfortable that she was keeping secrets from him. 'Yeah. I've been meaning to get Whistler on to it for ages. I think it's time we flushed out whoever it is who keeps passing on sensitive information to the press.'

'With respect, guv. Is that the best use of his time at the moment?'

Phillips clenched her toes in her boots as she attempted to ground herself and keep the tension she was feeling from appearing on her face. She hated lying to her closest ally. 'I've told him it can't get in the way of the investigations, but it's still something we need to do – and the sooner we find out who it is, the better.'

Jones drained his cup and tossed it in the waste bin. 'You're the boss.'

Desperate to change the subject, Phillips stepped up from her chair. 'We may as well head over to the hospital. I don't want to get caught in traffic.'

'Sure,' said Jones, getting up. 'I'll get the car keys.'

Jack Todd's post-mortem took over three hours to complete, in part due to the length of time it had been exposed to water in the shower cubicle at Alerton Hall. Once it was complete, Phillips and Jones sat with Chakrabortty in her office as they discussed her findings.

'In my opinion,' ventured Chakrabortty, 'there's little doubt Todd was killed by the same person and weapon as Venables. The wounds and bruising on both were pretty much identical.'

Phillips folded her arms across her chest. 'So a retired judge and an ex-chief constable were both strangled by a ligature made from horsehair.'

'Symbolism at its finest,' said Jones.

'The killer is clearly sending a message of some kind. But what's he trying to say?'

Chakrabortty sat forward and linked her fingers together on the desk. 'That's your department, but I can tell you that whoever did it is physically very strong. Todd and Venables were big men even at their ages, and judging by the marks on their fingers and hands, they both fought hard to stay alive. That would have been challenging for the killer: fighting them off whilst pulling the ligature around their neck long enough to incapacitate them and eventually kill them.'

'That makes sense,' said Jones. 'We have some CCTV footage of the man we think's responsible, and he looks pretty tall and well built.'

Phillips said nothing as she processed what she was hearing. 'Last time we were here, you mentioned your husband had heard rumours about Venables influencing juries when he was on the bench.'

'Yeah. Tom mentioned it to a few others at work to see what they thought of him, and they all said the same: Venables was a law unto himself for years.'

'Do you know if Tom ever came across Jack Todd at all?'

Chakrabortty's brow furrowed. 'He's never said anything to me about him. Why do you ask?'

'Just something I heard: that Todd and Venables were close back in the day. I wondered if there was anything in it.'

'I can ask him tonight if you like?'

'Yeah, may as well,' said Phillips before changing the subject. 'So can we expect the full report today?'

'Hopefully,' Chakrabortty replied. 'As ever, we're mad busy, but one of the support team should be able to finalise it this afternoon and send it over.'

'If they could, it'd be a real help,' said Phillips.

Chakrabortty smiled. 'If it's not with you by three, I'll give them a nudge.'

Phillips returned her smile. 'Thanks, Tan.' She turned to Jones. 'We should get going.'

Chakrabortty remained seated as she scrutinised her computer screen for a couple of seconds. 'Right, no rest for the wicked,' she said, stepping up from the chair. 'Post-mortem number two for the day awaits. Come on, I'll walk you out.'

Ten minutes later as they walked side by side back to the multi-storey car park of the MRI, Jones lightly touched Phillips's wrist. 'Back there you said you'd heard something about Venables and Todd being close. That's new. Where did that come from?'

Phillips continued walking at pace. 'Oh, yeah. Just someone I bumped into over the weekend.'

'Really, who?'

'An old mate, no one you'd know.'

Jones didn't respond.

Phillips could feel her stomach churning, and it took all her strength to not blurt out every detail of her meeting with Townsend on Saturday night. Yet, despite the temptation to come clean, she could hear Carter's words ringing in her ears: it was to stay between them. Suddenly she stopped in her tracks.

'What's up?' asked Jones.

'We're desperate to find a link between Todd and Venables, right?'

'Yeah.'

'And we know Nic Johnson worked for Venables in the CPS.'

'So?'

'So it's just occurred to me – she may well have worked with Todd at the same time, when he was still chief super.'

'It's possible, but I'm not sure at what level. She was pretty junior back then.'

'True,' replied Phillips, 'but even if she didn't deal with him directly, she probably spent a lot of time with those who did. And as we well know, lawyers love to gossip. It's gotta be worth a try.'

'Yeah, absolutely.'

Phillips checked her watch; it was approaching twelve thirty. 'Come on, her office is only a few minutes away.'

27

Phillips and Jones approached the same smiling receptionist who had greeted them on their previous visits. They knew by now her name was Chloe.

'Is Nic Johnson available?' asked Phillips, feeling no need to show her ID.

'I'm afraid not; she's in court all day with her senior KC, Ruben Cole.'

'We really need to speak to her.' Phillips drummed her fingers on the reception desk as she considered their options. 'Do you know what time they'll be breaking for lunch?'

'Today's the first day of trial, so I'm not sure, but I do know she's asked her clerk, Ian, to head over with some paperwork at one. You could always try to catch her then.'

Phillips and Jones exchanged glances and nodded in unison.

'We'll do that. Which court is she in?' asked Phillips.

'I'll just check for you.' Chloe tapped into her keyboard and scrutinised the screen. 'Looks like it's court four.'

'Thank you,' said Phillips, then turned and headed for the elevator.

The time was approaching 1:13 PM when they arrived at the Crown Court located in the centre of Manchester. The court building itself was well known to them, so it took very little time to find court four. Just outside the entrance – as Chloe had suggested – Ian was standing next to a sitting Johnson, who was furiously scribbling on documents resting on her knee.

'Have you got a minute?' asked Phillips as she approached.

Johnson glanced up and frowned. 'Do I look like I do?'

'It won't take long.'

'Good,' said Johnson as she passed back the paperwork to Ian before standing. 'Because I haven't got long.'

'Five minutes and we'll be out of your hair,' replied Phillips.

Johnson checked her watch. 'We're back in at two, and I need to get some lunch. You can walk with me to the deli if you like.'

'Sounds good.'

Johnson led them out of the court and down the side of the large red-brick building along a cobbled backstreet away from the lunchtime trade making their way towards Piccadilly Gardens.

'There's a little Italian deli down here that does the most amazing espressos,' said Johnson. 'Really helps with the focus when you have an afternoon session like the one waiting for me when I get back.'

'I must try one,' said Phillips, walking alongside, with Jones next to her.

'So what do you need?' asked Johnson, striding along.

'I'm sure you've heard about Jack Todd's death.'

'I have. Came as quite a shock, that one, especially so soon after Venables.'

'I'm sure,' said Phillips.

'So, are you treating it as suspicious?'

'You know I can't tell you that, Nic.'

'I'll take that as a yes, then,' said Johnson. 'And are the two deaths connected?'

'Again, that's not something I can share right now.'

'Which means they are.' Johnson flashed a knowing smile as she continued at pace.

'When you were in the CPS, did you ever come across Todd when he was the chief superintendent of Serious Crimes?'

'Not directly, no. Conversations with him were way above my pay grade. But I was involved in some of his cases. Filings and paperwork et cetera. Why?'

Jones cut in now. 'Was he close to Venables when he ran the CPS?'

'God, yeah. Thick as thieves, those two. Todd insisted on Venables handling all his cases personally.'

Phillips took the lead again. 'I have it on good authority that when Todd was running Serious Crimes, he didn't always play with a straight bat.'

'Now there's an understatement if ever there was one,' Johnson said, chuckling.

'What do you mean?'

She glanced right at Phillips. 'There was never any proof, of course – he was too smart to leave a trail – but the rumours were rife that Todd was a master of evidence planting. If he liked someone for a crime he was investigating, he'd do whatever it took to make sure they went down for it. Guilty or not.'

'So are you saying some of the people he secured convictions against were actually innocent?'

'Again, there's no proof, but if the rumours were true – and there's no smoke without fire in this game – then they had to be.'

'But how did he get away with it?' Jones cut in. 'Planting evidence is virtually impossible.'

'Nowadays maybe, but the law was very different back then. Yes, we had DNA, but it was very much in its infancy, and the checks and balances that are required to provide a safe sample today simply didn't exist in those days.'

'I always thought he was dodgy,' said Jones. 'But evidence planting?'

Johnson continued, 'Again, no proof, but I was once told by someone in his team that Todd had worked out how to harvest and plant DNA samples from his targets in order to make any conviction a slam dunk, innocent or not.'

They turned a corner, and the deli came into view.

'And was Venables aware that this was going on?' asked Phillips.

'He'd have to have been blind not to be,' Johnson replied. 'My guess is they were probably in it together. They were both racist, sexist bigots who enjoyed putting people they didn't like in prison. They got a kick out of it. You'd always see them together in the pub. Either celebrating or more likely plotting.'

'But if everybody knew about it,' pressed Phillips, 'why did nobody stop them?'

'Because they couldn't. Like I said, it was a very different world. No email trails or text messages. Very little usable mobile phone data, and social media didn't exist. The internet was in its infancy. It was their word against anyone who dared challenge them. And anyway, who do you think people would believe? Some lone activist fighting for justice, or a chief superintendent and the head of the CPS? It was a closed shop, and they knew it. They held all the power.'

'That's so messed up,' said Jones, shaking his head.

Johnson shrugged as they reached the entrance to the deli and stopped. 'That was just the way it was.'

'Do you remember any specific cases of Todd's that stood out as false convictions?' Phillips asked. 'Maybe someone he put away who might want revenge?'

'Todd, no, but last night I was thinking about our previous conversation about Venables and any cases he might have influenced. Nothing jumped out when he was a judge, but there was one that came back to me, when he was in charge of the CPS.'

'Which was?' asked Phillips.

'It was 1999. Venables was hell-bent on prosecuting the case, even though the accused had a strong alibi. The guy's name was Jerome Grant, and he was supposed to have murdered his girlfriend. However, the evidence was purely circumstantial when Todd first brought the case to Venables. I know because I had to log it on the system. Then suddenly and against the run of play, forensics found some blood in the boot of Grant's car that belonged to the dead girlfriend. The conviction was a slam dunk after that. Grant got life with a minimum of twenty years. Depending on how he served his time, he could well be out on license by now. He'd be someone you could talk to.'

Jones pulled out his notebook and scribbled inside.

Johnson looked at her watch. 'Right, I'm running out of time, and I've got a very hungry King's Council back at court. If you don't mind, I need to get some food ordered.'

'Of course,' said Phillips.

'Seriously, take a look at the Grant case. There could well be something in that,' said Johnson, then stepped inside the deli.

Phillips and Jones set off walking back towards the court.

'By the way,' Johnson shouted after them, 'you should speak to the chief constable about Todd,' she called out, from the doorway into the deli. 'After all, she was his bag man back in Serious Crimes.' Johnson gave them the thumbs-up, then stepped back inside.

Jones locked eyes with Phillips, his eyes narrow. 'Is she talking about Fox?'

Phillips nodded.

'Fox was Todd's number two when all this was going on?'

'Seems that way, yes.'

'So *she* could have been involved in what Todd and Venables were up to?'

'Potentially.'

Jones's face wrinkled. 'You knew about this?'

'Yes.'

'Since when?'

Phillips swallowed hard. It was time to tell him. 'Saturday night. Don Townsend told me.'

'Don Townsend? How the hell does he know about Fox's past?'

'Someone he's good mates with worked at the *MEN* when it was all going on. That same mate knew all about what they were doing, apparently.'

'And I'm just finding out about this now?' Jones's nostrils flared. 'So is Townsend the person you were talking about back at the PM? The friend you bumped into at the weekend?'

'Yeah.'

Jones bit his top lip. 'So why didn't you tell me about all this on Sunday when we were in the office?'

'Carter wanted it kept quiet for now.'

'*Carter* knows?'

'I briefed him on Sunday morning.'

'When? He wasn't even in that day.'

'I met him at Heaton Park before I came into work.'

Jones ran his right hand through his thinning hair. 'This just gets better.'

'I wanted to bring you into the loop, Jonesy, I asked him, but he said we should keep it to ourselves.'

Jones was incredulous. 'What? Does he not trust me or something?'

Phillips shook her head. 'No, he said he wanted to let you and the team run with the investigation unhindered.'

'That's as may be, but I'm *your* DI now, and I *should* have been told.'

'You're right,' said Phillips, 'and I'm sorry. I really am. I almost spilled the lot back at the hospital. It took all my strength to stop myself.'

Jones glared back at her but said nothing.

'I'm sorry I kept it from you, but Carter gave me a direct order.'

'Since when has that ever stopped you?'

Phillips nodded. He was right. 'I guess I deserve that.'

Jones's posture softened. 'Sorry. That was out of line.'

'No, you're right, I should have told you. Like you say, you're my second in command. You have every right to know.' Phillips continued, 'But I do agree with Carter that Bov and Whistler don't need to be brought in on this. Not yet anyway. Not until we have proof. We need them focused on the investigation – not worrying about the moral compass of the top brass.'

Jones shook his head. 'I dunno, boss. Keeping them in the dark could easily come back to bite us. Trust is at the core of MCU. If we lose that, we're finished.'

'I know that, but these are serious allegations, Jonesy. Without proof, there's no way we can wander round Ashton House telling everybody that Fox was potentially involved in securing false convictions back in the nineties. If that got out, we'd all be finished. No, the less the guys know, the better protected they are from all this.'

Jones exhaled sharply. 'This is seriously fucked up. I don't want to believe it's true, but we both know Fox, and I definitely wouldn't put it past her.'

'Me either.'

'So what happens if we start digging and find out she *was* involved?'

'Then we throw the book at her,' said Phillips. 'A crooked cop is a crooked cop, regardless of rank.'

Jones ran his fingers through his hair again as he locked eyes with Phillips. 'I have a really bad feeling about how this is all gonna end, guv.'

'Me too, Jonesy.' She patted him on the arm. 'Me too.'

28

Phillips could feel the weight of the world on her shoulders as she and Jones walked back into MCU. She just couldn't shake the feeling this business with Fox could spiral out of control at any moment.

As usual, Bovalino and Entwistle were at their desks, focused on whatever tasks they were doing related to the investigations.

'How did the PM go?' asked Bovalino as Jones dropped into his chair, and Phillips took a seat at the spare desk.

'Chakrabortty's convinced whoever killed Todd murdered Venables, as well,' Phillips said.

Entwistle sat back in his chair. 'No surprises there, then.'

'Not at all,' replied Jones. 'The bruising and marks on the bodies were pretty much identical, as we expected they would be.'

Phillips linked her fingers together on the desk. 'As we were in the city, Jones and I paid another visit to Nic Johnson at the Crown Court. She confirmed that Todd and Venables were well connected in the nineties, when Todd was chief super and Venables was running the CPS.'

'Connected in what way?' asked Bovalino.

Phillips glanced at Jones before choosing her words very carefully. 'Looks like they were both involved in what could have been a less than sound conviction.'

Jones cut in, 'A guy called Jerome Grant. He was convicted of murdering his girlfriend in 1999, even though he had a decent alibi.'

Phillips nodded. 'Johnson says rumours at the time suggested that Todd had potentially planted blood and DNA in Grant's car to secure the conviction.'

'*Jesus*,' said Bovalino. 'How the hell did he get away with that?'

Phillips shrugged. 'Different times and the protocols around evidence preservation weren't as stringent as they are today.'

'That's insane.' Bovalino shook his head. 'And how long did Grant get?'

'Life with a minimum of twenty years,' replied Phillips. 'So there's a good chance he's out by now.'

Entwistle began typing into his laptop. A minute later he found what he was looking for. 'Here he is. Jerome Grant. Convicted of murder, June 10, 1999. Sentenced to a life term, with a minimum of twenty. Released eighteen months ago. Looks like he's living in Wythenshawe.'

Phillips got up from the chair and moved behind Entwistle's shoulder. 'Can you show me his mugshot?'

Entwistle obliged, and the picture of Grant filled the screen. He was a mixed-race man, in his thirties when the photo had been taken.

'Judging by that, he's just over six feet two,' said Phillips. 'Can you pull up the stills from the CCTV at Venables's house and Alerton Hall?'

'Yep, give me a second.' Entwistle began clicking through folders on his computer. 'Here you go,' he said eventually.

Phillips stared down at the screen as Jones moved next to her. 'It's hard to tell because the picture quality isn't great, but that could be Grant, couldn't it?'

Jones leaned forward to get a closer look. 'I think so, yeah.'

Entwistle tapped the screen with his pen. 'Grant is mixed race, but the CCTV footage on both cameras is in black and white, so there's no way of telling whether the killer is or isn't. So that could well be him.'

Phillips felt a renewed energy rushing through her as she turned to Jones. 'I think we should pay Mr Grant a visit.'

Jones nodded and grabbed his car keys.

'While we're out' – Phillips pointed at the screen – 'I want a full background on Grant, and see if you can get hold of the case notes for his trial. We need to take a closer look at the evidence against him.'

'I can do that.' Bovalino made a note in his pad.

Phillips turned her attention to Entwistle. 'Any luck tracking down the source of the horsehair?'

'I spoke to the two retailers in London, and they both confirmed there's an online site that has started selling to the UK in the last twelve months. Problem is they're based in China, and the person in the office over there doesn't speak great English – and my Cantonese is non-existent. So I'm waiting on one of the custody translators to come back to me. I'm hoping they can speak to them on my behalf.'

'Great,' said Phillips. 'Let's make that happen today.'

'I'll chase up the translator again now.' Entwistle picked up the phone on his desk.

'Before you do that, can you write down Grant's address for us?' said Phillips.

Entwistle replaced the receiver and pulled across a yellow Post-it note. After scribbling down the details, he passed it over.

Phillips grabbed it and turned to Jones. 'Let's go.'

Jerome Grant's flat was located on the third floor of a block of flats situated in the densely populated suburb of Wythenshawe. It was one of the largest areas of social housing in Europe and had been built during the 1920s and '30s when Manchester had attempted to provide suitable homes for families relocated from the slum terraces that had dominated the industrial areas of the city. Nowadays it was a mix of privately owned and council properties. Grant's front door opened out onto a shared walkway that overlooked the sprawling estate below.

Jones banged on the door, and they waited. With no response forthcoming, he tried again, harder and louder this time.

A second later the front door to the adjacent flat opened, causing Phillips and Jones to turn.

A young woman with peroxide blonde hair peered out, holding an unlit cigarette in her left hand, a lighter in her right. 'He's not in,' she said in a thick and nasally Mancunian accent.

Phillips locked eyes with her. 'Is this Jerome Grant's flat?'

'I don't know his last name, but Jerome sounds about right.' She placed the cigarette between her lips and lit it, blowing out plumes of smoke a second later.

'Do you know where he is?' said Phillips.

The woman shook her head as she took another drag. 'So what's he done?'

'How do you mean?' Jones cut in.

'Two plainclothes coppers banging on his door. He's clearly been up to summat.'

'Who says we're police?' asked Jones.

The woman chuckled. 'I can smell it a mile off. Coppers stand out round here, mate. So what's he done?'

Phillips ignored the question. 'When did you last see Jerome?'

'I can't remember.' The woman blew smoke from her nostrils as she spoke. 'I just know he's a noisy bastard when he is here. Has the bloody telly on full volume all hours of the day and night.'

'I see,' said Phillips. 'Do you know if he has a job?'

'I wouldn't have a clue.' She took another long drag on the cigarette. 'The only time I've ever spoken to him is to tell him to turn his TV down – and even then he never talks back. He just grunts and shuts the door. Proper fucking weirdo if you ask me.' The woman continued unabated. 'I've complained to the council about him, but they've done bugger all.'

Phillips glanced at Jones, whose expression matched her thinking. *This is getting us nowhere.*

'Well, thank you for your time,' said Phillips, then turned and headed back along the walkway.

'We need to find out if Grant has a job,' said Phillips as they descended the concrete staircase at the end of the block.

'As he's a lifer, he'll still be under license. I'll get Bov to speak to probation and find out what he's been up to since he got out.'

'Good idea,' said Phillips as they reached the ground floor.

'So where now, boss?'

'Let's get back to base. See if Bov and Entwistle have come up with anything this afternoon.'

29

Nigel Duval signalled a right turn, then pulled the massive Range Rover off the main drag and onto the dirt track that would lead to the location of tonight's activity. He'd had a very full-on, stressful day in the office and was in need of a release – quite literally – to help relieve the tension that had been building in his neck and shoulders. He also had reason to celebrate this evening, having just brokered a deal with one of the UK's most revered TV actresses, Michelle Nightingale – she had agreed to star in the lead role of a gritty medical drama that would begin shooting in November. All of which was reason enough for him to drive all the way out here to Manchester's most notorious dogging spot. He'd often wondered where the term *dogging* had come from. Had it been coined by people pretending to take the dog for a walk, when actually they were out searching for sex with strangers? In public car parks no less. Or was it because most of the people you encountered at spots like this behaved like dogs in heat? Either way it was an odd term, and he much preferred to label his own regular activities at this location as *seeking out free love.*

As he reached the end of the dirt track, he turned into the small makeshift carpark and spotted two cars parked about twenty metres away. A rush of excitement and anticipation surged through him, but his hopes were dashed as the drivers of both vehicles switched on their ignitions and headlights and set off towards him. The occupants were obviously on their way out, and he'd clearly missed whatever they had just enjoyed. From his vantage point sitting in the driver's seat of the large SUV, he stared down into the cars as they passed and was more than a little disappointed that the driver of the lead car was a very attractive blonde woman who looked to be in her early thirties. Just his type.

The driver of the second car was a much older man who grinned like a Cheshire cat as he passed by.

'Lucky bastard,' he muttered, then watched in his rear-view mirror as both vehicles disappeared back down the dirt track.

Nudging the Range Rover forward across the now empty carpark, he reversed under the overhanging branches of a large oak tree and turned off the engine. The clock on the dash showed it was approaching nine o'clock, and he hoped he would not be alone for long. He'd been coming to this spot for nigh on five years, and he was yet to leave without some form of action.

Pulling out his phone, he decided to pass the time watching a little mobile porn. He was as horny as hell and figured it would do for the time being – and if all else failed, he had a pack of Kleenex in the glove box.

For the next five minutes, he amused himself by scanning through a variety of short movies until the glow of headlights in the distance caught his attention. 'Please be a woman, and please be hot,' he mumbled into the semi-darkness of the car. If truth be told, the porn had got him so tightly wound by now that as long as they were female, whether he found them attractive or not was immaterial. He was having sex tonight, no matter what.

The car pulled in through the entrance to the car park and stopped directly opposite him. Under the glare of the headlights, it was difficult to see who was driving and whether the occupant was male or female. The tension he felt was almost unbearable.

The car moved slowly across the gravel and, just as he had done, reverse parked so the headlights remained clearly visible. A second later, the lights went out, and to his delight, he could see the driver was a woman.

'Get in,' he whispered, then flashed his headlights.

A few seconds passed before the headlights opposite flashed back.

'We're in,' he said with a chuckle before opening the driver's door and dropping down onto the rough but dry ground below.

After running his hand through his thick hair, he strolled casually across the car park, a wide grin spreading across his face as the driver's face came into focus. Auburn hair, early thirties and pretty – she would do very nicely indeed.

The driver's window whirred slowly down as he approached. 'What's a beautiful girl like you doing all the way out here?' He bent down so his face was level with hers and placed his left hand on the roof. 'You lost or something?' he said playfully.

The woman smiled coyly. 'Just looking for a bit of fun and heard this is a good spot.'

He nodded. 'You've definitely come to the right place, love.'

She grinned as she looked him up and down. 'Yeah, looks like I have.'

'So,' he said, eyeing inside the car. 'Could be a challenge doing anything in there, but there's plenty of room in mine.'

'I'm more of an outdoor girl myself,' she replied.

He grinned. 'Oh, really? Like it in the trees, do you?'

'I like it anywhere I can get it,' she said with a giggle.

He clapped his hands together. 'Now that's what I'm talking about.' Standing straight, he opened the driver's door and offered his hand. 'This way, my lady.'

Taking it, she stepped up and out of the car. 'A gentleman? I like it.'

'I've been called many things, my dear, but a gentleman is not one of them.' As she moved forward, he closed the car door behind her, then crooked his left arm so she could link into it. 'So what do I call *you*?'

'Whatever you like.' She chuckled. 'The naughtier, the better.'

He raised his eyebrows. 'After the day I've had, *you* are just what the doctor ordered.' He said, then led her off towards the nearby tree line.

It had been relatively easy to follow Duval this evening, even though at times he'd struggled to keep up with the Range Rover on the moped he'd recently hired. He definitely hadn't expected to have to travel such a distance out of the city, and for long sections of the journey he'd wondered where on earth Duval was headed. However, as soon as he'd indicated a turn and pulled the large SUV off the main drag down the dirt road, he suspected he knew the location of Duval's destination. It was perfect, really, and he couldn't think of a more fitting place for such a stain on humanity to meet his maker – Manchester's most notorious 'dogging' spot. And whilst few people would ever lay claim to having used it, almost everybody in the city seemed to be aware of its existence and location.

Having parked the moped out of sight, he set off on foot with his backpack slung over his shoulder and his face partially covered with a light scarf. This far out into the Cheshire countryside, he was surrounded on all sides by fields and forest, with no sign of life in any direction, aside from Duval. A few minutes later he made his approach to the patch of wasteland that doubled up as a car park and was just in time to see two smaller cars making their way past Duval's now parked vehicle. A few seconds before the cars moved alongside him, he ducked down to hide in the long grass that ran along the side of the dirt track. He waited until both cars were safely out of sight, then straightened up. Over in the distance Duval reversed his Range Rover into position so that it now faced the entrance to the carpark, then switched off the engine and killed the headlights.

He decided now was as good a time as any to make his move.

The night sky was drawing darker with each minute that passed, and with the nearest street lighting at least half a mile away back down the track, he soon found himself surrounded on all sides by almost total darkness. The only other light visible was coming from inside Duval's vehicle as he stared down at his phone.

The sound of a plane flying towards Manchester airport caught his attention, and for the next few seconds he stared up at the stars, wondering where it had flown from and the journeys the passengers on board were making. Were any of them at peace in their lives? Or like him, were they reaching the end of the line? In truth, he would never know the answer.

Suddenly he spotted the lights of another vehicle, which had turned off the main road and was heading down the track towards him. He needed to hide. As quietly as he could, he moved deeper into the shadows of the trees, out of reach of the probing headlights. A few minutes later, the car swept through the entrance to the car park and stopped directly opposite Duval's vehicle. It remained motionless for a short time before the driver maneuvered backwards into position so the headlights remained facing Duval. Duval flashed his own headlights. The car opposite did the same, and shortly afterwards he watched as Duval opened his driver's door and jumped down onto the ground. Duval held his position for a second as he appeared to be coiffing his hair, then made the short walk across the car park, where he stopped to bend down and talk to the occupant. Standing in the shadows of the trees, it was difficult to make out what was being said, but he could hear a woman laughing.

The conversation continued a minute more before Duval straightened and opened the driver's door and helped a woman up from her seat. There was more banter between them before they linked arms and strode off into the trees on the opposite side of the car park, giggling as they went.

Luckily, in his rush to satisfy his perverse sexual desires, Duval had forgotten to lock his vehicle, and he now had the perfect opportunity to effect his plan. Moving with stealth, he was standing next to the Range Rover a minute later. Checking around to ensure Duval was nowhere in sight, he pulled off his backpack, then opened the back door and slipped inside, where he tucked himself in the very generous footwell behind the two front seats. He quickly removed the horsehair cord and placed it within easy reach, then made himself comfortable. Checking his watch, he could see it was 9:17 PM. Now all he had to do was wait.

Lying in the darkness, his mind wandered to Danni and the many hours they'd spent together; the reason he was here tonight. Such a wonderful woman who had been through so much pain at the hands of Duval, a vicious and sadistic narcissist, who cared for nothing and no one but himself.

Somehow Danni had managed to rebuild her life since the attack. A life that she had dedicated to helping people in pain just like him. She had become a beacon of light in the dark world he had been forced to inhabit for so many years. Tonight was his gift to Danni. His way of saying *thank you* and giving her the one thing she craved the most: peace at last.

Just then he heard laughter from outside the car and could easily make out Duval's voice saying goodbye – and that he 'needed a piss'. He listened on and soon after heard the woman fire her car's ignition, followed by the sound of tyres rolling over the gravelly ground below. Then the car revved loudly, and she set off back down the track, the sound of her engine getting quieter as she moved away towards the main road.

Silence descended as he lay motionless in the footwell, but his heart felt like it would burst through his eardrums as he waited.

Thankfully he didn't have to wait long, and a minute or so later, the driver's door opened, and Duval jumped in, causing the large SUV to loll left and right as he did.

'You dirty daaawg, Nigel,' Duval said to himself, clapping his hands with delight. 'You dirty fucking daawgg!'

Taking a deep breath, he grabbed the cord in both hands, then pushed himself up on the seat behind Duval.

'What the fuck?' Duval spun in his seat, trying to get a look at him.

But he was too quick, and a split second later he wrapped the cord around Duval's throat, yanking his head backwards against the headrest before dropping into the rear seat and using all his bodyweight to tighten the ligature. 'This is for Danni, you horrible cunt,' he spat out, staring into Duval's bulging eyes in the rear-view mirror.

Just as the others had, Duval's fingers grabbed at the cord, and his legs kicked out as he attempted to free himself, a guttural rasping sound escaping from his lips.

Jamming his feet against the back of the driver's seat, he locked his knees straight and further tightened his grip on the cord as the last remnants of air escaped from Duval's throat, and he finally stopped moving. Taking no chances, he held his position and yanked with every ounce of energy he had left for a further minute before finally letting go.

He watched with delight as Duval's body slumped to the side in the seat in front. As before, the level of adrenaline rushing through him was off the scale, and the familiar feelings of satisfaction and excitement returned.

Releasing the rear door, he jumped down to the ground and quickly pulled the driver's door open. Staring at Duval's body, he resisted the overwhelming urge to spit on him. That would be a fitting way to finish this encounter, but he knew that doing so would leave DNA samples behind, and that would never do.

Moving back to the rear door, he gathered the horsehair cord and folded it back into his backpack, then returned once more to gaze at Duval. 'Justice is done, you bastard,' he said before slinging the backpack over his shoulder. 'May you rot in hell for eternity.'

With one last glance around to ensure he was alone, he closed both doors of Duval's Range Rover, then set off back towards his moped.

30

Phillips wrapped the towel around her and made her way back into the bedroom. Adam was already dressed, perched on the end of the bed, putting on his Nike Air trainers. She glanced at the bedside clock: 6:07 AM. 'What time will you be back tonight?'

'Not sure,' said Adam. 'My shift is supposed to finish at seven thirty, but we're short-staffed again, so I may need to stay on a little longer. I can let you know for sure later, once I know what's happening.'

Phillips nodded.

'Sorry, babe. I know we hardly ever see each other at the minute.'

'It can't be helped,' replied Phillips. 'And right now, I need as much time as I can in the office myself. We seem to be taking one step forward and then two steps back. So not having to feel guilty for working late is fine by me.'

Adam stepped up from the bed and kissed her on the forehead. 'You're such a romantic.'

Phillips laughed. 'God, I know. I'm terrible, aren't I?'

'Right, well, if I want to beat the traffic, I'd better be going.'

Just then, Phillips's phone began to ring on the bedside table. Walking over towards it, she could see it was Jones. 'Calling at this time can't be good news.'

'I'll leave you to it,' said Adam with a wave.

Phillips waved back absentmindedly, then picked up the phone. 'Jonesy? This is early even by your standards.'

'Guv, you're gonna wanna see this.'

'See what?'

'Another strangulation.'

'Do we know who?'

'Not yet, but the body was found in a notorious dogging spot out past Alderley Edge. I'm on my way there now.'

'Have you called in CSI yet?'

'Yeah. Evans is meeting me there.'

'Send me the postcode, and I'll meet you there in an hour.'

'Will do,' replied Jones.

Phillips ended the call and quickly got dressed.

Saying goodbye to Floss as she headed out the front door, she had a strong feeling she wouldn't be back home for quite some time.

PHILLIPS ADORED the tiny green Mini Cooper her dad had loaned her whilst he recovered from an epilepsy diagnosis, but it had never been designed to tackle the bumpy terrain she found herself navigating, having turned onto the dirt track that led to the location of the victim. The sun was almost up, but the flashing lights of the paramedics and uniformed police team vehicles parked on the track up ahead still cast red and blue hues across the morning sky. After carefully bumping her way down the track for close to five minutes, she was somewhat relieved to pull the Mini alongside Jones's squad car. He was standing beside it.

'Morning,' she said as she climbed out of the tiny car.

Jones nodded in the direction she had come from and smiled. 'That looked like fun.'

'Try telling that to my backside,' she replied, then turned to face the car park to their right. 'Ok. So what have we got?'

'Male, IC1, strangled in the front seat of his Range Rover from what we've seen so far.'

'Are CSI here yet?'

'Yup,' said Jones. 'Working over the car as we speak.'

'So this is a so-called dogging spot, is it?'

'What, guv? You saying you've never been?'

'No, I bloody haven't, you cheeky sod.'

'Only kidding,' he asserted. 'But in answer to your question, yes. Apparently if you want sex with a stranger and no strings, then this is the place to get it.'

'God, I can't think of anything worse.'

Jones's nose wrinkled. 'All too messy for my liking.'

'Right,' said Phillips. 'Let's take a look.'

Jones led the way as they stepped under the blue and white police tape, and as they entered the car park, the large silver SUV came into view. It had all five doors open, and Evans and his team were crawling over it like huge white ants in their billowing forensic suits.

'So who found him and when?'

'A jogger out for an early morning run.'

'Must have been a bloody early riser,' replied Phillips. 'I mean, *you* called me just after six.'

'The guy's name is Henry Pollard. Reckons he's training for a triathlon, so he needed the early start. Apparently, he'd planned a twenty-five-mile ride after his early morning run.'

'Has anyone taken his statement?'

'Uniform are talking to him as we speak.'

Phillips said nothing as she surveyed the scene in front of her, then felt her brow furrow. 'How tall is he?'

'Well over six feet,' said Jones. 'Probably the same size as Bov, I'd say.'

'Really? In that case, check him out. Our killer seems hell-bent on staying off the radar, so I doubt you'll find anything, but belts and braces and all that.'

'Of course,' said Jones. 'I'll get one of the guys onto it as soon as they get in.'

Phillips moved close enough to the vehicle to be able to see inside, but far enough away so there was no need to put on forensic overalls. As Jones had described, the victim was sitting in the driver's seat, slumped slightly to the left over the central armrest. Like Venables and Todd, his eyes stared out in death, and a thick two-inch bruise ran around the front and sides of his neck. 'Looks identical to the others.'

Evans turned to face them and pulled his face mask down. 'Does, doesn't it?'

'Any fibres on the neck?'

'I haven't checked yet, but if there are, I'll get them tested as a priority.'

'Thanks, Andy.'

'We did also find what looks to be semen on his trousers, just around the zipper.'

'So he was here for sex.'

'Based on the location,' said Evans, 'I think that might be safe to assume.'

Phillips shook her head. 'How does everyone know about this place apart from me?'

'Must be your innocent Hong Kong upbringing,' said Jones wryly.

'Yeah, maybe. Any ideas on time of death, Andy?'

Judging by the state of the rigor, I'd say somewhere

between ten to twelve hours, but Chakrabortty will be able to confirm that for you.'

'What about ID?' asked Jones.

'I think Clara has just bagged a wallet.' Evans turned back to the car. 'Clara, was there any ID in the wallet?'

A tall woman in a full forensic suit, which covered most of her face, walked around from the other side of the vehicle. As she reached them, she held up a clear evidence bag containing a plastic driving licence. 'I found this in his wallet.'

Phillips pulled a pair of blue latex gloves from her pocket and slipped them on. She took the bag and examined the contents. 'Says his name's Nigel Duval.' Glancing into the car, she could see the picture ID was a match for the victim. She passed the bag to Jones. 'So who the hell is Nigel Duval?'

Holding the bag in his gloved hands, Jones scrutinised the picture. 'Never heard of him.'

'Certainly appears to be a man of means,' added Evans. 'There's a Rolex watch on his wrist that I reckon must have cost about the same as my car.'

'And these aren't cheap, either,' said Jones, pointing to the Range Rover.

Evans nodded. 'Over a hundred grand brand new.'

Phillips fished her phone from her pocket and took a picture of the driving licence. 'I'll ping this over to Whistler and see what he can find out about our victim.' She took a moment to send the email, then turned her attention back to the car. 'If we're looking at this being the same guy who killed the other two, then we have to assume Nigel Duval is somehow connected to Todd and Venables.'

'Makes sense,' said Jones, 'but how?'

'Hopefully Whistler can shed some light on that too.' Phillips checked her watch. It was approaching eight o'clock. 'He must be in by now.' Scrolling through the favourites in her phone, she tapped on Entwistle's number. A moment later as it began to ring, she activated speaker mode so Jones could hear.

'Morning, guv,' said Entwistle.

'Have you seen my email?'

'Just opened it this second.'

'We've got another strangulation. The victim's name is Nigel Duval. Can you check him out? Hopefully the address on the licence I sent through is up to date.'

'Give me a second, boss.'

They could hear him typing into his laptop.

'Clean record by all accounts.'

'Has anyone reported him missing?'

'Let me check the mispers log from last night.'

Again, they could hear him typing. About a minute later he returned to the call.

'Nothing on the mispers log from last night, so I'm guessing not.'

'Any idea who this guy is?'

More typing on the other end of the line. *'I've just Googled him, and his LinkedIn page says he's a senior talent executive in TV. Runs his own production company, by the looks of it, but used to work for various national TV networks before that.'*

'Find out if he has any connections to Todd or Venables.'

'I'll do a full background now.'

'Great,' said Phillips. 'We also need next of kin if possible.'

'I'll get straight on to it and text it across.'

'Thanks, Whistler. As soon as you can.' Phillips ended the call and turned to Jones. 'So what connects a TV exec to a Crown Court judge and an ex-copper?'

'God only knows, boss.'

31

After digging into Manchester's council tax records, Entwistle had concluded that Duval lived alone at the address on the licence in the affluent Cheshire village of Brammall, and having searched through his various social media profiles, his next of kin could only be his ex-wife, Angela. There was little evidence he was in a relationship or had any kids or parents who were alive. So an hour after leaving the crime scene, Phillips and Jones arrived outside Angela Duval's address, a city centre penthouse apartment in the recently constructed South Tower of Deansgate Square, Manchester's tallest building.

After parking up on a nearby street, Phillips and Jones made their way inside the plush modern-looking lobby. They identified themselves to the concierge who was sitting behind a minimalistic curved reception desk, a smartly dressed man whose name tag said he was called Aziz. After calling through to Angela's apartment to announce them, Aziz guided them to the elevator, and a minute later they stood side by side inside as the doors closed in front of them.

'Must cost a few quid to live here,' said Jones out of the side of his mouth.

'Yeah,' said Phillips. 'We're talking serious money for this kind of gaff.'

It didn't take long to reach the sixty-fourth floor, and as the elevator doors retracted, they stepped out into a brightly lit hallway. The walls around them were painted white and emblazoned with large golden numbers indicating they had arrived at floor 64 – the top floor.

Angela Duval's apartment was situated in the left corner of the building just ten feet from the elevator, and as they reached her double-width oak front door, Jones pressed the buzzer fixed to the wall next to it. A minute or so passed before the door opened, and an elegant woman with dark shoulder-length hair and striking features peered out, her brow furrowed.

Phillips presented her ID. 'Angela Duval?'

'Yes.' She nodded. 'Aziz told me you were coming. Can I ask what this is about?'

'We need to speak to you about your ex-husband. May we come in?'

Angela's brow wrinkled further before she nodded and opened the door wide.

They followed her inside the gargantuan open-plan apartment, which was reminiscent of a Manhattan playboy's residence: floor-to-ceiling glass windows lined almost every wall, and perfectly buffed oak parquet flooring covered every inch under foot.

Angela guided them into the living area, which featured a mezzanine floor above, and gestured for them to take a seat on one of the oversized cream, curved couches that took centre stage in the space. 'So what's Nigel been up to now?' she asked when they were all seated.

Phillips sat forward on the edge of the sofa. 'I'm sorry to

have to tell you this, Angela, but we found a body this morning, and we believe it to be Nigel.'

Angela pursed her lips and nodded. 'I see.'

Phillips was taken aback by the coolness of Angela's reaction, and as she scrutinised the woman's face intently, she could have sworn they'd met before.

'How did he die?' Angela asked flatly.

'At this stage we can't give you the specifics, but we believe it was suspicious.'

Angela let out a sardonic chuckle. 'Suspicious in life, suspicious in death. Sounds like Nigel.'

'You seem to be taking this very well,' said Phillips. 'I take it you weren't close, then?'

'Once upon a time I thought we were, but I've woken up since then. You get close to Nigel Duval at your peril.'

'What do you mean by that?' said Phillips.

'Nigel was a man who liked to play games. Spend too much time with him, and before you know it, your life is not your own.'

Phillips locked eyes with her. 'So he was controlling?'

Angela scoffed. 'A master gaslighter if ever there was one.'

'Could you expand on that a little?' said Phillips. 'To help us get a better understanding of who Nigel was.'

'I can tell you *exactly* who – or rather *what* – he was: a cheat and a liar. The king of mind games and manipulation. Before I met him, I was a confident, happy young woman. By the time we divorced, I was in therapy twice a week.'

'Was he ever abusive towards you?' Jones cut in.

'Emotionally, yes, from the moment we met, but the problem was I didn't realise it. I thought he was being charming, but looking back, he was just doing what he did with everybody and getting inside my head – breaking down my barriers so he could take control of every part of my life.

Before I knew it, he was telling me how to behave, who I could speak to, and what to wear each day.'

'That must have been very difficult for you,' said Phillips.

'It was. He got so far inside my mind, it got to the point where I had no idea who I was. For five years he mentally and emotionally controlled me before I finally started to see what I'd become and what he had done to me.'

'And how did that come about?' Phillips asked. 'The realisation, I mean.'

'Therapy. After only a few sessions, my psychiatrist was quite certain I was living in an abusive relationship, and with her help, over time I worked out how to escape from him. If she hadn't intervened, I'm scared to think what might have happened to me or what he might have done.'

Phillips nodded softly. 'I'm sorry you had to go through that.'

Angela sat back into the sofa and folded her arms against her chest. 'Anyway, that's all in the past now. I stopped letting Nigel Duval hurt me a long time ago.'

'When did you last see him?' asked Jones.

'In person?'

'Yes.'

'Must be a couple of years ago now. Just before the divorce was finalised, I think.'

Jones continued, 'And have you communicated in any other way?'

Angela laughed. 'I'd get late-night texts from him every now and again. Usually when he was drunk and needed someone to bark at. He begrudged handing over half of everything when we split; said I was a leech and a parasite. He would regularly message to threaten me with going back to court to get our divorce settlement overturned and all his money back.'

'Was Nigel a wealthy man?' asked Phillips.

'On paper, yes,' replied Angela. 'But all his money was tied up in the business and property. There was a bit of liquid cash, but not enough to call himself a millionaire.'

Phillips cast her gaze around the opulent space. 'This place can't be cheap. Did the divorce pay for it?'

Angela shook her head. 'It's rented, and my settlement meant I got half of his businesses, so dividends each year as opposed to cash reserves. Like I said, his money was all tied up.'

'And what do *you* do?' said Jones.

'Aside from my share of the profits, I'm an actress. I was in a TV series a few years ago that was recently picked up by Netflix. My monthly repeat fees pretty much cover the cost of living here.'

Phillips's eyes narrowed as she studied Angela's face again, suddenly realising why she looked so familiar. 'Was it a show about gangsters in sixties London?'

'You saw it?'

'I did – the first series at least. I thought it was very good.'

Angela smiled. '*Killer Streets* – I played one of the gangsters' wives, Tessa Mitcham.'

'I thought you looked familiar.' Phillips smiled. 'Do you know if Nigel had any enemies?'

'Why do you ask?'

'As we said, we're classing his death as suspicious.'

'You mean he was murdered?'

'We're looking at all possibilities,' replied Phillips.

Angela nodded silently.

'So can you think of anyone who might want to harm him?'

'The way he went about business, I'm sure that's very likely.'

'What do you mean by that?' said Phillips.

'Nigel was completely obsessed with a novel called *The Art of War* – by Sun Tzu.'

'I'm familiar with it,' said Phillips. It was a book Fox greatly admired and had coerced her into reading a number of years ago.

'In that case, you'll know it talks about ancient Chinese warfare and how you beat your enemy not by fighting them head-on, but by attacking them cut by cut. Weaken them over time without them realising, and then take them out when they can no longer fight back. It's how he ended up with his own production company.'

'Really? How so?' Jones asked.

'When he was running the network, he used to commission Big Bear Productions to make shows for him. Those shows made a lot of money, and Nigel wanted a piece of it. He asked for a cut in return for more shows, but the owner, Shaq, was having none of it. So Nigel, being Nigel, came up with a plan to get the whole thing for nothing. Over the next eighteen months he commissioned Big Bear to make dozens of shows. So many shows they needed to invest heavily in infrastructure. When they were up to their eyes in debt, Nigel pulled the plug on every single project, and Big Bear had no way of covering their overheads. They filed for administration six months later.'

'And let me guess,' said Jones. 'Nigel bought the company?'

Angela flashed a thin smile. 'Exactly – for just one pound.'

'So could this guy, Shaq, have an axe to grind with Nigel?' said Phillips.

'Not unless he killed him from the grave. Shaq died last year. Cancer. I know his wife well, and she said she believes the cancer was brought on by the stress of losing everything. It was a terrible shame.'

Phillips hooked her hair behind her right ear. 'Can I ask where *you* were last night?'

Angela's face wrinkled. 'Why? Am I a suspect?'

'Merely procedure,' Phillips replied.

'I was here all night with Zane.'

'Zane?' asked Phillips.

'My partner.'

'Can he vouch for you?'

Angela got up from the sofa and wandered over to the edge of the mezzanine, where she craned her neck. 'Zane!'

Phillips glanced at Jones, who raised his eyebrows.

A tall, dark-haired, muscular man wearing a tight-fitting white T-shirt and gym shorts, who looked to be in his early thirties, appeared on the small balcony a moment later. 'Yeah?' His accent was thick Australian.

'The detectives want to know where we were last night.'

Zane frowned. 'Why?'

'It seems Nigel is dead.'

'Really?' Zane appeared unmoved. 'Couldn't happen to a nicer bloke.'

'We were here all night, watching TV together, weren't we?'

Zane took a moment to answer. 'Yeah, that's right.'

Angela turned back to face Phillips and Jones. 'Happy?'

'Sure,' Phillips said, 'but we'll need Zane's details, of course. Just for our records.'

'Zane Toohey.'

Jones pulled out his notebook. 'Date of birth?'

'Twelfth of August, 1989.'

Jones scribbled down the info.

Angela remained standing.

Phillips took the hint and stood. 'Well, thank you for your time. You've been very helpful.'

'Not at all. Happy to be of service.'

'One last thing,' said Phillips. 'We need someone to formally ID Nigel's body. Would you be up for doing that?'

'After everything that happened, I'd rather not. His sister, Sarah, would probably be the best person for that.'

'He has a sister?' said Jones.

'Yes,' replied Angela. 'Lives in London. Battersea if I remember rightly. Goes by Sarah Preston since she got married.'

Jones opened his notepad again. 'Do you have an address?'

'No. We lost touch after the divorce.'

Phillips eyed her for a moment. 'Not to worry, I'm sure we can find her on the system.'

Angela flashed a thin smile. 'If there's nothing else, I have a lot to do today.'

'Of course,' said Phillips. 'Thanks again.'

A few minutes later as the elevator doors closed, Jones turned to her. 'You thinking what I'm thinking, guv?'

'That Zane looks the right height and build to be our guy?'

'Totally.' Jones nodded. 'And she was definitely coaching him on their alibi.'

'Yeah. I saw that too. Plus, there wasn't the slightest hint of surprise on her face when we told her Nigel was dead. Same with Zane.'

'True.' There was a long pause before Jones continued, 'Look, I get why she'd want her ex dead, but what's the connection to Venables and Todd?'

'That's the bit I'm struggling with too.' Phillips glanced up towards the roof of the elevator and noticed the CCTV camera positioned facing the doors. She pointed up to it. 'We're going to need copies of all the CCTV from last night. See if they really did stay in like she claims.'

'I'll speak to the concierge.'

'And we need a full background on Zane Toohey.'

'Yeah, Bov can sort that,' replied Jones.

The elevator stopped, and the doors opened. 'You get the video, and I'll call Carter. He'll want the heads-up on Duval before Fox gets wind of a third strangulation.'

'If she hasn't already.'

'True.' Phillips pulled her phone from her pocket. 'Her bloody spies are everywhere.'

32

On the return journey to the station, Phillips had called ahead and requested Bov and Entwistle set up the MCU conference room so they could debrief on everything they had so far. There was lots to get through, and she felt a more formal setting would help keep them focused. She'd also asked Bov to organise lunch for everyone on the department's tab. It'd been a long morning, and she knew everyone would need refuelling to make the afternoon as productive as possible.

As Phillips and Jones walked into the conference room forty minutes later, Bovalino was placing hot drinks and a variety of sandwiches on the conference table.

Phillips grabbed a coffee, then selected a ham and cheese before taking her seat as each of the team collected their own food and drink. For the next few minutes the room fell silent as they tucked into their lunch.

Finally, with half a sandwich remaining, she began the debrief. 'So, according to Duval's ex-wife, he was an abusive, coercive gaslighter who ruined her life.'

'Sounds charming,' Bovalino said through a mouthful of food.

Phillips continued, 'She works as an actress, and it seems they met when she starred in a TV show called *Killer Streets* that was based on London's gangland culture around the time the Krays were at their peak.'

Entwistle placed what was left of his sandwich on the table and began tapping into his laptop, which, as usual, was being projected onto the big screen.

Phillips looked on as he pulled up IMDB – the movie and TV database – and typed in the name Angela Duval. A second later, the woman they had just spoken to appeared on-screen, albeit clearly a lot younger in the featured headshot.

Entwistle scrolled down and found the details of her past roles. 'You're right. Looks like she played Tessa Mitcham.'

Phillips took a sip of her coffee. 'She painted quite a picture of her ex, Nigel, didn't she, Jonesy?'

'Too right,' he shot back. 'Sounds like a right bastard, by all accounts, who used his power and influence in the TV industry to get what he wanted, whenever he wanted it.'

'Which means' – Phillips sighed – 'that the potential list of suspects who could want him dead could be as long as those of Venables and Todd.' She took another bite of her sandwich and turned her attention to Bovalino. 'I want you to check out Angela Duval's boyfriend, a guy called Zane Toohey. He's a physical match for the backpack guy on the CCTV footage, and both he and Angela seemed less than convincing when asked about their whereabouts last night.'

'How you spelling Toohey, boss?'

'T-double O-H-E-Y.'

Bovalino scribbled in his pad.

Jones passed over a pen drive to the big Italian. 'This is a copy of the CCTV from the apartment block where she lives.

I got the concierge to download all the folders and cameras from the last twenty-four hours. We need to know if Angela and Zane were in all night as they claim to have been.'

Bovalino examined the small drive, then made another note in his pad.

'I also want all ANPR footage within a five-mile radius of the murder scene,' added Phillips. 'Let's start with the hours leading up to and after Duval's death.'

'Not a problem,' said Bovalino.

Phillips focused on Entwistle. 'Any progress on the horse-hair supplier in China?'

Entwistle glanced down at his notes, then back at Phillips. 'Right, so the translator managed to speak to them, but even when talking in Mandarin, she said they seemed reluctant to help. So I contacted a guy at the Chinese embassy in London, a fella called Myles Lazenby. He said he could try to intervene with the officials over there on my behalf but didn't offer much hope that it would make any difference. Apparently the Chinese embassy over here has very little appetite to help in these kinds of situations. They claim all Chinese nationals are free to run their businesses without interference from the government.'

'Yeah, right,' scoffed Jones. 'China has the most controlling government on the planet. Their new social credit system is the epitome of big brother is watching you. Very George Orwell and *1984*. It's bloody terrifying.'

Chinese politics was not a rabbit hole she wanted the team to get lost down at this moment. 'So we're no further forward with tracking down where these fibres came from?'

'No, sorry, guv,' replied Entwistle.

Phillips exhaled loudly, struggling to hide her growing frustration. 'What about the fibres we found on Duval? Any update from Evans on those?'

Entwistle shook his head. 'Not as yet.'

'Can you chase him on it?'

'Will do.'

Phillips continued, 'We need to know for certain if they're a match. Having seen the state of Duval and the crime scene, I'm pretty sure they will be.'

Bovalino finished his sandwich and sat forward. 'I did manage to track down the mysterious Jerome Grant though.'

Phillips raised her eyebrows. 'Oh really?'

'Yeah, on the way into work this morning. I was passing his address, so I thought I'd chance it. He was half asleep and not very happy that I'd woken him up, but then I also think he was stoned: the stench of cannabis from inside the flat was really strong.'

'So what did he have to say for himself?' Jones asked.

'He claims he was working in the warehouse at the Tesco in Parrs Wood on each night of the murders.'

'Can anyone verify that?' said Phillips.

'Gave me his manager's number to call.' Bovalino opened his notepad. 'A woman called Wendy Li. He said she can confirm it, as he has a digital fob that he uses to clock in and out and access secure areas around the building, which will prove he was there. I tried getting hold of her this morning, but I was told she's not back in until five in the afternoon, so I'll try her again after that.'

Phillips placed her hands flat on the conference table. 'If Grant does have a solid alibi, then Zane Toohey could well be our only suspect right now. So checking the CCTV from Angela's building has to be a priority.'

'I'm on it, guv,' Bovalino assured her.

'And check the council cameras around the apartment block too.'

The big man nodded.

Phillips continued, 'Let's also get Nigel Duval's phone

records over the last month and check his finances. See if he owed anyone money.'

'I'll do that,' said Entwistle.

Phillips stared at the big screen on the wall ahead and Angela Duval's headshot, which was still visible. 'I keep coming back to the same question: what connects a Crown Court judge, a retired chief constable, and a TV executive?'

Jones sat forward. 'I've been thinking about that since you asked me this morning, and the only thing I can think of so far is sex. I mean, we *know* Venables was a big fan of the Purple Door, and Duval was murdered in a notorious dogging spot.'

'But what about Todd?' asked Bovalino. 'There's nothing to suggest *he* was into that sort of stuff.'

'Nothing so far,' Jones shot back. 'Doesn't mean we won't find something once we start digging a little deeper.'

'Jones makes a good point,' replied Phillips, 'but if it *is* sex that connects them, how did it get them killed?'

The room fell silent, and each of the team appeared deep in thought.

Phillips turned to Bovalino. 'Speak to the manager at the Purple Door. See if Duval was a customer, and check for Todd too. If either of them was, that could be our connection right there.'

'Sure.' Bovalino made another note in his pad.

Phillips drained her coffee, then turned to face Jones. 'I think it's time we had a look around Nigel's home. See if that can give us any clues as to why someone might want to strangle him.'

'Want me to drive?' Jones asked.

'Yeah, and book a tactical team to meet us there. His front door keys were bagged and tagged at the scene by forensics, so unless he keeps one under the mat, we're probably going to need the big red one to get in.'

'I'll call them now.'

'Great,' said Phillips as she stood up from the chair. 'We've a lot to do, guys, so let's get cracking.'

33

Duval's palatial Brammall home was a sight to behold, a huge flat-roofed single-storey building with glass walls on all sides that gave the structure an almost weightless appearance. It was set back from the main road, which ran straight into the village one mile away, on what Phillips guessed was probably five or six acres of land. As the squad car moved along the gravel drive, she gazed in awe at the architecture on display. It was quite unlike anything else she'd seen in Manchester before today.

'Clearly made a few quid, then,' said Jones as he pulled the car up next to the tactical team's vehicle.

'Looks like it. Either that or he was mortgaged up to his eyeballs. We'll know either way once we get sight of his financials.'

It was another warm afternoon as Phillips and Jones crunched across the gravel drive towards the head of the tactical unit, Sergeant Louise Andrews. Andrews stood at six feet with a athletic frame. Over the years she had developed a fierce reputation for getting into any locked building the

GMP required access to. She and her team were the go-to unit at times like this.

'Afternoon, ma'am.' Andrews thumbed towards the house behind her, where a couple of members of her team stood next to the front door. 'We've checked for any spare keys knocking about the place, but I'm afraid we've drawn a blank.'

'So it's the big red key, then, is it?' asked Phillips, referring to the red, handheld battering ram her team used to break open doors.

'Yep. Lewis and Podgorski are ready and waiting. All we need is your approval.'

'In that case, go for it,' said Phillips.

Andrews turned to face her team and signalled with her hand to execute entry.

The two officers gave her the thumbs-up, then prepared to take aim. A split second later the red battering ram connected with the heavy wooden door, which splintered around the lock but remained closed.

'Well-made door, that,' remarked Jones.

A second blow landed, and this time the door flung open on its hinges.

Andrews produced a wide grin. 'But still no match for the big red key.'

'Nice work,' said Phillips.

'Shouldn't take very long to secure the building,' Andrews added before marching off towards the house.

Under normal circumstances when a tactical team entered an unknown building, Phillips and Jones would have waited outside – just in case any suspects tried to fight their way out – but today, knowing Duval was dead and expecting that his property was empty, they followed closely behind Andrews, stepping inside the large hallway as the tactical unit swept the house.

The interior was just as impressive as the exterior, clean lines, open plan, and minimalistic design in every direction.

'It's like a bloody morgue in here,' said Jones with disdain.

Phillips chuckled. 'You're not a fan of modern design, then?'

'No. Not at all. Too bloody hard to keep clean. Especially with teenage daughters to contend with.'

At that moment Andrews reappeared from one of the adjoining rooms. 'The house is empty as expected, ma'am. But we have found a locked door off the main bedroom. No idea what's behind it, but we can break it down if you'd like.'

Phillips was intrigued. 'Can you show us?'

'This way.' Andrews turned and headed back into the main block of the house.

A minute later Phillips and Jones followed her into the main bedroom, a gargantuan space with 270-degree views of the garden and outdoor pool beyond.

'It's this one.' Andrews tapped on a door to the side of the bed. 'Want us to smash it down?'

'Yeah,' replied Phillips.

Once again, Andrews gave the order, and in a flash Officer Lewis thrust the big red battering ram against the lock. This time there was no resistance, and the door caved in on itself like a piece of cardboard.

Phillips stepped forward and peered inside. 'Jesus. Look at this little lot.'

Jones appeared at her shoulder, then stopped in his tracks. 'Bloody hell. It's like a flaming sex shop.'

Moving inside, Phillips examined the contents of the shelves that lined both sides of the long narrow room. Covering almost every available space was a wide selection of sex toys of various sizes and complexity, as well as leather and rubber outfits and a host of whips and chains, which hung from the walls.

'Well, the minimal look seems to have gone out the window in here,' quipped Jones.

Phillips gazed all around, then turned back to Jones. 'Sex *has* to be how Duval's connected to Todd and Venables. Looks as if they both had a taste for the exotic.'

'Is that what they call it?' said Jones.

'Let's see what else is hidden in here.' Phillips moved deeper into the room. 'You take that side, and I'll take this.'

Jones pulled a pair of latex gloves from his pocket. 'Think I'm gonna need disinfecting after this.'

For the next fifteen minutes, they searched the shelves item by item, looking for anything that might help explain why Duval had been targeted, but all they found was more evidence of his extreme fetishes.

'What the hell is this?' said Jones, holding up something that resembled a large torch with what looked like an oversized tulip on the end.

Phillips stepped closer to get a better look, and her eyes narrowed. 'I can't be certain, but I think that's what they call a flashlight.'

'A what?'

Phillips flashed a coy smile. 'Blokes use it.'

Jones stared down at it. 'For what?'

'You're the detective.' Phillips chuckled. 'You figure it out.'

Jones wrinkled his nose, then placed it back on the shelf, and they continued their search.

With the examination of the shelves soon exhausted, Phillips moved to the corner of the room where she'd spotted two large plastic storage containers sitting on the floor. She removed the lid of the first one she came to and placed it against the wall. The box was full of what appeared to be old camcorder tapes. 'Have a look at these,' she said, examining one at close quarters.

Jones joined her and pulled out a couple of tapes himself.

Phillips stared down at the handwritten label: 'Natasha – March 2005 – threesome.'

Jones did the same. 'Marsha – September 2004 – blindfold.'

'Looks like he kept souvenirs,' said Phillips.

'There must be over a hundred tapes in here, guv.'

'Yeah, and we need to see what's on all of them.'

'But how? This technology's obsolete.'

'Hold this for me, will you?' Phillips handed across the tape in her hand and pulled the lid off the second box. 'Seek and ye shall find.'

Inside the box was a medium-sized camcorder about the size of a small brick – the kind that were popular in the nineties before the proliferation of cameras in mobile phones. Reaching in, Phillips pulled it out and attempted to switch it on.

'Looks like the battery's flat,' said Jones.

Phillips spotted the charging block in the box. 'Let's get this back to base and see if Whistler can get a tune out of it. We'll need all the tapes too.'

Jones put the tapes in his hands carefully back in the box.

Phillips did the same with the camera, then turned to survey the room once more. 'There's a reason Duval kept that door locked up tight, and as weird and wonderful as these sex toys and outfits are, I don't think the extra security was for their benefit.'

'I think you're right, guv.' Jones glanced round the space once more and shuddered. 'Even so, I'm definitely going to need a shower when I get home.'

34

Early next morning the team reconvened in the conference room. Once again Entwistle had sourced the tech needed to view the videos found in Duval's secure room. The tapes had been unpacked and were now stacked on the conference table.

'Right.' Phillips took a sip of hot coffee and nodded toward the screen. 'Let's see what's on these things.'

Entwistle picked up the closest tape to him. '*The Beast Masters*,' he said, reading the label on the side before inserting it into the adapter provided by the tech team the previous evening. A second later he pressed play, and the big screen burst into life as a grainy video appeared in front of them. Initially the footage appeared to show a man's bare feet and legs from above as he walked across a thick carpet, but the camera soon lifted, revealing a group of middle-aged men and much younger women having sex in what appeared to be a substantial living room. Mounds of white powder could be seen on various tables and flat spaces around the room.

'Jesus,' muttered Bovalino. 'Those fellas look old enough to be the girls' dads.'

'Recognise anyone?' asked Phillips.

Jones squinted as he stared at the footage. 'I can't say I do, but like Bov says, each of the guys must be in their fifties or sixties.'

The tape played for another five minutes, and the orgy and drug-taking continued, but nothing much changed.

'I think we've seen enough of that one for now, Whistler,' said Phillips. 'Let's try another.'

Entwistle picked out the next tape and replaced the previous video on the big screen. A similar scene appeared. This time a different group of similarly aged men were having sex with young women and snorting cocaine. The camera operator was laughing and providing commentary on the activities on show in front of him. The location appeared to be the same room as the last video.

'What's this one called?' asked Jones.

Entwistle picked up the empty cassette case. '*Beast Masters Two*.'

'So can we assume these old boys, like the last lot, are the Beast Masters?' said Phillips.

'It's an appropriate name if they are,' Jones shot back. 'Those girls look a similar age to my teenage daughters.'

'Duval's yet to make an appearance,' said Entwistle.

'I'm thinking he must be the one behind the camera,' Phillips replied. 'Any sign of Venables or Todd?'

'Not yet,' Entwistle said, shaking his head.

'So who the hell are these guys?' Phillips asked, frustrated.

Jones sat forward. 'Whoever they are, like you said, Duval kept these videos hidden for a reason.'

Phillips locked eyes with her second in command. 'Looking at this lot, I'm even more certain that sex is the link between Venables and Duval. The Purple Door, the dogging spot, and now these tapes, but we still have nothing concrete on Todd.'

Silence descended before Bovalino spoke. 'So, taking Todd out of the equation for the time being, if sex connects Venables and Duval, could it also be their connection to the killer?'

'It would be the obvious link,' Phillips conceded, 'but in what way? From what we've seen so far, Venables and Duval were vehemently straight – as was Todd – and our killer's clearly male.'

'A jealous boyfriend?' Entwistle ventured.

'Well, you'd know all about that,' said Bovalino with a grin.

Entwistle rolled his eyes. 'Yeah, yeah, very funny.'

'Bov makes a good point though,' said Jones. 'Maybe he's connected to one of these girls on the tapes?'

'Or.' Phillips pursed her lips. 'Maybe the killer actually *features* in one of these videos? Maybe he's trying to remove all links back to himself.'

'If that's the case, then why not just go after the tapes?' said Bovalino.

'Maybe he planned to eventually,' Jones ventured. 'And we beat him to it.'

Phillips turned to Entwistle. 'Who have we got in the support team who can help us view them?'

'PC Lawford is close to finishing logging the ANPR footage around Venables's and Todd's houses, and I've been very impressed with her eye for detail.'

Phillips took another drink of coffee. 'In that case, let's get her started on these as soon as she's finished. We're looking for any males who match what we have from the CCTV so far.'

'I'll brief her as soon as we're done.'

'I also want to see the contents of Duval's mobile ASAP. If he was this fond of filming, I'm sure his phone will be full of videos.'

Entwistle nodded. 'I'll speak to digital forensics.'

Phillips turned her attention to Bovalino. 'Any updates from the ANPR cameras around the Duval murder?'

'Yeah.' The big man passed across a pen drive to Entwistle. 'Stick that on the screen, will you?'

A moment later, a number of folders appeared.

'Open folder nineteen,' added Bov. 'It's cued up where I want it.'

Entwistle did as requested, and the footage played.

Bovalino narrated what they were watching. 'This is the camera at the junction just down from the turn-off to the dogging spot.'

'Wow. That's a lucky break,' said Jones.

'Totally.' The big man grinned. 'Made me laugh. All these people sneaking around in the woods for sex, not realising their cars and reg plates are logged every time they do it.'

'I shudder to think who we might find on those tapes,' said Phillips.

Bovalino continued, 'On the night of the murder, we see Duval's Range Rover passing the camera just before nine. Shortly afterwards, this moped passes the camera. A few minutes later we see these two cars travelling in the opposite direction, then two more, a couple of minutes apart. Because it's a main road and we don't have sight of the dirt track, we have no idea if any of them came from the dogging spot.' He turned to Entwistle. 'Fast-forward fifteen minutes on the time stamp, will you?'

'Sure.'

Soon after, Bov took the lead again. 'Now, at approximately 9:06, this blue Kia Sportage passes the camera, heading west towards the crime scene. The same car comes back east forty minutes later. Fast-forward to 9:56, will you, Whistler?'

Again, Entwistle obliged, and the footage played once more.

'Ten minutes later, the same moped passes the camera, but this time heading back towards Manchester. All other vehicles logged around the hour Duval was killed go either east *or* west. The Kia and the moped are the only ones that go in *both* directions.'

'So who's the driver of each?' asked Phillips.

Bov looked down at his notes. 'The Kia is registered to a Nigel Tanner of Urmston. No record, works on the railways as an engineer.'

'Could he be our guy?' said Jones.

'I've had a quick look at his social media profiles, and if I've found the right Nigel Tanner, then he fits the profile. Tall, slim build, recently ran the Boston Marathon, so he's physically fit.'

'What about the moped driver?' asked Phillips. 'Who's the registered keeper of that?'

He glanced down at his notes again. 'Kingsway Rentals.'

'It was hired?'

'Looks that way, guv.'

'A rented vehicle spotted in the immediate vicinity of a murder scene – well, that's a red flag for a start. Get onto Kingsway and find out who hired it that day.'

Bovalino nodded.

'And while you're doing that, me and Jonesy can go see Nigel Tanner.'

Bov handed across a yellow Post-it note. 'His address in Urmston.'

'Are we done with the ANPR footage?' Entwistle asked.

'Yeah, that's it for now,' said Bovalino.

'Just before you go, boss.' Entwistle opened another folder on the screen. 'I checked the cameras from Angela Duval's apartment, and it seems she's either lying or has a case of amnesia. Check this out.'

The big screen was filled with yet more CCTV footage, this time showing the inside of what appeared to be an underground garage. 'This was captured at eight fifteen the night Duval died. Just watch the bottom of the screen.'

The team watched on as the video played, and a man and a woman appeared in the shot, walking towards a large silver Mercedes with their backs to the camera.

'Is that Angela?' asked Phillips.

'Yep.'

'How can you tell? Her back's to the camera,' Jones cut in.

'Not for long,' said Entwistle.

A moment later, as suggested, the woman turned as she opened the passenger door of the Mercedes, and Angela Duval's face appeared on-screen.

Jones pointed at the footage. 'I knew their alibi was a load of shit.'

The video continued, and a minute later, the Mercedes pulled out of the parking space and headed for the exit.

Phillips gazed at the screen. 'So if they left the apartment at 8:15, that gives them plenty of time to get to the crime scene.'

'But there's no sign of them on the ANPR cameras,' said Bovalino.

'True.' Phillips nodded. 'But if they're smart, they could have used a different route to avoid them. Made their way to the final location on foot.'

'It's certainly possible,' Jones added.

'Bov, check the ANPR cameras around the apartment

block,' said Phillips. 'See what direction they went. Follow them if you can.'

'Will do.'

Phillips glanced at the Post-it note in her hand, then across at Jonesy. 'Let's go see what Mr Tanner has to say for himself.'

35

Tanner's home was located in Urmston, a densely populated suburb four miles west of Manchester; it was a recently built three-storey, red-brick town-house with a small driveway that connected the property to the pavement. Before knocking on the front door, Phillips bent down and took a long look inside the blue car, noticing the rosary beads hanging from the rear-view mirror. Nothing else of note stood out. Straightening, she turned to Jones and nodded in the direction of the front door.

He rapped on it three times, then stepped back as they waited.

A minute or so passed before a petite woman with auburn hair opened the door, a quizzical look on her face. 'Can I help you?'

Jones took the lead and held up his ID. 'DI Jones and DCI Phillips. We're looking for Nigel Tanner.'

The woman frowned. 'Nigel? Why? What's wrong?'

'Do you live here?'

'Yes. I'm his wife.'

'And what's your name?' said Jones.

'Emily. Look, what's this all about?'

'We really need to speak to your husband, urgently,' Phillips cut in.

'He's away for a few days on a golfing trip in Portugal.'

'Really? Since when?'

'Sunday afternoon.'

Phillips turned towards the car. 'Is this Nigel's?'

'Er, yes. Why?'

'It was spotted on our automatic number plate recognition cameras on Monday night,' replied Phillips, 'near the scene of a serious crime, and we were hoping Nigel could have witnessed something.'

'Does anyone else drive the car besides your husband?' Jones asked.

'No.' Emily's neck appeared to flush slightly.

Phillips locked eyes with her. 'Are you sure? Because we can easily trace the car's movements across the ANPR network and find out where the vehicle came from.'

'On some of the cameras, we can even see who was at the wheel,' Jones added.

Emily glanced at the car, then blinked furiously. 'Er...'

'Who *else* drives the car, Emily?' asked Phillips.

'I do.'

'And were you driving it last night?'

'Yes.' The flushing on her neck had spread to her cheeks now.

Phillips took a step forward. 'I think we'd better come inside, don't you?'

Emily nodded silently and opened the door.

A few minutes later they each sat down in the small, smartly decorated lounge to the rear of the house.

Jones took out his notepad.

'Can you tell us what you were doing on the road to Alderley Edge around nine on Monday night?' asked Phillips.

'Nothing much, really. I just fancied a drive.'

'So at which point did you turn around and head back to Manchester?'

'Erm, I don't really remember. I wasn't paying attention.'

'Did you by any chance turn into the Peak View car park?' asked Phillips.

Emily bit her lip and took time to answer. 'I might have done. I don't know the area very well.'

Phillips and Jones exchanged glances.

'The thing is, Emily, a serious crime took place in that car park around the time you were in the close vicinity. A man died.'

Emily's mouth fell open, and her eyes widened like saucers.

'We've studied the ANPR footage around the area, and it seems your vehicle is one of only two that could have pulled into the car park at the time that crime took place.' Phillips locked eyes with her. 'So I'll ask you again, did you use the Peak View car park around nine on Monday?'

Emily closed her eyes for a moment, then nodded.

'And what were you doing up there at that time of night?' Jones asked.

'I went for a walk.'

'So you got out of the car?'

'Just for a few minutes, yeah.'

Jones scribbled in his notebook. 'And did you see anyone when you were out for your walk?'

Emily rubbed the back of her neck. 'No.'

Phillips studied her body language. It was obvious she was hiding something. 'The thing is, Emily, the Peak View car park is a notorious dogging spot. People don't generally go there to walk.'

'Dogging?' Emily straightened. 'I'm afraid I don't know what that means.'

Phillips folded her arms and stared at her in silence for a long moment. 'Why do I get the feeling you know *exactly* what it means?'

Emily stared back but said nothing.

'Here's what I think happened,' said Phillips. 'I think you pulled into the Peak View car park that night, looking for sex.'

'That's ridiculous,' Emily scoffed.

Phillips continued unabated. 'And judging by how long it took for your car to reappear heading back west on the ANPR cameras, I'm guessing you succeeded in your quest. Am I right?'

Emily laughed nervously. 'I don't know what you're talking about.'

'A man died, Emily,' Phillips said. 'So I need you to *seriously* think about what you're saying to us.'

The room fell silent.

'We don't care what you were doing up there,' said Jones. 'We just need to know the truth.'

Emily dropped her chin to her chest.

Phillips pulled her phone from her pocket and scanned through the photos until she found the screenshot of Nigel Duval that Entwistle had sent to her on the drive over. She presented it to Emily. 'Did you meet this man in the car park?'

Emily lifted her head and stared at the screen for a long time before finally answering. 'Yes.'

'And have you met him before?'

'No.'

'So you don't know who he is?'

'No. He didn't tell me his name.'

'Did you have sex with him?' asked Phillips. 'And remember, we can run tests that will tell us if you did.'

'Oh, God.' A tear streaked down Emily's cheek as she nodded.

Jones cut in now. 'We believe he died in his car. Is that where you two were intimate?'

'No,' said Emily, wiping her nose with the back of her hand. 'He took me into the woods.'

'So how long were you together for?' Jones asked.

'I dunno.' Emily shrugged. 'About twenty minutes, half an hour, maybe.'

'And what time did you last see him?' said Phillips.

Emily took a moment to answer. 'I honestly can't remember. I wasn't really thinking about the time.'

'Did you stick around when you returned to your car?' Phillips asked.

'I didn't, but *he* did. Said he needed the toilet.'

Phillips's eyes narrowed. 'Did you see him get back into his car before you left?'

'No.'

'And were there any other cars in the carpark at that time?'

'No. Just ours.'

'Was anyone hanging about on foot?' said Jones.

'Not that I saw, no.'

Phillips studied her face to see if she was lying and was confident she wasn't.

'How did he die?' asked Emily.

'I'm afraid we can't tell you that at the moment,' replied Phillips.

Emily wiped her eyes.

'Did you see a moped anywhere near the car park when you were there?'

Emily's brow furrowed. 'No. Not that I remember, anyway. It was empty apart from our two cars.'

'I see,' said Phillips.

Jones cut back in now. 'We're going to need you to come into the station to give a DNA sample.'

'Really, why? I didn't do anything.'

'It looks like you were one of the last people to see him alive,' replied Jones. 'And you were intimate with him not long before he died. That means currently you could well be connected to his death, and we're going to need DNA to understand to what extent.'

'But—'

'You can either come of your own volition this afternoon,' Phillips cut her off. 'Or maybe you'd prefer for a uniformed unit to come back when your husband's here and take you into custody. It's your call.'

Emily rubbed her hands down her face, causing her cheeks to redden.

Phillips glared at her. 'What's it to be?'

'I'll come in today.'

'Good.' Phillips stood.

Jones stepped up a second later.

'You won't tell my husband, will you?' said Emily. 'I don't make a habit of this kind of thing, you know.'

'What you do in your own time is none of our business,' Phillips replied. 'Unless, of course, it links you to Nigel Duval's death. That would be a different matter entirely.'

Emily nodded.

Phillips looked at her in silence for a long moment before finally speaking. 'I think we're done here, so we'll see ourselves out.'

Back in the car, Phillips called Bovalino.

'Hey, boss,' he answered.

'Turns out Turner's wife was driving the Kia up at the dogging spot, not him. Seems he's away on a golfing trip overseas. So finding the driver of the moped is even more urgent.'

'I've just this minute been speaking to the rental company, guv.

Apparently they've put in a new central booking system and are having a few teething problems.'

'Which means what exactly?'

'They can't tell me who hired the scooter at the moment, but they reckon the server will be back online in the next few hours.'

'Okay, stay on them. Looks like the rider might be our guy.'

'I'll call them back,' said Bovalino. *'Let them know just how urgent this is.'*

'Thanks, Bov, we'll see you when we get back to the office.' Phillips ended the call.

36

As Phillips and Jones walked through the doors of MCU, her mobile began to ring. Fishing it from her pocket, she could see it was Evans.

Jones continued towards his desk.

'Andy? What have you got for me?'

'The fibres on Duval's neck, Jane.'

'Yeah.'

'They're the same as those we took from Venables and Todd.'

'Figured they would be. Anything else of note?'

'As I mentioned at the scene we found traces of semen around the zipper of his suit trousers, along with vaginal transudate. So it looks as if he had sex not long before he was killed.'

'Any hairs or fibres?'

'Yes, but from a female.'

'What colour?'

'Auburn.'

'Makes sense. Anything else?'

'Not at the moment.'

'Okay. Thanks, Andy.'

'My pleasure.'

Phillips hung up and joined the rest of the team, who were in conversation at their desks.

'Just telling the team about Emily Tanner and Duval,' said Jones.

'That was Evans. Seems the fibres on Duval's neck are a match for the first two murders, so there can be no doubt we're looking for the same guy.'

Jones reclined in his chair. 'Based on the crime scene, we always knew that would be the case.'

Phillips turned her focus to Entwistle. 'What have you managed to find on Duval?'

'In regard to his background, nothing more than we already had: TV exec with his own limited company, divorced, financially stable, but with little liquid cash and a large mortgage on the house in Brammall.'

'Any ideas who inherits in his will?'

'Not yet, no, guv, but I've put a call into the national will register to see what they have on file.'

'Videos on his phone?'

'Digital forensics are going through it as we speak, and I've also managed to get his phone records, which I've passed to the support team to cross reference against Todd's and Venables's call logs. We're trying to find any common numbers, but so far we've drawn a blank.'

'And what about ANPR cameras further afield from the car park?'

'I'm still going through them, boss,' said Bovalino.

'Any joy with the moped rental company?'

'Systems are still down, but they've assured me as soon as they're back online, they'll get me the details ASAP.'

'Okay.' Phillips took a moment to reset her ponytail. 'We really need more intel on Duval, to see if we can figure out what connects him to the other two.'

'I hate to say it,' Jones ventured, 'because he's a total dick, but what about Townsend? With Duval's obvious media profile, maybe he came across him at some point.'

Phillips considered it as an option before pulling out her phone again. 'I have another idea.' Quickly scrolling through her numbers, she found what she was looking for and pressed dial.

After connecting, it rang a few times before it was answered. *'Jane, long time no speak.'*

'Marty, I need a favour.'

'Okay. So how can I help the Greater Manchester Police today?'

'Have you ever come across a guy called Nigel Duval?'

'That prick?' spat Marty. *'Sadly, yes. The man is a complete arsehole.'*

'Where are you now?'

'The golf club. Just having some lunch.'

'Which one?'

'Worsley. Why?'

'Can I come and see you?'

'Of course, but I'm only here for another hour or so before I head into the studio.'

'I'm on my way,' she replied before ending the call.

'Marty?' Jones stared at her with expectant eyes. 'As in Marty Michaels?'

'Yeah. Seeing as he's such a big fish in the TV industry, I figured if anyone could give us some insight on Duval, it was probably him. And we're in luck, seems he knew our murdered media mogul, so don't get comfortable, Jonesy. We're going to Worsley.'

WORSLEY GOLF CLUB was very similar in style to Alerton Hall, where Jack Todd had been murdered. The drive up from the main road was a little longer and the clubhouse grander, but there was little else to tell them apart.

The sun was shining as Phillips and Jones made their way into the empty clubhouse bar, where she could hear Michaels holding court nearby, and after a quick scan of her surroundings, she spotted him sitting outside on the terrace, his expensive-looking sunglasses glinting in the midday sun.

'Jane!' Michaels smiled widely as soon as they stepped outside, immediately standing and drawing her into a hug.

'You're still as loud as ever,' she said warmly.

'I wouldn't be Marty Michaels if I weren't.' He smiled wider and held out his hand to Jones. 'Jonesy, good to see you, mate.'

'Likewise,' replied Jones, shaking his hand.

'Please, let me get you a drink.' Michaels beckoned the waiter as they sat down around the table.

The waiter joined them a second later.

'What do you fancy?'

'Just a Diet Coke for me,' said Phillips.

Jones nodded. 'I'll get the same, please.'

'And I'll have another Grey Goose and tonic,' added Michaels.

The waiter scribbled down the order, then disappeared inside.

Michaels was the picture of success, and everything about him suggested he had wealth and no shortage of confidence. Despite approaching his fiftieth year, he looked ten years younger, and whilst his hair appeared wild and free, it had certainly been expensively coifed to look that way. His skin glowed, and his teeth sparkled almost as much as the Cartier watch on his tanned wrist. All of which was in stark contrast to a thick scar that ran down the left side of his neck. A constant reminder of the horrific events that had first thrown him and Phillips together almost five years ago.

'You're looking well,' said Phillips.

'What can I say, Jane? Life's good.'

'It would appear so,' Phillips said. 'Still busy?'

'Like you wouldn't believe.' He smirked. 'Getting accused of murder was probably the best thing that could have happened to my career.'

'I only wish your little dalliance with the law had been as good for me.'

'What do you mean?' Michaels feigned shock. 'You're famous now thanks to all that.'

'I was thinking more about the bullet I took on your behalf,' said Phillips sardonically.

At that point, the waiter returned and handed out their drinks before disappearing as quickly as he had arrived.

Phillips took a mouthful of Coke, then placed the glass, clinking with ice, back on the table. 'So, tell us about Nigel Duval.'

A wry grin spread across Michaels's face as he lifted his drink to his lips. 'What's this about? Finally been caught, has he?'

'He's dead,' Phillips replied without emotion.

Michaels sat to attention. 'He's what?'

'Dead.'

'Bloody hell.' Michaels sipped his drink. 'How?'

'Too early to tell,' Phillips lied.

'But it was murder, right? Otherwise, you two wouldn't be here?'

'Ever the journalist, hey?'

'Never leaves you, Jane.'

Phillips had no intention of sharing the details of Duval's death with Marty Michaels of all people. As close as they had become over the years since their near-death experience, he was a complete gossip and the last person to share confidential information with. 'What did you mean when you asked if he'd finally been caught?'

Michaels sniffed contemptuously. 'He was a bad man, Jane.'

'In what way?' asked Jones.

'Sexual predator. Used his position in the business to molest and abuse countless women over the years.'

Phillips took another drink, a blessed relief against the heat of the sun overhead. 'According to who?'

'According to *everyone* who ever worked with him,' Michaels shot back. 'He even tried it on with Becky back in the day.'

'Your ex Becky?'

Michaels nodded. 'Cheeky fucker crept up behind her in the office and grabbed her boobs. I wanted to kick the living shit out of him when I found out, but Becky was having none of it. Said it was just his way and the industry was like that. It was long before the 'Me Too' movement – boiled my piss, I can tell you.'

'If he was as prolific as you suggest,' said Jones, 'why has no one ever come forward about him?'

'They did, but they were given plenty of reasons to keep shtum.' Michaels rubbed his thumb and finger together. 'If you know what I mean.'

Phillips tilted her head to the side. 'His victims were paid off?'

Michaels cradled his drink in both hands. 'Naturally.'

'Any proof of that?'

'No, but believe me, it happened.'

'So who paid them off?' asked Phillips.

'The network. In fact, rumour has it that his behaviour got so bad they actually built a line into the company's P&L to cover the payouts each year.'

Jones's brow furrowed. 'But why would they do that? Why not just sack him?'

Michaels shrugged. 'Nobody ever knew, but the joke was he must've had photos of the network bosses shagging animals or something.'

Phillips and Jones locked eyes. *The videotapes.*

'That said,' Michaels continued, 'there was *one* incident that nearly finished him off.'

Phillips turned her attention back to Michaels. 'What was that?'

'Duval finally escalated to full-blown rape: a young runner starting out who worked with Becky at the time. Daniella Briggs was her name.'

'What happened?' said Jones.

'I'm not sure on the details, but I know he attacked her after the company Christmas party that year. Apparently he invited himself into her flat, forced himself on her, and when she tried to fight him off, he raped her.'

'And this was public knowledge at the time, was it?' Phillips asked.

Michaels took a mouthful of his drink. 'Again, nothing was ever proven, but it all came out a few months later when Daniella's dad turned up at the network, shouting the odds. Becky was walking through reception just as he arrived. He was ranting and raving, apparently, saying Duval had raped his daughter, that he wasn't going to let him get away with it, and he was planning on telling the police everything.'

'So what happened then?' said Phillips.

'As you'd imagine, news like that spread like wildfire all over town. Everyone was expecting him to be hung, drawn, and quartered and to finally get what was coming to him, but just like all the other incidents, it went quiet, very quickly, and before long, it went away completely.'

'What about the police?' Jones asked. 'Did they not look into it?'

'Not that I'm aware of.' Michaels sat forward and lowered his voice. 'It was weird. I mean, look, *I* know better than most you're guilty until proven innocent in the eyes of the media, but not one single outlet reported on the allegations. No TV, no radio, no papers, and, of course, social media didn't exist back then. Not one single story came out about it. That's unheard of. I mean, look at how much press there was around the allegations made against me. You couldn't move without seeing something about my apparent crimes. But with Duval, nothing, and after that, it seemed he was untouchable. That's certainly how he behaved, anyway.'

'Could it have been an injunction?' asked Jones.

'Nah,' replied Michaels. 'I've tried to get a few of those myself in the past. They're only good for a few days, then whatever it is you're trying to keep quiet always comes out one way or the other. No, something else was at play in this case.'

Phillips took a moment to process everything she'd just heard.

Michaels sat back again, drained his glass and looked at his watch. 'Do you need anything else? Only I'm due at the studio in half an hour.'

'No, no, you go. That's been very useful.'

Michaels smiled and grabbed his keys from the table. 'Look, you know where I am if you need anything else.'

'Thanks, Marty,' said Phillips as they all stood up.

'Right, one last hug and then I must dash.' He drew her in, then shook Jones's hand. 'Come again soon, yeah?'

'Sure,' said Phillips.

'We could even have a round if you like?'

Phillips laughed. 'I think I'll leave that to you.'

'Suit yourself,' said Michaels with a grin before stepping away from the table and heading back into the clubhouse.

Phillips turned to Jones. 'I think we need to have a closer look at Duval's videotapes. See if we can figure out who those blokes are.'

'I was just thinking the exact same thing.'

'They could well be the reason he was never outed in the press.'

'Friends in high places?' said Jones.

'More like blackmail. A motive for murder if ever there was one.'

37

He had marveled time and time again at how quickly people had expected him to move on after her death, to get back to normal and forget about what had happened that night. But that had been an impossibility. How could he? When those responsible for her murder and for destroying her memory were free to live their lives without consequence? Justice was hard to find; he had come to realise that over time. In fact, discovering just how corrupt the legal system had become was what had driven him to take matters into his own hands. This evening he would deliver on the promise he had made silently at her funeral: to make them all pay for what had happened exactly five years ago tonight.

Watching the house from the cover of the trees, he was reminded how long he'd fantasied about this moment. So much of his life over the last five years had been dedicated to meticulous research and planning in order to deliver his own brand of justice, deadly justice. With his face partially covered under a scarf and the backpack over his shoulders, he slipped on the latex gloves. Then, slowly, he moved around the perimeter of the garden, being careful to stay out of sight of the neighbours' overlooking windows, closer to the open French bi-folding doors that ran the length of the rear of the house.

Nic Johnson had taken the afternoon off to attend a hospital appointment, which had proven fortuitous for him, given his plans for her tonight. But after returning home, rather than rest, she had jumped on her phone and spent the last couple of hours talking to person after person, hardly drawing breath. It appeared she was a woman with little time for self-care and that the pursuit of money was her master.

Standing now to the left of the open doors, he took a deep breath to steady his racing pulse as he prepared himself for the task in hand and the long night ahead. It was time to deliver the final act of revenge for what they did to Sally. There was no time to waste, and the clock was ticking. It was now or never.

38

As they walked back to the car, they discussed the next steps.

'We should talk to Daniella Briggs as a priority,' suggested Phillips. 'See if she can corroborate what Marty said.'

'Makes sense. Especially as all we've got so far is media gossip, which is never the most reliable.'

Phillips pulled out her phone and called the office.

Entwistle answered, and after sharing the details of their conversation with Marty Michaels, she asked him to find a current address for Briggs. He promised to get straight into it and a few minutes later called back with the information.

'And how long has she lived there?' Phillips asked.

'Three years, by the looks of it.'

'Okay. Can you text me the postcode and full address?'

'I'll do it now,' he replied. *'Oh, and Bov says he needs to talk to you.'*

'No worries. Put him on.'

She waited as Entwistle passed over the phone to the big man.

'*Guv.*' His tone was urgent. *'I've got a name and address for the moped rider. A guy called Marcus Thomas.'*

'Great. Get over there and see if he can explain what he was doing out at Peak View on Monday night.'

'I'll go straight away.'

'Let me know as soon as you have anything, won't you?'

'Of course, boss.'

After hanging up, she turned her attention back to Jones. 'Bov's got a hit on the moped rider, a guy called Marcus Thomas. He's heading over to speak to him now.'

'And what about us?' he replied. 'Where are we going?'

'Withington.' Phillips glanced at the message from Entwistle. 'Maudleth Road.'

Jones pulled open the driver's door. 'I know it well. We can jump on the M60. Shouldn't take too long to get there.'

'Great.'

Thirty minutes later they walked up the steps to the Victorian townhouse, which had at some stage been converted into flats.

'It's number eleven, according to Entwistle,' said Phillips as they reached the oversized front door.

Jones ran his finger down the section of buzzers, then pressed the one marked eleven.

A second later, a voice came through the speaker connected to the buzzers. *'Hello?'*

'Daniella Briggs?' Jones asked.

'Yes.'

'I'm Detective Inspector Jones from the Major Crimes Unit, and I'm with my colleague DCI Phillips. Can we have a word, please?'

'What's this about?'

'I think it really would be better if we speak inside.'

'Can you put your ID in front of the camera, please?'

Jones obliged.

After a long pause, a buzzer sounded. *'Push it open and come up to the third floor.'*

Jones stepped inside, Phillips at his back.

A few minutes later, they turned up the final flight of stairs to find a short, slim woman with close-cropped black hair and thick black glasses waiting for them on the landing. 'Can I see those IDs again?' she asked as they reached her.

Jones presented his credentials for a second time, as did Phillips.

Daniella inspected them closely and thoroughly. 'Thank you, you can't be too careful these days. Anyway, you'd better come through.'

Inside, the flat was immaculately presented and almost military clean. The long hallway that led to the rear of the property was painted a bright yellow, with polished wooden floors.

Once they reached the living room at the back of the apartment, Daniella offered them seats, then took her own in an oversized beetroot-red–coloured armchair. Phillips and Jones sat opposite, side by side on the matching sofa.

Daniella's angular face was etched with tension as she folded her arms across her tiny frame. 'So why are two detectives suddenly knocking at my door?'

'I'm really sorry,' Phillips said softly. 'But we need to talk to you about Nigel Duval.'

Daniella's body visibly tightened, and she lifted her chin slightly. 'After all this time? Has he done it again?'

'No,' replied Phillips. 'He was found dead in his car on Monday night.'

Daniella remained stoic.

Phillips studied her reaction, but she was giving nothing away. 'We understand he assaulted you.'

'Bit late to the party, aren't you?' Daniella shot back.

'Agreed,' replied Phillips, 'and nothing I can say will make up for that, but as the assault was never reported, we do need to know about it from you.'

'Does it matter anymore? Now he's dead.'

Phillips shifted in her seat. 'Yes. I think it does. Just because he covered it up all those years ago doesn't mean it should stay that way.'

Daniella didn't respond.

'Having stayed silent about it for all these years, maybe talking about it with us might help.'

'I very much doubt it.'

Phillips remained silent.

'And anyway, I've been talking about that night for the last ten years.'

'How do you mean?' Jones cut in.

Daniella pushed her glasses back on the bridge of her nose. 'I run a support group for victims of physical and mental abuse, as well as sexual assault; my way of coming to terms with what happened to me. I've talked about it plenty.'

'I see,' replied Phillips. 'In that case, could you share what happened with us?'

'He raped me,' Daniella said flatly. 'What else is there to tell you?'

Phillips paused, then followed a different line of questioning. 'We understand your father made threats against the network after he found out what happened to you.'

'That's right. I asked him not to, but he was so angry with Duval he wouldn't listen to me or Mum.'

'Can you tell us what happened after he made those threats?' said Phillips.

Daniella cast her gaze to the floor. 'They came after us.'

'Who did?'

'The network and their team of lawyers.'

Phillips sat forward. 'When you say they came after you, what exactly did they do?'

'Threatened us mostly.'

'With what?'

'All sorts,' said Daniella. 'A long, drawn-out trial, including a full character assassination of me, suggesting I was promiscuous and had set out to seduce Duval and then, as she put it, "had suffered buyer's remorse" – not to mention the promise of a horrific cross-examination in the witness box. That lawyer of theirs said she'd easily be able to paint a picture of *me* as the one who had wanted sex – not him – and all because I had invited him into my flat late at night. As if by allowing him through the front door, he was entitled to have sex with me whether I liked it or not. It was outrageous.'

'That must have been very frightening for you,' Phillips said.

'It was, but nothing compared to what Duval threatened to do to me if I told anyone.'

'And when did he do that?'

'The moment he'd finished with me.'

'What did he say?'

'I was lying on the sofa in shock, and he stood over me, sneering as he got dressed. He told me to keep my mouth shut, or he'd kill me and bury me in the woods. He claimed no one could touch him, not even the law. Said he had so much dirt on the right people that he could literally get away with murder.'

'Do you know which people he was talking about?' Jones asked.

Daniella shook her head. 'I don't, but I believed him. That's why I begged my dad not to go after him, and I never said anything to anyone about it outside of my therapy group. What we speak about in there stays in there.'

'So how did your dad find out about the assault?' said Phillips.

Daniella exhaled sharply. 'After it happened, I shut down emotionally. I couldn't function and was missing work a lot. I tried my best to hide what was going on from everyone by staying in my flat all the time. Mum and Dad had always been regular visitors, usually a couple of times a week, so when I started avoiding them and kept them at arm's length for over a month, they suspected something was going on. Eventually, about three months after the attack, Mum and Dad confronted me because they thought my issues were down to drugs. I broke down and told them everything, and that's when he went to the network and started making threats.'

'And that's when the lawyers got involved?' Phillips cut in.

'Yes. Offered us a settlement to sign a gagging order. Dad wanted to fight it, but I just wanted it all to go away, so I agreed, and part of that agreement meant I had to leave the network, which, to be honest, was fine by me. I just wanted to get away from Duval.'

'And was that the last time you had any contact with him?' asked Phillips.

'No.' Daniella bit her bottom lip. 'When I left the network, my mental health got even worse. I was taking huge amounts of antidepressants and anxiety meds, which turned me into a zombie, and I had to move back in with Mum and Dad. I literally spent a month in bed, and Mum and Dad were really worried about me, so they decided to use the settlement money to buy a holiday cottage in Broxton as a place to help me recover. We used to go there as kids on holiday, and we'd always loved it as a family. It took a while, but eventually it really started to help me. The fresh air, being away from everything, I began to feel like I was coming back, but then he...' Her words tailed off as a tear streaked down her cheek.

Phillips sat forward. 'What happened, Daniella?'

'Duval showed up at the cottage one night when I was staying there on my own. I don't know how he found out about the place, but he turned up at the front door without any warning. He'd been drinking and said he'd been thinking about me and wanted to "pick up where we'd left off". He tried to force the chain to get inside, but I managed to shut the door and called the police. Naturally he disappeared before they arrived, but the damage was done. That house wasn't safe, so I got in my car that night, drove straight to Mum and Dad's and never went back. We sold the cottage soon after.'

'I'm not surprised,' said Phillips.

Daniella continued, 'Dad went ballistic when I told him what had happened. Told me he was going to sort Duval out himself. I was genuinely worried he was going to kill him, but thankfully Mum and I managed to calm him down and convinced him to leave it alone, eventually.'

'And where is your dad now?'

'He passed away, a massive stroke.'

'I'm sorry to hear that,' Phillips said.

'We could never prove it, but I'm convinced the stress of what happened to me caused the stroke.'

Phillips remained silent before changing tack again. 'You said the lawyer who threatened you was a woman. Do you remember her name?'

'Her surname, no, because I burnt all the letters she sent at the time – part of a healing ritual in the group – but I seem to recall she had a first name that could also be a man's.'

'How do you mean?'

'You know, like Leslie or Alex...but it wasn't either of those. Shorter, in fact.'

Phillips's eyes narrowed. 'Can you describe her?'

'Tall, jet-black hair, total bitch. Stinking of money with a huge gold Rolex on her wrist.'

Phillips looked at Jones, then back at Daniella. 'Was her name *Nic*?'

Daniella appeared deep in thought.

'Nic Johnson?'

'Yeah.' Daniella nodded. 'That's her.'

39

'So do you want to go see Johnson again?' asked Jones as they headed back down the stairs after leaving Daniella's flat.

'Seeing as she's somehow connected to all three victims, I think that's a very good idea. But I'm not risking being turned away again.' She pulled out her phone and searched for Johnson Law in Google. 'I'm going to make an appointment,' she said with a wry smile as she placed the handset to her ear.

The call was answered briskly: 'Johnson Law. This is Chloe speaking; how can I direct your call?'

'This is DCI Phillips. I'd like to speak with Nic Johnson, please.'

'I'm afraid she's not in the office today; can I take a message?'

'Do you know where she is?'

'I'm afraid that's confidential.'

'Not when it involves a police investigation.'

'I'm sorry, but her reasons for being out of the office are personal.'

Phillips's patience was wearing thin. 'Can you at least give me her mobile number?'

'I'm not supposed to give out personal phone numbers, so I'll need to check with one of the partners. Can you hold?'

Phillips opened her mouth to protest but was cut off by Vivaldi's *Four Seasons* as the hold music kicked in.

'She's not the easiest person in the world to pin down, is she?' said Jones.

Phillips shook her head, frustrated by the delay.

A minute later Chloe returned to the call. *'Hello again. I've spoken to Mr Edwards, one of the partners, and he says it's fine.'*

She listened intently as Chloe shared the number, repeating the digits out loud so Jones could note them down. 'Thank you,' she said finally, then hung up. She quickly dialled Nic Johnson's mobile, but after several rings, a recorded message kicked in. 'Voicemail. Damn it.'

She tried again two more times but got the same result with each attempt.

'So what now?' asked Jones.

Phillips tapped the phone against her teeth while she figured out the best way forward.

'I'll keep trying Johnson, but in the meantime let's get back to base and take a look at those videotapes of Duval's.'

'Sounds like a plan,' replied Jones, deactivating the squad car's central locking.

At that moment, Phillips's phone began to ring. Initially she hoped it was Johnson calling back, but when she glanced at the screen, she could see it was Bovalino. 'Did you find the rider of the moped?'

'Yes and no, guv.'

Phillips was in no mood for games. 'What the hell does that mean?'

'I spoke to Marcus Thomas at the address used on the rental agreement, but he's not our guy.'

'How so?'

'The Marcus Thomas I just met is in a wheelchair; he has cerebral palsy.'

'So the moped rider used a fake driving license to hire the bike?'

'Looks that way.'

'We need to find this guy. He has to be involved.'

'Now we know what we're looking for, I can try to track him on the other ANPR cameras once I get back to base.'

'Okay. We're heading to the office too. We'll see you there.'

'Cool, won't be long,' said Bovalino, then hung up.

On the drive back, Phillips reflected on how her growing sense of frustration was affecting not only her, but likely the team as well. She'd been pushing them hard for seven days straight without a break, and with so much video and ANPR footage still to check, today would likely require another late finish. In an effort to boost morale, when they arrived back at Ashton House, whilst Jones headed back to his desk, she made a quick detour to the canteen to sort out sandwiches, hot drinks, and a few sweet treats for the guys.

Ten minutes later as she negotiated the doors to MCU while carrying a tray piled high with food, she was delighted to see Bovalino making his way up the stairs.

'Need a hand, guv?' he said cheerfully.

'Please.'

He took the tray from her and used his right shoulder to open the doors.

Phillips followed him through.

'Look at this little lot,' said Bovalino in Jones's direction, beaming from ear to ear.

'You never see Bov as happy as when he's about to eat.' Jones smiled.

The big Italian placed the tray on the spare desk, and each of them picked out their preferred sandwich.

'Where's Entwistle?' asked Phillips, her eyes fixed on his empty chair.

'Been complaining of having a dodgy stomach earlier this afternoon,' Bovalino replied as he unwrapped his sandwich.

'I think there's a bit of gastro going round,' said Jones. 'Sarah mentioned a load of her workmates have gone down with it.'

'It's brutal, gastro,' Bov added. 'I had it once a few years ago; I didn't eat for a week.'

Jones laughed. 'And food vendors all over Manchester filed for bankruptcy.'

Bovalino grinned as he took a large bite.

Just then Entwistle stepped inside, his right hand placed against his stomach as he walked across the office.

'How's your arse, big man?' Bovalino teased.

Entwistle shook his head but remained silent as he dropped gently onto his chair.

'Bov tells us you're not feeling well,' said Phillips.

'Not sure if I've eaten something that didn't agree with me, guv.'

'I was just saying, gastro's going round at Sarah's work, could be that,' added Jones.

Entwistle wiped his brow. 'Well, whatever it is, *that* wasn't very pleasant.'

Bovalino laughed as he threw his sandwich wrapper in the bin. 'Shitting through the eye of a needle, hey?'

'Something like that,' Entwistle replied.

'Do you need to go home?' asked Phillips.

'No.' Entwistle winced slightly. 'I'll be fine. We've got too much to do.'

Phillips got up from the chair and moved across to the water cooler, where she filled a plastic cup, then handed it to Entwistle. 'Get that down you.'

'Thanks.'

'Right,' said Phillips, retaking her seat. 'Before Jones and I update you on our progress today, Bov, why don't you bring Entwistle up to speed on our moped rider, Marcus Thomas.'

Bovalino swallowed his latest mouthful, then wiped his mouth with a napkin. 'I visited Mr Thomas at the address registered on the hire agreement from Kingsway Rentals. It looks like our moped rider used a fake ID.'

'Which begs the question, why?' said Phillips.

'Because he knows we can track him through the cameras,' Bovalino replied.

'Exactly.' Phillips took a drink of coffee. 'Which makes him a credible suspect for Duval's murder. So I've tasked Bov with tracking him across the ANPR network. See if we can figure out where he went after Duval was killed.'

'Do we know how long he hired the moped for?' asked Jones.

Bovalino checked his notepad. 'Two weeks, it looks like. Picked it up on Monday morning.'

Jones placed his cup on the desk. 'Which means he could still be riding round on it as we speak.'

'True,' replied Phillips. 'Let's get the registration out to all officers. You never know, we might get lucky.'

'I've also asked for copies of the CCTV from the rental garage, boss,' Bovalino added. 'They're sending it over tomorrow.'

Phillips frowned. 'Can we not get it today?'

'A chunk of their system is still offline, their security camera files included.'

'We need it first thing tomorrow, in that case.'

'I'll make sure of it, boss.'

Phillips drained her cup and threw the remnants into the bin before focusing back on the team. 'So Jonesy and I had a busy afternoon. Firstly catching up with Marty Michaels and then a visit to a woman called Daniella Briggs.'

For the next few minutes Phillips and Jones shared the details of their afternoon's work with Bov and Entwistle. When they were finished, the room fell silent for a time.

'You said Duval had serious leverage on people in power,' Bovalino ventured. 'Are you thinking that could be the tapes?'

'Exactly that' Phillips replied.

Jones nodded. 'It would certainly explain why he kept them locked away like he did.'

'So he was blackmailing people?' asked Entwistle.

Phillips nodded. 'It's certainly possible.'

'Now we just need to find out who,' added Jones.

'The other angle we need to explore urgently,' said Phillips, 'is that Nic Johnson was connected to all three victims. She worked for Venables and alongside Jack Todd when she was starting out in the CPS, and a few years later when she moved into private practice, she made Daniella Briggs's rape allegations go away on behalf of Nigel Duval.'

'Are you saying *she's* involved in all this?' asked Bovalino.

Phillips folded her arms across her chest. 'Involved? No, but connected in some way? It's a definite possibility. I've been trying to get hold of her for the last hour but keep getting her voicemail.'

Grabbing her phone, she pressed redial, but again, there was no answer from Nic. 'Okay, until I can speak to Johnson, our focus has to be on checking the tapes and the ANPR system. So, Whistler, let's you, me and Jones move into the conference room and take a closer look at of those videos, and, Bov, you get on with tracking that moped.'

A few minutes later in the conference room, Entwistle reconnected his laptop to the big screen, along with the camcorder adaptor. 'That seems to be working okay. I'll just fetch the tapes.' He headed out the door.

Phillips turned to Jones. 'I really need to update Carter on all this.'

'If you want to do that now, I can make a start on these with Whistler?'

'Might not be a bad idea, actually.'

At that moment the door to the conference room opened, and Entwistle stepped back inside. His face was ashen, almost grey.

'You okay, Whistler?' asked Phillips. 'Is your stomach bothering you again?'

He shook his head. 'No, it's the tapes, guv,' he mumbled.

'What about them?'

He appeared to be lost for words before finally answering, 'They've gone.'

Phillips did a double take. 'What do you mean they've *gone*?'

'They're not there anymore.'

'Not where?' asked Jones.

'Where I left them in the main office. Next to the filing cabinets in the storage box. I put them there this afternoon, ready for PC Lawford to start going through them tomorrow. When I went to get them just now, the box has gone.'

Phillips jumped up from the chair and marched towards him. 'Show me.'

Entwistle nodded as he turned on his heel and headed back to the office.

A second later, Phillips stood at his side as they stared at the empty space on the office floor next to the filing cabinets. Jones and Bovalino appeared soon after.

Entwistle pointed. 'The box was there.'

'When did you last see them?' said Phillips.

'I could have sworn they were there when I went to the toilet earlier.'

'Could Lawford have taken them?'

'I don't think so; like I say, she's due to start on them tomorrow.'

'You'd better check just in case.'

Entwistle pulled out his phone and made the call.

Phillips turned to Jones. 'You didn't see anyone knocking about when you came into the office, did you?'

'No. Not a soul.'

Entwistle returned, his shoulders sagging. 'As I thought, she's been finishing up the ANPR checks we gave her around the first two crime scenes. She's not been anywhere near the tapes.'

'Fuck.' Phillips exhaled loudly. 'Have we got any CCTV cameras in the corridor?'

'No, guv,' replied Jones. 'Just the main reception and custody suite.'

Phillips rubbed her face with the palm of her hand. 'This is all we bloody need. If Fox finds out we've let someone walk off with vital evidence, we're all in deep shit.'

'But who would take the risk?' asked Entwistle. 'I was only gone for ten or fifteen minutes, and the building is crawling with coppers.'

'Yeah, it is.' Phillips nodded. 'And we know at least one of those coppers could well be working against us – the same person who's feeding inside information to Don Townsend.' She turned to Entwistle. 'Have you got anywhere with that list yet?'

He shook his head. 'No, sorry. I've been busy with the investigation.'

Phillips could feel her jaw clenching as her stomach churned. 'We need to find those tapes, guys, so drop everything else and start looking.'

40

Having had no luck tracking Nic Johnson down on the phone, Phillips had decided that trying to catch her at home was the next best option. After sourcing Johnson's address on the system, she had left the guys to continue their search for the missing tapes, hoping beyond hope they would have found them by the time she returned to the office later that day.

As usual she had laboured through the heavy traffic that always seemed to surround West Didsbury. It always amazed her that no matter what time of day she attempted to navigate the popular village, the roads were always jammed full. Finally, after what felt like an eternity, she pulled left down Clyde Road, creeping along as she searched for Johnson's house, number 59. She found the large red-brick semi-detached Victorian villa a minute later and turned the Mini Cooper onto the empty gravel drive.

It was another warm evening as she made her way to the front door and pressed the video doorbell attached to the wall. There was no reply, so she tried again with the same result. Pulling out her phone, she pressed redial, and as the call connected, she could hear Johnson's ringtone nearby. Phillips frowned as she set off towards the ringing phone. Heading down the side of the house, the ringing became louder. It was then she spotted the spots of blood on the path and stopped in her tracks. Her pulse quickened as Johnson's phone defaulted to voicemail. 'What the hell?' she whispered as she crouched down to get a closer look. The blood was fresh.

Standing up, she dialled Johnson's phone a second time and again followed the ringing. Moving quietly to the end of the path, she stopped and peered round the corner of the building. The garden was empty and the back of the house open. She walked towards the ringing and vibrating handset, which she spotted lying on the patio just outside the kitchen. Ending the call, she put her own phone back in her pocket. She pulled on a latex glove and picked up Johnson's handset, which she could see was also splattered with blood. Turning to look inside the house, she could see paperwork and legal files were strewn all over the floor – it was clear a struggle had taken place recently.

'Nic!' Phillips cried out. 'Nic, can you hear me?'

There was no answer. Phillips stepped inside, careful not to disturb anything, and placed Johnson's phone on the long dining table. Next, she headed back to the front of the house and took a closer look at the driveway. She'd noticed some gravel had been displaced when she got out of the car, but hadn't given it much thought on arrival. Looking at it now, it appeared as though someone had left in a hurry, kicking up stones and leaving a deep skid mark. There was also a series of indentations in the gravel that looked about the size of an adult shoe.

It was time to call Jones.

He answered quickly. *'Hi, guv. If you're calling about the tapes, we still haven't found them, I'm afraid.'*

'Never mind the tapes,' Phillips shot back. 'I think Nic Johnson's been abducted.'

'She's what?'

'I've just arrived at the house, but there's no sign of her, and it looks as if there's been a struggle. There's blood splatter on the path to the side of the house, and she's left her phone behind. Plus, there's a bloody great hole in the gravel drive where someone has left in a hurry and what looks like heavy footprints. Given her connection to all three previous victims, I'm worried she's next on his list.'

'Oh shit. So what do you want us to do?'

Phillips glanced at the driveway again. 'If I remember rightly, Johnson drives a bloody great big Mercedes, doesn't she?'

'Rings a bell, yeah.'

'Well, it's not at the house, so that could be a good place to start. Get her registration, and let's see if it's popped up on any of the ANPR cameras around here.'

'I'll do it now.'

Phillips turned round to face the house, and her eye was drawn to the Blink doorbell. 'I'll stay on the line, and while you're doing that, I've had another idea.' Rushing back to the kitchen, she picked up Johnson's phone. The passcode screen appeared, and she began typing in the most obvious combinations, 0000, 1111, 1234, 9999, but to no avail. She let out a frustrated growl.

'I've found the registration, guv.'

'What is it?'

'N5 JLL.'

'Can you dig out her date of birth as well?'

'Sure, give me a sec,' said Jones, typing at the other end before rejoining the conversation. *'The twenty-fifth of May in 1974.'*

Phillips keyed 250574 into the phone. It opened instantly.

'Bingo,' she said loudly.

'What's going on, boss?'

'Johnson has a Blink video doorbell at the front of the house – Adam and I had one installed after he was attacked. If she's as paranoid as I am, she'll have the motion detector switched on, which means if someone *did* snatch her, then it'll have been recorded on her phone.' She scanned through the various apps on Johnson's home screen until she found the Blink app. Clicking on it – and to Phillip's great delight – there were a number of clips logged, the most recent of them capturing her arrival and movements since, but more importantly, a clip had also recorded twenty minutes previously. 'I've got video.' She pressed Play and watched in silence as the footage unfolded. A man, almost certainly the same person captured at Venables's home and Alerton Hall golf club, was dragging Johnson down the front steps and across the gravel drive. He was wearing a baseball cap, and his face was partially covered by a scarf. 'It's the same guy, Jonesy. He's bundling her towards her own car.'

'Can you see his face?'

'No. He's got his back to the camera, plus it's half covered, but the cap and backpack appear the same. It has to be our killer. Let's get an alert out to all officers. We need to find Johnson's car.'

'I'm loading it into the system as we speak.'

As the footage continued, it was evident Johnson was not going down without a fight, her arms and hands flailing around as the man opened the car's large boot and attempted to force her into it. Johnson lashed out, grabbing at the scarf, which fell from his face. A second later he punched her hard in the nose, knocking her back, before bundling her into the boot.

'Turn to the camera, you bastard,' Phillips muttered, willing him to show his face.

At that exact moment, as the man slammed the boot shut, he looked left and right to check he had not been seen and then back towards the house and the doorbell.

'Got him!' said Phillips. 'He just looked at the camera.'

'Do you recognise him?'

Phillips stared at the screen for a long moment before answering, 'I don't believe it.'

'What?'

'It's her bloody assistant.'

'Who?'

'The guy we met the first time we went to Johnson's office. Ian, I think he said his name was. He was in court with her too.'

'That long streak of piss, you mean?'

'Yeah. That's him,' replied Phillips. 'Is Whistler there?'

'Sitting opposite me.'

'Put him on.'

Jones obliged, and a second later, Entwistle appeared on the line. *'Hi, boss. Look, I'm really sorry about the tapes—'*

'Don't worry about them right now. I need you to find out everything you can on a guy who works for Nic Johnson.'

'What's his name?'

'Ian.'

'Do you know his last name?'

'No. But he's one of her clerks, and he's just forced her into the boot of her own car.'

'He's done what?'

'Jones will explain. Just get me what you can on him as quick as you can, and we're also going to need a uniform team to secure this place.'

'I'm on it.'

With that, Phillips ended the call.

Desperate for answers, she opened the browser on her phone and Googled Johnson's Law. Frustratingly it seemed to take an age to display the search results. Finally, they appeared; she clicked on the top link. Just as the website began to load, the screen changed as her phone began to ring. It was Jones. 'Jonesy, what have you got?'

'Whistler checked Johnson Law's website—'

'I was just trying to do the same thing.'

Jones continued, *'—turns out the guy's name is Ian Crowther.'*

'Crowther? You mean like *Sally* Crowther from the domestic abuse murder?'

'That occurred to me too. So I got him to check the guy's social media pages to see if we can connect them.'

'And?'

'Sally Crowther was Ian's older sister.'

'Fuck! How did we miss that?'

'To be fair, boss, we had no reason to believe Sally had any siblings. I mean, when we spoke to her mum and dad, they never once intimated they had another kid. The way they talked, it was just Sally.'

'I don't believe this. He's been right in front of us this whole time.'

'There's more. Looking at his social pages, he's certainly not prolific and rarely posts, but a year ago today he put something on Facebook about the fact it had been four years to the day since his sister was murdered, and that more needed to be done to protect women from abusive partners.'

'So today's the *fifth* anniversary of Sally's death?'

'Yeah.'

'Oh shit. That's all we need, a killer with a deadline.'

'The alert on Johnson's car has just gone live across the force – we'll start scanning the ANPR cameras looking for it immediately.'

'Okay.' Phillips cast her eyes to the tyre tracks in the gravel. 'I'm gonna call the Crowthers. See if they can shed any light on what the hell is going on with their son.'

41

He steered the Mercedes through the gate and down the lane towards the cottage, the only house within a square mile – the perfect location for him to finally fulfil his promise. After parking up outside the holiday home, he climbed out and moved round to the rear of the car. Opening the car boot, he stared down at a bloodied and terrified Johnson blinking furiously as her eyes adjusted to the sunlight. 'Show me your hands,' he barked, pointing the large kitchen knife at her.

Johnson obliged.

'Link your fingers together and stick your hands in the air.'

Again, Johnson did as ordered.

In one fluid movement he slipped a cable tie around her wrists and pulled it tightly together, locking them in place, then reached in and dragged her out of the boot.

'What the hell's going on, Ian? Why are you doing this?'

'Shut up,' he snapped back.

Spinning her round, he marched her towards the cottage, the knife pressed into the small of her back.

'Please don't hurt me, Ian.' Her voice was panicked.

'I said be quiet,' he growled as he keyed in the combination that opened the front door. 'Get in.' He pushed her forward.

Marching her along the dark corridor, they soon found themselves in the large farmhouse kitchen at the rear of the house, where thick oak beams crisscrossed the pitched roof.

He pulled out a kitchen chair. 'Sit down.'

Johnson followed the instructions.

Taking a knee behind her, he wrapped duct tape around her ankles, securing them to the chair, then stood and walked round to face her.

'What's this all about, Ian?' Her nose and top lip bore the marks of their recent scuffle.

He stared at her in silence for a time, savouring the fear in her eyes. 'Justice, Nic. This is about justice.'

'I don't understand.'

He flashed a smile. 'That's probably the most truthful thing to ever have come out of your mouth.'

'What are you going to do?'

He leaned forward so their eyes were on the same level. 'I'm going to kill you.'

Johnson's eyes bulged.

'Just like the others.'

Johnson was breathing heavily now. 'What others?'

'Venables, Todd, Duval.'

'Nigel Duval is dead?'

A satisfactory smile spread across his face. 'As of last night, yes.'

'And *you* killed him?'

He straightened. 'Yes. I killed them all.'

'I don't understand. Why, Ian?'

'Like I said, justice.'

'Look, you don't need to do this. Please stop,' she pleaded. 'No more killing.'

'It's too late to stop now. I need to finish this before they catch me.'

'I can help you, Ian.' Johnson's words shot out in a flurry. 'Let me represent you; we can plead mitigating circumstances. I can use my connections to get you a reduced sentence in a decent prison.'

'Quiet!' He struck her across the face with the back of his hand.

Johnson's nose began to bleed again as her cheeks reddened.

'Sally took a lot worse than that before she died.' He pulled up a chair and took a seat opposite her. 'You just can't help yourself, can you? Always trying to manipulate the situation to your own end.'

As blood dripped from her nostril, a tear streaked down her flushed cheek. 'I don't want to die, Ian.'

'Neither did Sally, but that made no difference to you lot.'

Her chest was heaving with panic now. 'What are you talking about? I don't know any Sallys.'

He laughed sardonically. 'You really don't remember her, do you?'

'No. Should I?'

'Of course you should.'

'Why, who is she?'

'My *sister*.'

'And what's she got to do with me?'

'She was murdered. Beaten to death by her boyfriend.'

'I'm confused.' Johnson blinked furiously. 'How is she connected to me?'

'Does the name Paul Stillwell ring any bells?' he asked.

Johnson's brow wrinkled as she shook her head. 'No, it doesn't.'

He folded his arms and sat back in the chair, glaring at her as he did. 'He killed Sally.'

'I don't know him.'

'Really?' he shot back. 'Because *you* defended him in court.'

'Did I?'

'How can you not remember? He beat my sister to death!'

'And I truly am sorry about that, Ian, but I've worked a lot of cases over the years. I can't recall them all.'

'That's right. Clients are just numbers on a spreadsheet to you, and their victims never even enter your thoughts, do they?'

Johnson swallowed hard. 'I think I remember it now; it was a domestic violence case, wasn't it?'

He nodded as he stood up from the chair. 'Do you know the police had been called to their home three times before he killed her. *Three times* they let Paul off with just a warning. No arrests were ever made, and instead they just told him to treat her better. *Treat her better?* He treated his dogs better than he treated Sally, because he knew full well he could keep getting away with it. And then finally he went too far. That night he beat her so badly the doctors needed her dental records to identify her.'

He wandered over to the window and gazed out across the sprawling field adjacent to the cottage garden. 'Her face was so badly damaged, I never got a chance to say goodbye to her in the funeral home. The undertaker told us it would be better for us to remember her as she was.'

'Oh, God, I had no idea. I'm so sorry, Ian. I really am.'

He turned and locked eyes with her. 'You will be.'

42

Having been unable to get hold of the Crowthers on the phone, Phillips had activated her mobile lights and siren, speeding to their home in the hope of catching them there. Luckily, when she arrived, she found Jonny Crowther unpacking groceries from the car.

'Back so soon?' he asked as she approached.

There was no time to waste. 'I need to know where I can find your son, Ian.'

'Ian?' Crowther frowned. 'I'm afraid I've not seen him in years.'

'Can I ask why?'

Crowther's shoulders sagged, and he suddenly appeared older. 'He had a breakdown not long after Sally's funeral and ended up being sectioned.'

'I see,' said Phillips.

Crowther continued, 'It was for his own safety, apparently, at least that's what the doctors said. He was suffering from delusions and psychosis.'

'Which hospital was he treated at?'

'Parkside. He was in there for about twelve months. His

mum and I visited him as often as we could to begin with – back when he was heavily medicated – but as he started to come out from under the drugs, he became very aggressive towards us both. He seemed to think we could have done more to protect Sally. I tried to tell him I did what I could, but Ian wasn't having any of it. After that, the visits became less and less frequent.'

'Why didn't you mention any of this the other day when DI Jones and I were here?'

Crowther frowned. 'My wife and I lost both our children when Sally was killed. We've done everything we can to block out the pain, and that means blocking out what happened to Ian, too. We tried to be there for him, but he made it clear he wanted nothing to do with us. So we moved forward without him in our lives. It was the only option we had left, Inspector.'

Phillips nodded. 'So when exactly was the last time you saw him?'

'I think it was probably about six months after the funeral,' said Crowther. 'So a long time ago now. Last we heard, he was out of Parkside and had his own flat and a job working as a clerk for a law firm in town. That gave me and his mum some comfort at least. We did try reaching out to him on an email address we managed to get hold of from one of his friends, but he wanted nothing to do with us.'

'I see.'

'Why the sudden interest in Ian, anyway?'

Knowing the pain he and Linda had already suffered over the years, Phillips considered whether to tell him the truth or simply avoid the question altogether, but in her heart she knew she had little option but to share what was going on with his son. 'Look, this isn't something you'll want to hear, but we strongly believe Ian has just abducted his boss.'

Jonny did a double take. 'He's done what?'

'Tonight is the anniversary of Sally's death, isn't it?'

He nodded sombrely. 'She was pronounced dead at ten o'clock on that evening. Some things you never forget.'

'For reasons known only to Ian, in the last hour he was captured on video forcing his boss into the boot of her car before driving away with her in it.'

'Oh, my god. You can't be serious.'

'I'm afraid I am,' replied Phillips. 'I've seen the video myself. It was definitely him.'

'But why would he do that?'

'That's what I need to find out.'

Crowther's exhaled deeply. 'We always worried he'd do something stupid if he stopped medicating. He never could deal with what happened to Sally; he was so angry all the time. Her death haunted him.'

'It's imperative we find Ian as quickly as possible before he does anything else stupid. Do you have any idea where he might have taken Nic?'

'I'm sorry I don't. In fact, I wouldn't know where to start. Like I said, we've had no real contact with Ian for years now, and he's not the boy we raised. His whole personality changed after Sally died. Sadly, he's pretty much a stranger to us.'

'Okay,' said Phillips, handing across her card. 'I know it's a long shot given what you've just told me, but if for some reason he decides to get in touch, call me on that number immediately.'

Crowther held up the card. 'We have one of these inside.'

'I know, but at least it's close to hand.' Phillips turned and began walking down the path towards the Mini, which was parked on the road.

'He's not a bad boy,' Crowther shouted after her.

Phillips span back to face the house.

'He's just very damaged,' he added.

'I know,' said Phillips. *Killers usually always are,* she thought as she turned away again.

Back in the car she called Jones.

'I was literally just about to call you, boss,' he said. *'We've got a hit on Johnson's car.'*

'Really? Where?'

'It was captured on the M56 a number of times in the last hour heading west towards Cheshire, then again on the A41, and was last seen on a camera just outside the village of Broxton about half an hour ago.'

'Broxton?'

'Yeah. It rang a bell with me, too. Why do I know that?'

'Daniella Briggs told us she used to holiday there as a kid, and it's the village where she had the holiday home. Remember?'

'The place where Nigel Duval turned up and tried to force his way in?'

'That's the one,' said Phillips.

'Looking at the map, Broxton has one road that runs the length of the village. Seems there's an ANPR camera on the south side of the village, and so far he's not passed that, so we can probably assume he's stopped somewhere off that road.'

'So why Broxton?'

'God only knows. I've given up trying to second-guess the motives involved in this investigation.'

Phillips glanced at the clock on the dash. It was approaching 9:05 PM. 'How far is Broxton from the Crowthers' house in Denton?'

'Give me a sec. I'll google it.'

She could hear Jones typing on the other end of the call.

'If you whip round the M60 and then switch to the M56, you're looking at about forty minutes in light traffic.'

'Right. I'll head there now.'

'But there's no guarantee that's where he's gone, guv. You could drive all that way for nothing.'

'I know, but it's the only lead we have so far, and I can't just sit around waiting for him to show up on the next ANPR camera. At least if I'm over that way, I'll be closer to his final destination.'

'In that case, I'm coming too,' said Jones. *'I can be there in an hour.'*

'Okay, but before you leave the station, call Daniella Briggs and get the address for the cottage.'

'What, you think he might have taken Johnson there?'

'Maybe.'

'But how would he know about that place?'

'I honestly have no idea, but everything seems to be somehow linked in this case. My gut's telling me that if Ian's in Broxton and Daniella Briggs once had a house here, we should check it out.'

'I'll call her now.'

'Thanks, Jonesy. As quick as you can.' She ended the call and fired the ignition. A second later she pulled the Mini away from the kerb and gunned the accelerator.

Fifteen minutes had passed by the time Jones called back. 'Did you get the address?'

'Yeah, apparently it's on the opposite side of the village to the exit from the A41,' he replied. *'I'll text the postcode to your phone.'*

'Thanks.'

'Daniella reckons it's an Airbnb now, so I had a look online, and she's right, it is. It's also unavailable today and tomorrow.'

'So it's already been booked?'

'Looks like it, and based on the conversation I've just had with Daniella, I'm starting to think the cottage could be exactly where he's going.'

'What did she say?'

'She knows him, guv.'

'Ian?'

'Yep. Apparently, he's a regular at her group for people affected by abuse. Been going for a couple of years now.'

'Jesus. This investigation just keeps throwing up surprises.'

'She said she knows all about Sally and what happened to her. She said Ian also knows about what she went through with Duval, including the fact he turned up at the cottage that night, trying to get in.'

'I need to find that cottage, Jonesy.'

'I agree, but not on your own. Bov and I are heading there now to back you up.'

Phillips moved the car left towards the exit for the M56. 'I think I'm about half an hour away. It'll be an hour before you reach me, so I need you to call in a firearms unit to meet me at the cottage. Just in case I need more urgent help.'

'I'll sort it now.'

'Thanks, Jonesy.'

'Be careful, guv.'

'I will,' she said, then ended the call.

43

Darkness descended across the fields to the rear of the house as the sun finally set. Checking his watch, he realised he had just over half an hour to finalise the preparations. Heading to the car, he returned a few minutes later with the backpack in hand, which he placed on the kitchen table next to Johnson.

She stared at him, wide eyed. 'What's in there?'

'You'll find out soon enough.'

Johnson's nose had finally stopped bleeding now as she shifted in her seat. 'Come on, Ian. Stop this.'

He stayed silent as he unzipped the bag.

'There's no way you can get away with it. You left so much evidence behind at my house, the police will soon figure out it was you.'

He locked eyes with her and produced a wicked grin. 'They'd have to *find* me first, and there's no way they'll be able connect me to this place in time to save your neck. Plus, we're a mile from our nearest neighbours, so no one will have seen us arrive.'

She swallowed the lump caught in her throat.

'By the way, I meant to ask,' he said nonchalantly. 'What do you think of the place?'

Johnson didn't reply.

'It's an Airbnb. Quite reasonable, actually. Just under five hundred quid for two nights.' He pulled out a long length of horsehair curled into a loop and laid it on the table. 'Actually, the house used to belong to Daniella Briggs. I bet you don't remember her either.'

Johnson stared back at him but didn't reply.

'You don't, do you?' He shook his head. 'You really are a piece of work.'

'I don't know what you want me to say. I see so many people on a daily basis, I can't remember them all.'

He sat down opposite her again. 'Well, let me remind you, shall I? Danni was raped by Nigel Duval about ten years ago, and *you* made sure she stayed silent.'

A dawn of realisation flickered across Johnson's face.

'Coming back now, is it?'

She nodded.

'Danni told me *all* about how you threatened to drag her name through the mud and painted a terrifying picture of her being cross-examined in court by your barrister. Not to mention the fact she'd have to face Duval at the trial, day after day after day. I took the liberty of reading through your notes in the file back at the office, and everything Danni told me rings true.' He sat forward on the chair and pointed his index finger directly at her. '*You* helped Duval get away with rape – and all because he paid you handsomely for the privilege. How could you do that?'

'I was doing my job,' replied Johnson. 'It was nothing personal.'

'Of course it was personal,' he spat back. 'It was nothing *but* personal, it was Danni's life, her state of mind, her self-worth, her *everything,* and you took all of that away from her with your threats and your inflated chequebook.'

Johnson opened her mouth to speak but seemed to think better of it.

He continued, 'Have you any idea what that poor woman went through? Have you?'

Johnson shook her head.

'Being violated by a monster like Duval, and then bullied into silence by you and your mob of expensive lawyers.'

'But that's the law, Ian. Sometimes we have to do things we don't like, defend people we know are guilty.'

'Don't give me any of that bollocks.' He stepped back up from the chair. 'D'you know what Danni did with the money?'

'No, I don't.'

'She bought *this* cottage.' He cast his arms out wide. 'Strictly speaking, her parents did – to provide a safe space where she could try to come to terms with what happened to her. And it worked for a time too, until Duval showed up one night, that is – drunk – banging on the door and trying to force his way in.'

Shock was etched on Johnson's face. 'I had no idea he did that.'

'Of course you didn't, because once the deal is done, you move on to the next case, don't you? On to the next big money offer. No thought for the actual victims of the crimes you help your clients walk away from.'

'That's not true, Ian.'

'Don't make me laugh! You're all the same. Venables, Todd, Duval, none of them cared about anyone but themselves, just like you. I couldn't let that stand. Someone had to speak up for the victims – for Sally and Danni – someone had to get them justice.'

'And how does killing me get justice?'

'You'll finally pay for what you've done,' he said calmly. 'Just like Todd and Venables did, just like Duval.'

'You're sick, Ian. Anyone could see that. You need help.'

He could feel his jaw clenching. 'Don't presume to tell me what I need!' Picking up the horsehair, he began to unfurl the thick rope.

Johnson stared at it.

'Impressive, isn't it? It's made of horsehair. The same stuff I used to strangle the others with.' He smiled. 'Poetic justice, you might say.'

She couldn't take her eyes off it.

'But I have something slightly different planned for you.'

Beads of sweat had formed on Johnson's brow.

He next made a loop in one end of the horsehair rope and tied a thick knot, then bent down and looped the other end around the leg of the large oak kitchen table before tying a second knot. 'This bit can be quite tricky,' he said before stepping back slightly and launching the loop up and over the beam positioned directly above his head. A second later it tumbled back down and came to a stop just in front of Johnson, her eyes wide with fear. Holding the looped horsehair in both hands, he tested its strength. 'That should do it.'

'Please, Ian.' Her voice cracked. 'Don't do this. I wasn't responsible for Sally's death, and I didn't rape Daniella Briggs.'

'No, but you defended the two monsters who *did* – which makes you just as guilty.' He retook his seat opposite her and checked his watch: 9:40 PM. *Not long now.* 'You should know I also read the case notes on Paul Stillwell's trial – that's my sister Sally's killer in case you've forgotten him already.'

Johnson remained silent.

'Do you remember what Venables said in his chambers?'

Johnson blinked furiously and appeared to be trying to remember.

He folded his arms across his chest and his right leg over his left knee. 'He said if Sally was stupid enough to stay with Paul after the first few beatings, then she got what was coming to her.' His nostrils flared as he struggled to control his rage. 'Can you believe that? My beautiful sister – who was beaten senseless on a weekly basis and lived in fear of what would happen if she tried to leave her abuser – she *got what was coming to her*.'

'I remember,' whispered Johnson.

'I thought you might, because according to your own handwritten notes in the case file, you actually pulled him up on those comments, but rather than ask him to recuse himself, you let it slide and "banked it for use at a later date".'

Johnson closed her eyes as a tear escaped down her cheek.

'Walter fucking Venables should never have been anywhere near that trial – you knew that. And *you* had the chance to make sure he wasn't – but you let him get away with it because you also knew, from the moment he made those comments about Sally, he was essentially on your side and could help you sway the jury.'

'But we lost that case; Paul Bennett was found guilty.'

'Of manslaughter!' He growled as he jumped up from the chair. 'A plea that *you* brokered with the CPS. That bastard will be out in a couple of years when he should have gotten life for murder.'

More tears streaked down Johnson's cheeks. 'I'm sorry, Ian. Please, you must understand, I was doing what I thought was best for my client.'

Standing over her, the rage in his stomach burned like a wildfire. 'Sally was pronounced dead at exactly ten o'clock five years ago tonight.' He looked at his watch, then prodded the noose hanging between them. 'And in fifteen minutes, you'll die too.'

44

After struggling to locate the address, it was dark by the time Phillips found the entrance to the long track that led from the main road up to the cottage. In the distance she could see light emanating from within the house, about a hundred yards away. Parking the Mini out of sight, she switched her phone to silent mode, then jumped out into the warm evening air and set off on foot in search of Ian Crowther and Nic Johnson. As she moved closer to the house, she spotted the Mercedes parked to the left of the house, and her pulse quickened. The section of the cottage closest to her appeared empty, but light was bleeding through the frosted glass in the front door. *They must be round the back*, she reasoned. Taking short, soft steps, she headed down the path to the side of the building, stopping at the end of the wall. Voices filtered out through an open window – a man and a woman – but from where she stood, she couldn't make out what they were saying. Taking a couple of steps forward, she craned her neck to peer into the kitchen. Ian was standing with his back to the window, holding a large kitchen knife in his right hand. Johnson was sitting on a chair in front of him, her wrists cable-tied together, a large noose hanging from the ceiling between them. 'Shit!' she said to herself as her adrenaline spiked. Her heart began pounding so loudly in her head, it almost seemed they could hear it inside the cottage.

Checking her watch, she could see it was 9:48 PM. With just over ten minutes left before she believed Crowther planned to kill Johnson, she considered going in without backup, but she knew that was a high-risk strategy. He was a big man in possession of a large blade, and he could potentially kill them both. Just then, the phone in her pocket began to vibrate. Praying it was the firearms team, she retraced her steps and moved back to the front of the house, whispering as she answered it. 'This is Phillips.'

'Ma'am, Sergeant Rhodes.'

Armed backup. Thank God.

'We're approaching your location. ETA is three minutes.'

'Okay, I have eyes on the suspect, and he's armed with a large knife. Park up by the Mini Cooper at the end of the lane. I'll meet you there when you arrive.'

'Got it.'

Phillips rang off and made her way back up the track.

A couple of minutes later as she approached the Mini, she spotted the headlights of the tactical firearms unit's BMW X5 on the main road. She watched as the large SUV pulled in next to her tiny car, and the four-strong team decamped.

Sergeant Rhodes – nicknamed Dusty because of his greyish, ginger hair – made a beeline for Phillips. 'Ma'am.' He was a big man with broad shoulders who cut an intimidating figure in his black combat gear, carrying a Heckler & Koch G36 assault rifle. 'I understand we're dealing with a potential kidnapping.'

Phillips nodded. 'Our target, Ian Crowther, IC-one male, is positioned at the back of the house in the kitchen. Earlier today he abducted his boss, Nic Johnson, IC-one female. She's in the kitchen with him and looks to have been restrained at the wrists. When I last looked, she was sitting in a chair with a noose hanging down in front of her, and Crowther was standing over her with a knife. He's already killed three people in similar circumstances, and we believe he plans to kill Johnson at 10 PM. She glanced at her watch. 'So we need to get in there right now.'

'How do you want to do this?' asked Rhodes.

'We know Crowther's armed, and he has a history of psychosis and paranoia. So we go in fast and hard, okay?'

Rhodes smiled. 'Just how we like it.' He turned to one of the team next to him. 'Keano, get the big red key.'

Keano nodded, then marched to the back of the X5, where he opened the boot and pulled out the red mobile battering ram, returning a minute later.

'Right, guys,' said Rhodes. 'We all know the drill, so let's go.'

The TFU team armed their weapons, then set off at pace towards the cottage, with Phillips bringing up the rear.

45

'It's almost ten o'clock,' said Ian, checking his watch theatrically, 'so it looks like your time is nearly up.'

'Please, Ian. Stop this madness, please!'

He laughed as he stepped closer. 'You wouldn't be the first person to think I was insane.'

'Ian, I'm begging you, please don't do this!'

He refused to engage with her, and instead grabbed the horsehair noose with both hands and placed it around Johnson's neck.

'Ian, please! I don't want to die!' she screamed, jerking away from the rope.

'Neither did Sally,' he replied nonchalantly as he forced the noose over her head and tightened it around her throat.

Suddenly the sound of trickling liquid filled the air.

He took a step back and glanced under the chair. 'Ah, now would you look at that,' he said playfully. 'You've wet yourself.'

Johnson began to sob like a child, and her whole body appeared to shake. 'Please, Ian, let me go. I'll give you anything you want, anything, just please don't kill me.'

He moved behind her chair and leaned in close to her left ear. 'What I want is to erase *you* from this planet, you bitch, and that's exactly what I'm going to do.' In a flash he stepped back, grabbed the back of the chair and flipped it forward.

Johnson fell into the noose. With her legs still tethered to the chair and her hands tied, the full weight of her body was now hanging from her neck as she began to choke, her face swelling with blood, eyes becoming bulbous as she writhed around.

'Goodbye,' he said, watching her struggle against the cord, his eyes wide with excitement.

THE TEAM REACHED the back door just as Ian flipped over the chair.

With no time to waste and his Heckler & Koch machine pistol at the ready, Rhodes gave the order to go, and a split second later two of his team smashed the kitchen door off its hinges.

Rhodes was first in, charging through the door. 'Armed police! Put the weapon down now!'

Ian appeared momentarily stunned as he stepped back and brandished the kitchen knife.

Meanwhile, Phillips, who had watched the horrific scene unfold through the kitchen window, rushed towards Nic Johnson, desperate to free her from the noose.

But before she could reach her, Ian grabbed her by the hair and yanked her back.

'Oh no you don't!' he said, wrapping his long arm tightly around her neck and pulling her against himself like a human shield, holding the kitchen knife against her back. 'Nobody move.'

Johnson, still hanging from the noose in the middle of the room, continued to choke as she wriggled and jolted.

Thrusting the blade under Phillips's chin, Ian sneered. 'Drop your weapons, or I'll slit her throat!'

Rhodes was standing in a firing position, staring down the sights of his assault rifle. 'You don't have to do this. Just put the knife down, Ian.'

Ian's eyes were wild. 'I mean it, drop your weapons. Or I swear to God I'll slit her throat – right here, right now!'

Rhodes hesitated.

'Put all of your guns on the table!' Crowther demanded.

'We can't do that,' replied Rhodes, the extended stock of his rifle pulled hard into his shoulder.'

'It's not too late to save Nic, Ian,' said Phillips over her shoulder.

'She's way past saving.' He cackled as he dragged Phillips back towards the obliterated back door, tightening his grip on her neck as he did. Instinctively her fingers grappled with his forearm to try to free herself, but he was holding her too tightly.

Rhodes maintained his position in the middle of the room, standing directly opposite Phillips with Ian directly behind her.

Phillips locked eyes with Rhodes, then winked to get his attention.

It worked as he held her gaze.

Still holding the knife to Phillips's throat, Ian took a step backwards, again dragging her with him. 'As much as I want to stay and watch Johnson die, I'm more interested in getting out of here.' He took another step backwards. 'I'm going to leave now with DCI Phillips, and you lot are going to stay *exactly* where you are.'

Phillips glanced at Rhodes's weapon and surreptitiously

made the gun symbol with her fingers, holding them against her chest.

Rhodes offered a micro nod of acknowledgement.

Ian moved back again. 'If any of you so much as blink in our direction, I'll slice her in two.'

Phillips glared at Rhodes, then held three fingers to her chest.

Again, he offered the slightest of nods.

Phillips now showed two fingers...then one. In that split second, she dropped her right shoulder slightly and rammed her elbow deep into Ian's groin.

Crying out in pain, he relaxed his grip.

It was enough. Conjuring every ounce of power she could muster, Phillips thrust her head backwards into his nose with a sickening crunch.

Stunned by the blow, he staggered backwards as Phillips threw herself to the floor.

In that instant two deafening shots exploded from Rhodes's rifle, launching Ian backwards like a rag doll.

With no time to waste, Phillips scrambled to her feet and rushed to lift the weight from Johnson's neck, ramming her shoulder under her chest and forcing her upwards to release the tension on the rope. Officer Keane arrived a second later and did the same.

Grabbing a carving knife from the block on the kitchen bench, Rhodes joined them and began frantically sawing at the horsehair rope.

Finally, a few seconds later, it gave way.

Phillips fell backwards under the weight of Johnson.

'Nic! Nic!' she shouted as Johnson landed on top of her, but she appeared unresponsive.

Sergeant Rhodes and Officer Keane moved in quickly, picking up Johnson's limp body before placing her gently on the floor.

'We've got a pulse,' said Keane, holding his fingers against her wrist. 'It's faint, but it's there.' Pinching her nose, he opened her mouth and started CPR.

Rhodes grabbed the radio attached to his chest. 'Control, this is Foxtrot-Charlie-three requesting an urgent heli-med.'

Keane began the chest compressions.

The response was instant. *'Foxtrot-Charlie-three, this is control. What is your location?'*

'Broxton Village, Cheshire. What-three-words reference blacken-juniors-rent.'

'Understood. Stand by.'

There was a long pause.

'Received, foxtrot-Charlie-three. Heli-med is on the way.'

'ETA?' asked Rhodes.

'Approximately fifteen minutes, en route from Broadgreen Hospital in Liverpool.'

Phillips glanced at Keane as he continued with the chest compressions. 'How's she doing?'

'Pulse is still faint, but it's there,' Keane replied before grabbing her nose and mouth once more.

Getting to her feet, Phillips made her way across the kitchen to the spot where Ian was lying on his back, thick purple blood had pooled under his back. As she bent down to check his pulse, his dead eyes stared back at her.

'I wasn't taking any chances, ma'am,' said Rhodes as he moved next to her.

'I know,' she replied, standing again. Turning to face him, she patted him on his thick upper arm, then looked down at Ian's body once more. In that moment her heart went out to the young man who had lost his beloved sister, whose grief and pain had become so overwhelming they had led him to seek the ultimate revenge for her death. Phillips could never condone his actions, but she could at least understand his reasons for taking the law into his own hands. The system had failed Sally Crowther just as it had failed so many others. Sergeant Rhodes had had no choice but to take those shots – she knew that – but she couldn't help thinking Sally's and Ian's lives could have been saved had more people stepped up when it really mattered.

46

ONE WEEK LATER

Jones wandered into Phillips's office with a steaming mug of coffee just as she was hanging up her coat. 'Made it myself, boss.' He smiled.

Phillips took a seat as he handed it over. 'You're a star, Jonesy.'

Holding a mug of his usual peppermint tea, Jones perched against the bank of drawers adjacent to her desk. 'So how was Johnson last night?'

'Still struggling to speak, but definitely on the mend. She's out of intensive care, which is great, and she reckons they could let her out as early as next week.'

'To be honest, I'm amazed she even survived, the way you described it.'

'Me too.' Phillips took a mouthful of coffee. 'The doctor who treated her at the scene reckoned just a couple of seconds more and she wasn't coming back, and if Keano hadn't been so sharp in administering CPR, I'm certain she'd have been brain damaged.'

Jones shuddered. 'Doesn't bear thinking about.'

'Listen, while I've got you, I wanted to talk to you about Whistler.'

'Really?' Jones raised his eyebrows. 'What's up?'

'Have you noticed he's been acting a little odd this last week?'

'In what way?'

Phillips shrugged. 'I dunno, just quieter than usual. He's hardly said a word.'

Jones took a drink of his tea. 'Now you mention it, he hasn't been his usual chippy self. I mean, there's been very little banter with Bov, which isn't like those two at all.'

'Yeah, that's what I was thinking.'

Just then Bovalino appeared at her door, grinning. 'Got something I thought might interest you both.'

Phillips reclined in her chair as she cradled her coffee in both hands. 'I'm intrigued.'

'There's mischief in your eyes, Bov,' added Jones.

The big man stepped inside. 'You remember Angela Duval and her fella, Zane Toohey, lied about being at home the night Nigel Duval was killed?'

'Yeah,' said Phillips.

'Last night I was filing the final reports from the past few weeks and spotted PC Lawford's map of her journey through the ANPR network that night. You'll never guess where she ended up.'

Phillips was intrigued. 'Where?'

'The Purple Door.'

Jones's face wrinkled. 'As in *the* Purple Door, in Whalley Range?'

'The very same.'

Phillips felt her brow furrow. 'What was she doing there?'

The grin on Bovalino's face reappeared. 'Turns out she was working there that night.'

Phillips and Jones exchanged glances, then turned back to face Bov.

'In what capacity?' said Phillips.

'She's a sex worker,' he replied. 'Goes by the name Angel Dupont.'

'Are you sure?' Jones asked.

'One hundred percent. A mate of mine is a regular there. I just called him and he confirmed it.'

'Oh, a mate of yours, was it?' said Jones grinning. 'You sure it wasn't you?'

'Give over,' Bovalino shot back. 'There's only one girl for me. Always has been, always will be.'

Phillips sat forward and placed her mug on the desk. 'So maybe it wasn't just the Netflix series that helped pay for that flash apartment.'

'Yeah, and no wonder she lied about what she was doing,' added Jones.

At that moment, Entwistle tapped on her door, his shoulders sagging. 'You got a minute, guv?'

'Sure, come in.'

'In private, if that's okay?'

'Of course.' Phillips nodded and shot Jones a look.

He took the hint. 'Right, better get back to it,' he said as he moved away and guided Bovalino out.

Entwistle closed the door behind them, then moved to stand in front of Phillips. He was holding a manila folder, which he passed to her. 'These are all the names of the people who attended each of the crime scenes where confidential intel was passed to Don Townsend.'

Phillips frowned as she opened the file and began scanning down the page.

Entwistle continued, 'It covers all departments: uniform, paramedics, major crimes and forensics.'

'So one of these lot could be our spy, then?'

'Yes, guv,' he replied sombrely.

Phillips continued checking the names for a time, then closed the file in front of her. Reclining in her chair, she folded her arms across her chest. 'What's going on with you, Whistler?'

Entwistle flinched. 'Sorry?'

'What's happening? Why have you been moping around so much this last week? You're like a man who lost a tenner and found a penny.'

'I don't know what you mean, boss.'

Phillips stared at him in silence for a long moment. 'Oh, come on. I've got eyes, Whistler. So what is it? What's going on?'

Entwistle swallowed a lump in his throat, then locked eyes with her. 'I think I should resign, boss.'

'Do what?' Phillips's brow furrowed. 'What's brought this on?'

'The lost videotapes, guv.'

'Don't be ridiculous.' Phillips waved him away. 'Sure, we lost some evidence, but we caught the right man and saved Johnson's life. It was a decent result. And besides, we all make mistakes in this job.'

Entwistle stared back in silence.

'As long as you learn from them, that's all that matters. Look, sit down, and let's talk about this.'

'I'd rather stand if you don't mind, guv.'

Phillips scrutinised his face. 'What are you *not* telling me, Whistler?'

He took a deep breath. 'I didn't lose the tapes, guv. I removed them from the department.'

Phillips's eyes narrowed. 'What exactly are you saying?'

Entwistle dropped his chin to his chest for a moment before returning his gaze to Phillips. 'I got rid of the evidence.'

She shook her head. 'And why did you do that?'

'I had no choice.'

'Really?'

'Yes, guv.'

'And what did you do with the tapes?' asked Phillips.

'I gave them to a senior officer.'

Phillips was incredulous. 'Which one?'

'Chief Constable Fox.'

Phillips opened her mouth to speak, but no words would come out.

'I'm sorry, guv.'

Phillips was struggling to understand what she was hearing. 'So what the hell did Fox want with them?'

'She wouldn't say. Just told me she wanted them, and if I had any ideas about being a copper in the long term, I had to hand them over immediately.'

Phillips sat back in the chair and folded her arms. 'So why d'you do it? You're as honest as they come. Why lie?'

'I can't say, guv.'

'Can't? Or won't?

'Bit of both, I guess.'

'Why didn't you come to me with this when she first asked you to do it? You know I would have had your back.'

'She gave me explicit instructions not to,' replied Entwistle. 'Said if I did, she would see to it that I was finished on the force.'

'I see.' Phillips stared him straight in the eye as she prodded the file on her desk with her index finger. 'So will I find your name in here, Whistler? Are *you* the mole?'

He shook his head vigorously. 'No! Absolutely not. This was a one-off. I would never betray your confidence.'

'But you did though, didn't you? You stood there and flat out lied to me and the guys about what happened to those tapes.'

Entwistle nodded. 'Look, I know I fucked up, and I wish to God I'd said no when she asked, but if I'd done that, she'd have…' His words tailed off.

'What was she threatening you with?'

'I really can't say.'

'Has she got something on you, Whistler?' asked Phillips. *'Leverage?'*

Entwistle took a moment to answer, then nodded.

'So what does she have?'

'I'm sorry, guv, but I can't tell you that.'

Phillips sat forward. 'Let me guess. Something from your past? Before you were a copper?'

'Yes.'

Phillips shook her head as she linked her fingers together on her desk. 'And *you* think walking away is the answer, do you?'

'What other option do I have?'

Phillips remained silent for a long moment, then picked up the folder. 'How about you help me catch the *real* mole. That could be a good place to start.'

Entwistle's face wrinkled. 'But like you said, I lied to you, boss. I lied to the team.'

'Yeah, you did. And as I also said, we all make mistakes. It's what we learn from them that matters.'

'I abused your trust, guv.'

'I know,' replied Phillips, 'but under duress from one of the most Machiavellian coppers ever to wear the uniform. *And* even though you knew it could be the end of your very promising police career, you did eventually own up to what you did. Which took guts.'

Entwistle swallowed hard again.

'I'm not accepting your resignation. Instead, here's what's gonna happen.' She handed back the file. 'You're going to go back out there and start looking into everyone on this list.'

He stared back in silence.

'You're going to say nothing of this to anyone, ever again. And you're going to tell me only the truth from now on.' Phillips locked eyes with him. 'But let me be clear: any more lies, no matter *how* small – and you're finished. Understood?'

Entwistle's eyes widened as he nodded. 'Yes, guv. I promise. I won't ever lie to you again.'

Phillips held his gaze.

'But what about Fox?'

'What about her?'

'Well, the tapes. She still has them.'

'And that's the way it'll stay...*for now*.' She straightened in the chair. 'But trust me when I say this, Whistler, if there's one thing I can't stand, it's bent coppers, no matter what their rank. So when the time is right, you can count on one thing.'

'What's that, boss?'

Phillips flashed a thin smile. 'I'm going to make sure Chief Constable Fox gets everything that's coming to her.'

ACKNOWLEDGMENTS

This book is dedicated in the loving memory of my friend Alan Smith, who died suddenly while I was writing *Deadly Justice*, aged just forty-eight.

Alan was one of the funniest, kindest and most caring people I ever had the joy of spending time with. His huge smile was infectious, and he had a gift for making anyone feel welcome and at ease in his company.

He was also a hugely talented music promoter who was responsible for helping so many bands across the UK find worldwide success, including Amy Macdonald, Sam Fender, Gerry Cinnamon, Dylan John Thomas and Nina Nesbitt.

Alan leaves behind an amazing body of work and a lasting legacy, not least his two beautiful children, Logan and Abbey, and his wonderful wife, Lynsey.

Sleep easy, my friend. You were definitely a bigger 'ginge' than me! ☺

I'd also like to acknowledge the support of so many people who made this book possible:

My wife, Kim, and my gorgeous boy, Vaughan.

Jan Smith.

Tahir Taj.

Bryn Jones.

Keith James.

Carole Lawford.

Lambo.

Donna and Cheryl from 'Now Is Your Time'.

My publishing team.

Finally, thank you to my readers for reading *Deadly Justice.* If you could spend a moment to write an honest review, no matter how short, I would be extremely grateful. They really do help readers discover my books.

ALSO BY OMJ RYAN

DEADLY SECRETS

(A crime thriller introducing DCI Jane Phillips)

DEADLY SILENCE

(Book 1 in the DCI Jane Phillips series)

DEADLY WATERS

(Book 2 in the DCI Jane Phillips series)

DEADLY VENGEANCE

(Book 3 in the DCI Jane Phillips series)

DEADLY BETRAYAL

(Book 4 in the DCI Jane Phillips series)

DEADLY OBSESSION

(Book 5 in the DCI Jane Phillips series)

DEADLY CALLER

(Book 6 in the DCI Jane Phillips series)

DEADLY NIGHT

(Book 7 in the DCI Jane Phillips series)

DEADLY CRAVING

(Book 8 in the DCI Jane Phillips series)

DEADLY JUSTICE

(Book 9 in the DCI Jane Phillips series)

Printed in Great Britain
by Amazon